ILLUSIONS

APPEARANCES 3

(A MATT & OLLIE ROMANCE)

I0767911

T. H. FOREST

Other books by T.H. Forest

Adult
Twinkies & Beefcake
Appearances (A Matt & Ollie Romance)
Foundations (Appearances Book 2)

Young Adult
Kelly's Folly

HP Copyright © 2025 by Holdorf Press, LLC
www.thforestauthor.com

Cover design: Sigrid Silberman
Images: Thomas Holdorf, Shutterstock
Illustrations: Sigrid Silberman

Paperback ISBN: 978-1-966065-04-3
Hardcover ISBN: 978-1-966065-03-6
eBook ISBN: 978-1-966065-05-0

This is a work of fiction. Unless otherwise indicated, all the names, characters, businesses, places, events and incidents in this book are either the product of the author's imagination or used in a fictitious manner. Any resemblance to persons living or dead is purely coincidental. The (often egregious) opinions expressed are those of the characters and should not be confused with the author's. No part of this book was created using AI, nor may any part of it be used to train AI.

All rights reserved. No part of this publication may be reproduced or transmitted in any form or by any means, electronic or mechanical, including photocopy, recording, or any information storage and retrieval systems, without permission in writing from the copyright holder.

Printed in the United States of America.

For my cousin Tom Holdorf,
Can you believe I'm still at it?

AUTHOR'S NOTE

Dear Readers,

Thank you for picking up a copy of Illusions! Please consider leaving a review when you have finished. As an indie press published author, I rely on my readers to help spread the word about my books. Perhaps it was reading a review that led you to me in the first place.

Did you know, if a book receives 20–25 reviews, Amazon will highlight the novel under the 'Customers Who Bought This Item Also Bought' and 'You might also like' section on a page. If a book has more than 50 reviews, Amazon will include the title in their newsletter and increase its visibility on the site with spotlights.

That would be HUGE for a non-traditionally published author like myself, and others like me. It doesn't take long, in fact, if you don't have time to write a review, all it takes is a click of the mouse on a star. I just ask that if you're on either end of the star spectrum, that you please leave a written review as to why you loved the book, or why you hated it. That way future readers can make an informed opinion.

Thank you and happy reading!
THF

CONTENTS

PART THREE

UNTIL THE END OF THE WORLD

PART ONE

MYSTERIOUS WAYS

———

1

———

Next to Me

September 2018

MATT WATCHED FROM INSIDE the dim interior of Ollie's Maserati as Ollie made his way down the steps of SharkFinn's Gulfstream jet. After nearly a week apart, Matt's hungry eyes took in Ollie's perfectly styled hair, his slightly rumpled linen suit, and his tired expression. Matt got out and took Ollie's wheeled suitcase from him with a smile.

"Did you get any sleep on the plane?" he asked as he put the suitcase in the open trunk.

"Some. Guy said to say hi," Ollie replied, his green-blue eyes catching the late afternoon sun and sparkling. "Made some of his usual comments about your cock and then spent the rest of the time lamenting the end of his fling with Finn."

Matt closed the trunk and made his way back to the driver's side as Ollie got in the passenger seat. He'd been horrified when he discovered that Ollie's cousin Guy had witnessed them having sex at Ollie's family's chateau in Lyon, France, but Guy had kept his mouth shut, other than the teasing remarks he cast Ollie's way that is, and since his

3

remarks were complimentary, Matt was more than willing to let them slide with a smile.

"I would've been perfectly fine with him moving here to be with her," Matt said as he pulled out of the parking space next to the hangar and made his way out of Hanscom Field. "He's the first, and only guy, or rather, *Ghee*," Matt clarified the pronounciation of Guy's name playfully, "I ever approved of; and it's only because he's your cousin that I did."

"He wasn't really being serious. Guy enjoys his bachelorhood too much to settle down just yet. And he knows all about you and your legendary protection of Finn." Ollie waved his hand dismissively. "Besides, he would never leave France, and you'd never let her move out of the States again. Not sure why she lets you have a say over her love life. I mean, yeah, you guys are besties or whatever, but you have to realize she *will* settle down someday."

Matt looked at Ollie with a frown and then merged onto the highway. "I owe everything that is phenomenal in my life to her, including you." Matt squeezed Ollie's thigh and then slid his hand higher into the heat between Ollie's legs. "She's too trusting. She only wants to see the good in people and I have to keep her safe. You might think I shouldn't meddle, but believe me, Ollie, I have kept more than one gold-digging shithead away from her and will continue to do so."

"Whatever. Just get me home so I can shower and, if I can keep my eyes open, let you fuck me." Ollie waggled his eyebrows and shifted in his seat so Matt's fingers grazed his crotch.

"Oh, I'll fuck you whether you can keep your eyes open or not, sleeping beauty. It's been nearly a week, and Little Matt has been at attention since the plane's stairs folded down."

Matt smiled and widened his legs as Ollie turned his head to stare at the bulge in his crotch. Ollie met his gaze with a grin and licked his bottom lip.

"There is nothing little about *that*, Lieutenant."

Just then Matt's phone rang through the car's audio. Ollie looked at the display and then at Matt who gripped the wheel tighter.

"Why is a *Star Wars* droid calling you?"

"He's a SEAL buddy," Matt replied as he contemplated letting the call go to voicemail. "Don't speak," He added and pressed the answer button on the steering wheel.

"R2D2!" Matt crowed. "How the fuck are ya?"

"Hey, Kool Aid! Not too bad," a deep voice with the barest hint of a accent replied. "You know, living the dream. Of course, not quite the actual dream you've been living, but I can't complain."

Matt chuckled and avoided Ollie's curious stare. "Well, it's more work than play, but I do alright. Where are you these days?"

"Mexico, mostly. But I happen to be stateside at the moment, DC specifically. But Paddy and Downtown are on the Cape this weekend at Downtown's in-laws. I've been invited but apparently, Paddy and I will be fighting for the couch because of all the kids." There was a pause. "Don't you have a place there?"

Matt felt as though he was straddling a continental divide. The coming weekend he'd promised Ollie they'd go to the beach and unplug, and yet he hadn't seen his SEAL buddies in years. He kept his eyes locked firmly on the road. "I do. You should all come; I have plenty of room. Without the kids I mean," Matt added in a rush. "Could Downtown get away, do you think?"

"Sweet!" R2D2 crowed. "I'm sure he can for at least one night. He's gonna be there all week but Paddy and I will just be in for the long weekend. I'll let the guys know and text you later. Send me the address. Looking forward to seeing your ugly mug again."

"Sounds good R2. See you this weekend."

Matt ended the call and took a breath before glancing at Ollie as he merged onto the Mass Pike. Ollie was looking at him with his eyebrows raised.

"Hey, *Kool Aid*. There's a lot to unpack from that conversation. I'm not sure where to begin. Should I start with the silly nicknames? Or should I start with where the fuck am I sleeping this weekend?" Ollie's tone went from teasing to pissy.

Matt swallowed and decided to ignore Ollie's irritation. "R2's real name is Arturo, but his whole family calls him Arturito. Plus, he's kinda like the droid. Playful and funny but don't underestimate him. Paddy, Joe's, last name is Fitzpatrick and is as Irish as they come. He was also our driver, for a little bit anyway." Matt glanced at Ollie who was looking at him with disbelief. "So, the other guys on our team began calling our transport the Paddy Wagon. Which is pretty racist, but Paddy didn't care." Matt exited the Pike and headed through the traffic snarl and onto Storrow Drive. "And Downtown's real name is Jules Brown, so he earned the nickname because, you know, MTV, and because he always goes on and on about how much he loves eating pussy."

Ollie made a sound of disgust. "Who are you? That is so crass."

"Hey, his words not mine." Matt held up his hand in defense.

"Regardless." Ollie shook his head and then sighed. "I don't see how any of that has to do with MTV, but whatever."

"Downtown Julie Brown? You've seriously never heard of her?" Matt stopped at a red light and scanned his eyes over Ollie for signs of recognition.

"No. What show is she on? Not that I even watch MTV. Is it still around?" Ollie scoffed.

"She was on in the eighties and nineties, but she's been referenced a bunch since then. Come on, you have to have heard the name."

Ollie rolled his eyes and smirked. "I wasn't even born yet, of course I don't know her. Christ, you're old. Have you received your AARP card yet?"

"I'm only five years older than you, Ollie." Matt poked Ollie in his side and smirked happily at the resulting shriek.

"Yeah, but your pop culture references are embarrassing." He squirmed out of reach and blocked Matt's hand.

Matt downshifted and turned into the alley entrance behind their townhouse on Marlborough Street. He pulled into the space next to his new Porsche 911 Turbo and the Range Rover they both drove and engaged the emergency brake.

"It's so good to be home," Ollie said softly. "But I'm really looking forward to the Cape this weekend."

Matt turned off the car and looked at Ollie. He saw a challenge in Ollie's eyes, along with a resigned sadness. Matt swallowed. He hated that look, but there was nothing he could do to fix it. Ollie knew the rules; he'd agreed to their secret arrangement, but that didn't stop him from working himself up into a mood apparently.

Matt exhaled and got out of the car without a word. There was no way they'd have the impending argument out in the open where people could see or hear. Matt got Ollie's bags out of the trunk and followed Ollie's stiff back to the door under the fire escape.

"You sure you don't want to go up to your townhouse," Ollie said in an irritated tone and gestured to the metal stairs next to them with his chin. "Wouldn't want anyone to get the wrong idea."

"Open the door," Matt ordered softly.

Ollie shot a dark look over his shoulder and put the key in the lock. Matt followed him into the narrow hallway that led to the elevator and the door to Ollie's garden-level condo. The condo Matt had given him when Ollie moved to the States. A condo Ollie never used. Ollie stopped in front of the door to said condo and reached for the knob with a key in his hand.

"Oliver." Matt put down the bags and stepped between Ollie and the door.

Matt cupped Ollie's scowling face in his large hands and forced his gaze. "I love you, and I've missed you. I know the phone call and weekend plans upset you, but you are not going in there." He angled his head to indicate the door behind him. "You are coming upstairs to our home, where I'm going to strip you down and wash your beautiful body in our shower. Then I'm gonna take you apart piece by piece in our bed." Matt dropped one hand and ran it down Ollie's body. "And then I'm gonna fuck you until you can't think about anything other than how much I love you."

Matt pressed his thumb under Ollie's jaw to tilt his head up and brushed a kiss on Ollie's thinned lips He continued to pepper kisses on Ollie's resistant mouth and jaw while squeezing Ollie's ass with his other hand, knowing just how and what to do to get through Ollie's defenses. He watched Ollie's eyelids flutter, and then close, with a triumphant surge in his belly that then radiated lower as he felt his dick swell.

Ollie finally opened his mouth to Matt's tongue as his arms came up around his neck. Matt deepened the kiss and pulled Ollie in tight with a moan that Ollie matched. He smoothed his fingers through Ollie's hair and pulled back to admire Ollie's kiss-plumped lips. He kissed Ollie's chin and licked the corner of Ollie's mouth.

"You're such a bastard. You know that right?" Ollie whispered and looked up at him with hooded eyes.

Matt curled one side of his mouth up in a grin. "But I'm your bastard. Now let's get upstairs and get you naked."

* * *

Ollie was exhausted and had fallen asleep the minute his head hit the pillow after Matt had wrung him out, first in the shower then later in bed. When he woke in the morning, he looked at the empty spot next to him and then at the note on the pillow.

Gone for a run xo—M

Matt didn't leave notes every morning, like he had when they'd first started dating. Now he did it when he wanted to remind Ollie of their early days, or when he was feeling contrite. Sometimes Ollie wished Matt would just say 'sorry' instead. He rolled over with a sigh and unplugged his phone.

He was scrolling through social media, something Matt hated, when Matt appeared in the doorway of their large bedroom, looking like a sweat covered god. Ollie raked his eyes over Matt's nearly naked body and felt the usual twinge in his cock. Something about that man, no matter how frustrating it was to love him, did something irrational to Ollie's insides.

"Morning, sleeping beauty," Matt said in his deep gravelly voice.

That was the gentle tone Ollie knew and loved, and it was so unlike the macho, bro-y one he'd used in the car with his former teammate. Matt had so many personas between family, and work, and with Ollie, now there was a new one that Ollie wasn't so sure he wanted to know. Ollie looked at the mug of coffee in Matt's hand and sighed.

"Thank you for the delivery."

"Who said this was for you?" Matt smirked and took a sip of the coffee.

"That's my bloody mug." Ollie raised his eyebrows, but he knew Matt was teasing.

Matt brought him coffee every morning without fail, and always in the mug Matt had given him for Christmas their second year together that said, *I love to wrap both my hands around it and swallow.* If that one was in the dishwasher, he'd bring coffee to Ollie in the mug from their third Christmas that said, *My sexual preference is… often.* Though that was the mug Matt used the most.

Ollie was always sure to hide those mugs when his parents came to visit.

Matt put the coffee on Ollie's side table and bent down to give him a sweaty kiss. One Ollie tolerated because with his own morning breath, he was in no position to complain.

"I love you. Remember we have that marketing meeting at nine thirty." Matt straightened and headed to the bathroom.

Ollie sipped his coffee and looked at his Rolex to see that it was just past eight. He picked up his phone and swiped into his email.

Twenty minutes later Matt was fully dressed in a charcoal Brioni suit with a white shirt and purple tie. His hair was perfectly mussed, and his jaw was smooth shaven, but it wouldn't be for long. Matt's five o'clock shadow always made an appearance by two-thirty or so.

Matt looked at his watch and then raised his eyebrows in that pissy, officer way of his. The way that made Ollie drag his feet and want to pull rank.

"I'm getting in the shower now." Ollie put down his phone, flung the covers back and rolled to his feet with a nonchalance he knew Matt wouldn't miss. .

He stopped to sniff Matt's neck and give him a kiss.

God, he smells like a dream, Ollie thought and then mentally smacked himself.

"You better hurry, or you'll be late," Ollie teased and skipped out of Matt's reach.

"I'll see you at nine-thirty, Oliver," Matt called after him.

You'll see me when you see me, Ollie thought rebelliously and turned on the shower.

Ollie strolled into the conference room with his laptop tucked under his arm and another coffee in his hand at quarter to ten and sat in his chair to Matt's right. He looked fucking gorgeous, and Matt didn't have the heart to admonish him for being late. Ollie was always late. Matt did, however, look meaningfully at his watch before turning back to Sandra, his VP of marketing, to indicate for her to continue.

Matt occasionally had to ignore when other executives were tardy (though those lapses were few and far between) in order to hide any show of favoritism toward Ollie. His team knew what was expected of them and they were paid quite well to focus on their jobs. As long as numbers were exceeded and there was no insubordination, his C-Suite pretty much had free reign to run their departments with little oversight.

The meeting progressed, and despite his tardiness Ollie was as incredibly well-prepared as usual. He asked all the right questions, questions that hadn't occurred to Matt, and had follow-up suggestions that went beyond his role as general counsel. Ollie proved yet again, that his worth to the company, *to Matt,* was immeasurable and totally worth the tardiness.

Matt let his gaze linger on Ollie's profile for a brief moment as Ollie conversed down the table with Sandra. His perfectly styled honey-blonde hair brushed the collar of his light blue Brooks Brothers shirt under his Tom Ford suit jacket, and his ear was the most intriguing blend of delicate and masculine. Ollie's lashes were long and the color of Cape Cod sand, and his nose was small and straight with a pointed tip Matt loved to kiss.

Matt blinked and looked away with measured boredom, careful not to be caught staring by anyone else in the room. He sat up and closed his laptop, which drew everyone's eye except Ollie's.

"Everything looks great. I look forward to the campaign and the sales it will bring in." Matt stood with a nod and left the room.

He made his way past the elevators to the suite of offices that he shared with Ollie and their assistants. The double glass doors at the end of the hall were framed on either side by white walls with the company logo on one side, and a large painting of the ocean Ollie had bought in Provincetown on the other. He strode through the entrance and nodded at Stacey, his steadfast, long-time assistant, who was seated at a large, sleek desk offset from the solid door to Matt's office, and then at Kerry, Ollie's loyal and equally long-serving assistant who sat at a matching desk outside Ollie's solid door. There was a floor to ceiling window next to Stacey's desk that overlooked the buildings along the waterfront of the Seaport and a row of cabinet doors in the wall to her right.

"Bob Almy's assistant sent over a revised contract," Stacey said and handed Matt a thick packet of paper held together with a large binder clip, "and your eleven o'clock got pushed to eleven fifteen. Do you want refreshments?"

"Thank you." Matt took the pages and crossed the room to his door. "And yes, the usual assortment of drinks, and please send someone to get those pastries I like from that bakery off Hanover."

"Will do."

Matt closed the door after flashing Stacey a smile. He depended on her almost as much as he depended on Ollie. He loved that he never needed to be specific with her, nor have to remember things like the name of the bakery or which restaurants he liked for which type of meeting or meal. She knew everything from his favorite foods to his biggest pet peeves to who in the company (and beyond) had access to how much of his time, and he compensated her handsomely for it.

Matt put his laptop and the papers from Stacey on his desk and woke his computer up with his password as he sat down in his chair. The sun was streaming in the massive windows behind his desk and Matt took a moment to admire the view of the harbor. Being on the water, even twenty-five stories up and behind a wall of glass, was calming and grounding to Matt's soul. The connection he'd had his whole life, to the ocean, or any body of water, ran deep into his marrow.

Looking out at the bustling harbor and the wide variety of boats sailing, speeding or trudging by, reminded him of the coming weekend and he blew out a breath. His SEAL team had been like a family. Most of the guys he loved like brothers, and a few he barely tolerated, but they had worked together and didn't let the bullshit get in the way of their missions. He was looking forward to seeing the three guys he'd been closest to, but why did it have to be at the expense of the one man he loved with all his being?

Because they would ridicule you for being gay. The whole world would judge you for it. You're a successful businessman who built a company from one idea, and if you were out, all that would go away and you would be reduced to the 'gay CEO, in love with his General Counsel.'

Matt clenched his jaw and turned back to his computer.

"What are you doing this weekend?" Ollie asked Naomi, his best girl-friend (the woman who acted as his 'beard' when Matt required it), as he looked at the harbor out the window behind his desk. He had checked through the glass door that connected his office to Matt's that Matt's office was empty before calling her.

"Well, I had a date, but he canceled. So, I was just gonna work on some ideas for Bill's guest cottages on Nantucket."

"Well, it just so happens some bloody moron did the same thing to me. So, what should we do to make it right for ourselves?"

"Oh no," Naomi commiserated. "Was it work again? I know you'd been looking forward to unplugging at the Cape."

"No, he's got some of his SEAL buddies coming to the beach house for the weekend. I can't really be mad, can I? He never sees them. In fact, he never talks about them." Ollie looked into Matt's empty office again. "Maybe he never does because the nicknames they have for each other are *too* ridiculous to repeat. What is it with *bros*?"

Naomi chuckled. "I suppose that is a good excuse for canceling, but you still have every right to be disappointed. Should we go to a spa? You can tell me all about their ridiculous nicknames while we're away. There's a new one in Ogunquit I've been hearing amazing things about."

The gay scene in Ogunquit was something Pedro, Ollie's hairdresser, had gone on and on about the last time he was in his chair. Ollie thought maybe they should go. Something about this weekend really itched under Ollie's skin in a way that being in the closet with Matt these past years hadn't before.

"Is it an overnight place? Or should I have Kerry find us something?"

Naomi squealed happily. "They have accommodations, but I think it's a dry venue, so let's find something on the water so we can have cocktails. I'll look at the menu of options and some restaurants for the rest of our time there and send them to you. We're gonna have so much fun!"

Ollie smiled at Naomi's enthusiasm, feeling his own spirits lift. "I'll buzz Kerry now. Love you."

"Love you too, Ollie." Naomi blew a kiss and ended the call.

Ollie put down his phone and reached for the handset on his desk as Matt appeared in the doorway between their offices. Matt had taken off his suit coat and cuffed his sleeves at some point in the day and Ollie paused to admire his muscled and veiny forearms.

"Hey," Matt said in a soft voice.

Ollie straightened in his chair and swiveled to face Matt. "Hey. What's up?"

Matt came to lean his hip against Ollie's desk and looked down at him with his arms crossed. "I want you at the Cape this weekend. I spoke with Chuck and if you don't mind too much, you can stay at her place. Bring Naomi," he said, using the nickname for Finn that he'd given her in their youth.

There was something in Matt's expression that tugged at Ollie's heart, but he was still feeling a little petty.

"Naomi and I are going to Ogunquit for the weekend. I was just about to have Kerry book us a house on the water."

Matt's eyes narrowed as he studied Ollie. "Ogunquit?"

It was clear from the look on Matt's face that he knew all about Ogunquit.

"Naomi heard about some spa there. Supposed to be amazing. Don't worry. I'll decline the happy ending of my massage."

Matt's jaw ticked and he ran a hand disgruntledly through the short waves of his hair. "No way, Oliver. You're not gonna have some *gay* man run his hands all over you. Tell Naomi that plans have changed and you're coming to the Cape." Matt stepped away from the desk and put his hands on the arms of Ollie's chair. "I promise I'll make it worth your while."

Matt leaned down and kissed Ollie so hard Ollie's head thumped into the cushioned back of his chair. His tongue breached Ollie's lips like a running back through a defensive line and then swirled around Ollie's tongue like a salsa dancer. It was a stunned moment that turned heated in the blink of an eye. Ollie found himself gripping the back of Matt's neck as he sucked Matt's bottom lip into his mouth. This was a full-on assault that Ollie quickly lost himself in the defense of. If Matt wanted to lay claim, Ollie was going to make him work for it. Ollie matched Matt kiss for kiss and felt his stomach swoop with want.

Why do I find his commands so hot? Why can't I stay mad?

They were questions Ollie had no answer for, or rather he knew the answers but was loathe to admit them to himself. He was smart and self-possessed; he knew his worth, but when it came to Matt, he was all too eager to hand over control. If Matt didn't already praise those independent traits of Ollie's, if Matt wasn't already more than fully aware of just how much he depended on Ollie for almost everything in his life, Ollie would be a puddle of shame at his lack of control.

Ollie felt Matt's fingers tighten in his hair and wondered just when it was that Matt had even put his hand there. He reached out and gripped

Matt's hips and pulled him forward, ready to unzip Matt's fly and get his mouth on Matt's cock.

Matt pulled away with a moan and pressed his forehead to Ollie's as he caught his breath. Ollie bit his lip and whimpered at the sudden loss of Matt's mouth. He looked at his computer and saw that nearly ten minutes had passed since Matt came into his office.

How was it that he always lost track of everything when Matt's lips and hands were on him?

Ollie shifted his gaze to Matt's mouth and saw that his lips were plump and glistening with saliva. His cock strained against his zipper with the knowledge that it was his tongue and his kisses that made Matt look so undone.

"I have a meeting in fifteen minutes." Matt adjusted himself in his pants and licked his lips. "We can save all of this for later." He swept his hand in a circle in front of Ollie. "Call Naomi back. Let her know of the change in plans."

Matt passed through the glass door between their offices with one last heated glance over his shoulder at Ollie. Ollie sat back in his chair, ran his fingertips over his lips and turned his attention to the latest draft of the employee sexual harassment document that Barbara, their head of human resources, had sent over, which deflated his erection in a heartbeat.

He mulled over the change of plans. Part of him wanted to go to Ogunquit just on principle (and to be a brat), but the other, larger part, really wanted to lay eyes on Matt's fellow sailors.

Ollie picked up his phone and tapped Naomi's name.

"That was fast!" Naomi answered.

"Hi. There's been a slight change of plans. How about our favorite spa in Wellfleet instead? I'll book us a couples massage and anything else you want. It's going on Matt's card, so pick whatever," Ollie said with a grin.

"Oh? What changed Matt's mind?"

"Honestly, I'm not sure. But perhaps he saw the error of his ways. We have to stay at Finn's, but it's no hardship really. Whoever designed that place did an amazing job. It's like five-star resort," Ollie teased. "It more than makes up for the fact I won't be sleeping in my own bed."

"Thank you. Though after designing your house, I see things I should've done differently at Finn's."

"Nonsense, it's perfect. And *Boston Magazine* agreed," Ollie praised.

"I am very grateful that Finn and you guys allowed them to photograph your homes. That feature brought in so much business I've hired four more designers."

"It didn't take Matt too much convincing. He got free publicity for SharkFinn out of it as well."

The eight-page feature was a huge hit, and while Ollie was happy for the exposure it brought Naomi and her design company, he resented being left out of the article and resented how the write-up alluded to Matt and Finn being romantically involved. Of course, Matt wouldn't have allowed the truth of his relationship with Ollie to be discovered and certainly not in a magazine spread, but it still chafed.

You agreed to be a secret, his brain reminded him.

And Matt had bent over backwards to make it up to him after the article came out, knowing that Ollie had been miffed (it wasn't like Ollie had hidden his displeasure). There had been a long weekend in Quebec, where Ollie had discovered his flawless *Metropolitan* French stood out like a sore thumb with the *Québecois*, and then a business trip to Bermuda where they rented a two-bedroom house on the water but shared the primary suite.

"Anyway," Ollie shook himself out of his musings, "I'll find out when we're leaving, and let you know."

"Sounds good. See you tomorrow!"

———

2

———

No Ordinary Love

MATT'S CELL PHONE BUZZED in his pocket the whole way home. Apparently, the group chat among the guys had been resurrected, and with a vengeance. By the time he reached the townhouse his phone was practically a vibrator, having gone off over thirty times at a near constant pace. When he finally checked, most of the texts were absolute nonsense, as usual, and the rest were planning the weekend.

> R2D2: The Kool Aid Man's hosting!

> Paddy: Sweet! Thx KAM

> Downtown: I gotta ask the missus

> Paddy: Ask? More like
> don't ask don't tell, amiright?

> Downtown: First of all that's gay
> and second of all I gotta clear it

with her, that's why I'm married,
and your 2x divorced

Paddy: *you're

R2D2: Quit your bickering. KAM, what's
the address? R u near the beach?

Paddy: Why? You gonna storm it?
KAM, plz don't let him turn this into a
mission. I just wanna drink - r u near
a bar?

Downtown: Not sure how many bars
are out that far. He's in no man's land
At least that's what my FIL said

Paddy: Wait, where is his place?

There were eleven more texts about the geography of the Cape and the distance between Downtown's in-laws' in Sandwich, and Matt's place in Truro. That quickly devolved into several more texts regarding the location of Provincetown, not only in relation to Truro, but also in relation to its location at the tip of the flexed-arm shape of Cape Cod. Matt winced at the fisting jokes and gay slurs and scrolled until he got near the end.

Downtown: Kool Aid- u there?

R2D2: U guys know he hates
the chatter. He prob muted us.

Paddy:

Matt leaned against the kitchen island and typed out his response.

> Are you kids FINALLY done?
> My house is on the beach.
> There's a bar you'll like the
> next town over. See you Fri.

He typed in his address and then muted the conversation. He put down his phone, stripped off his suit coat and tie and crossed to the fridge with his stomach growling. By the time he'd pulled out the shrimp, tomatoes, zucchini, garlic, and a can of white beans, and made himself some cheese and crackers, Ollie was walking through the doorway from the stairs. He watched Ollie scan his eyes over him and then put his laptop folio on the counter against the far wall they used for mail and things.

"Are you making dinner?" Ollie asked in a teasing tone. "Shall I get the fire extinguisher?"

Matt grabbed Ollie by the waist as he came closer and nuzzled into his neck, inhaling the soft and expensive scent that was exclusively Ollie. He smelled like sandalwood and sunshine and something underneath that was indescribable and irresistible to Matt. Matt placed a kiss on Ollie's jaw, near his ear and pulled back.

"No. But this is what I want for dinner, and you had the ingredients." Matt smiled and sat in a barstool at the island. "I will chop and dice whatever you need me to."

Ollie ran his hand through Matt's hair and then turned to leave the kitchen. "Mince four cloves of garlic and get the zoodle maker out of the cabinet, unless you want the zucchini in chunks. Oh, and thaw the shrimp in a colander under cold water. Just going to change, I'll be right back."

Matt stuffed the last bit of cheese and crackers into his mouth and grabbed the chef's knife from the block on the counter. He set about the tasks Ollie had given him and then stepped aside to let Ollie take over when he returned wearing snug grey sweatpants and one of Matt's well-worn US Navy t-shirts that was a size too big on him.

Someone's looking for some action tonight, he thought to himself as he palmed Ollie's ass on his way back to the barstool.

Matt knew Ollie was very aware of how much he loved seeing Ollie in his t-shirts, not to mention those joggers that molded around the perfect c-curve of Ollie's ass. Matt sat back with his glass of water and watched Ollie's muscles flex as he worked the zucchini through the zoodle maker.

Ollie looked over his shoulder. "Don't just sit there drooling, peel the shrimp." He nodded to the sink.

Matt smirked and crossed the kitchen to turn off the water and set about his assigned task. They discussed work and travel as they prepped the ingredients, Ollie always one step ahead and somehow miraculously transforming said ingredients into a delicious meal. Soon the kitchen was filled with the aroma of sauteed garlic, sizzling shrimp and fresh herbs.

Matt washed his hands and came up behind Ollie at the stove. He rested his hands on Ollie's hips, teasing his thumbs under the hem of his shirt to touch Ollie's soft skin and leaned in.

"The difference between eating in a restaurant and eating here is the added ambiance," Matt said before dipping his face into Ollie's neck and breathing deeply. "Food just tastes better when you make it. Smells better too." Matt bit the soft flesh where Ollie's neck met his shoulder and rolled his hips against Ollie's ass.

Ollie chuckled and shrugged his shoulder to nudge Matt away. "Have a seat, you can grope me after my conference call."

Matt watched as Ollie dished out the meal onto two plates, one heaping for Matt, and one half-full for himself. They sat at the kitchen island and ate quietly as Ollie prepped for his meeting. Matt scrolled through emails on his phone while watching Ollie chew carefully as he typed one-handed on his laptop.

Matt finished his dinner well before Ollie and stole a shrimp off Ollie's plate before getting up to clean the kitchen. Ollie left his nearly empty plate on the island with a kiss for Matt and took a dress shirt and tie into his home office for a video call with SharkFinn's legal team in Palo Alto.

Matt watched him leave the kitchen and thought of all he and Ollie had been through over the past few years as he loaded the dishwasher, before turning his thoughts to the upcoming weekend. He and his SEAL team had been close, they had to be in order to work as well as they did together, but they never really knew Matt. Not truly. It wasn't because he was an officer and they were enlisted, those lines blurred in a group as small as theirs. There were twelve men on his team, unlike regular military platoons where there could be five times that. No, they never knew Matt, because hardly anyone knew him. In fact, Ollie was the only one who did, and Finn was a close second.

When Matt had realized he was different from his peers, that his interest in other boys in high school was something to hide at all costs, he crafted a persona and lived it so convincingly that he almost fooled himself. In fact, before he met Ollie, there had only been one other man that he had sex with: a teenager when Matt was a teenager.

And that had ended badly.

Matt turned his focus back to the weekend and to developing a plan of how he would get to see Ollie and his SEAL buddies without any overlap or hurt feelings. He slid the dishwasher drawer closed and headed to his home office overlooking Marlborough Street.

"What on earth is this ancient music, Lieutenant? The *Gilligan's Island* theme song?" Ollie asked as he walked into Matt's home office a few hours later. He was fresh from the shower though his hair was dry. He had changed back into the Navy t-shirt and grey joggers.

Matt looked up from his CFO, Fred's, email and paused to run his eyes over Ollie, before shaking his head with a laugh. "*Never My Love*, by the Association. You don't know it?" he asked incredulously.

"No, Matt. I don't even listen to the Beatles."

Matt crossed the room to stand in front of Ollie. "My father would pull my mother away from whatever it was she was doing when this song came on," Matt exhaled with a small sound, "and make her dance with him. He loved this kind of music, and Sinatra and Tony Bennett, of course." He put his hands on Ollie's waist as Ollie put his arms around Matt's neck. Matt smiled softly and began to sway to the music, his hips rolling into Ollie's groin suggestively. "I think of you now when I hear this song." He kissed Ollie. "I love you."

Ollie hummed with pleasure. "I love you too. This song was nice," Ollie said as the song faded into the next one. Maroon 5 blared jarringly through the speakers in contrast to the soft tones of the Association. "Now this song, I know. I remember you chasing me around your flat in the North End to this song. But please tell me your playlist is on shuffle, and not that you mixed it like this, Deejay Dion. Horrible contrast," Ollie said with a laugh. "Don't give up your day job."

Matt smiled and raised his eyebrows as he poked Ollie's tickle spot. "Yes, it's on shuffle, but the universe must have known, because I will be preying on you tonight. You know I get so high when I'm inside you."

Ollie bit his lip and hummed. "Let's go to bed. It's late, you need to stop working. That's why I was coming in here in the first place." He paused. "Or, you could fuck me in here. Surely you have one of your ever-present bottles of Swiss Navy handy." He licked Matt's bottom lip. "You have one of those things stashed in every room, you horny perv."

Matt grinned against Ollie's mouth. "I have to. Jesus, you claw at me non-stop."

Ollie rolled his head back with a laugh. "You're the insatiable one. Christ, why do you think I have to sleep so much?"

Matt kissed the column of Ollie's throat, sending shivers down Ollie's spine. "Who's the one who came in here looking to get laid?" Matt asked raising his eyebrows while lifting Ollie's shirt over his head.

Goosebumps erupted over Ollie's skin as Matt ran his warm hands up his sides. He circled Ollie's pebbled nipples with his thumbs as he continued to place open mouthed kisses on Ollie's neck and shoulder.

"I live with the most gorgeous man, who has the most magnificent cock, and he fucks me like a god. Surely, I'm not expected to keep my hands to myself," Ollie replied softly and closed his eyes in response to the feeling of Matt's tongue on his jaw. "Christ, how did I get so lucky?"

Matt's hum was like a growl as he kissed Ollie and guided him backwards. Ollie felt the hard edge of Matt's desk against his thigh and looked over his shoulder to watch Matt lift the lid of a box next to his computer. Matt paused with a grin, a small clear bottle in his tight grip. His eyes skimmed heatedly over Ollie's hairless chest, leaving a trail of fire in their wake.

Matt claimed Ollie's mouth with unrelenting passion, his lips firm and his tongue tender, as Ollie lifted the hem of Matt's shirt and ran his fingertips up Matt's solid body. Matt kissed from Ollie's lips to his neck and murmured endearments in Italian into Ollie's ear. The heat in Matt's words, and the grip he had on Ollie's waist had Ollie fumbling with the waistband of Matt's lounge pants with clumsy and tingling fingers.

Matt gripped Ollie's wrists. "Take off your sweats, then turn around and spread your legs," he commanded huskily.

Ollie whimpered and dropped his pants without hesitation.

"Commando, huh? What a needy slut you are, Oliver," Matt murmured with a grin.

Ollie turned around with a smirk and then yelped when Matt's hand came down with a loud smack on his ass cheek. He grabbed the edge of the desk with both hands and then shuddered reflexively when he felt Matt's hand run slowly down his spine and then up between his thighs. Matt knees creaked slightly as he knelt down and ghosted his nose up the crack of Ollie's ass. Ollie heard Matt's deep inhale just before he felt Matt's teeth nip the soft flesh of the roundest part of his cheek.

He squeaked and jerked away, which earned him another sharp crack of Matt's palm on his other cheek.

"Don't move. I can do whatever I want to this perfect ass. It's mine," Matt stated in his gravelly voice and gripped both of Ollie's cheeks in his hands to spread Ollie open.

Ollie felt the warm press of Matt's tongue a moment later as he licked a stripe from his taint to the top of his crack.

"Mmmm," Matt hummed happily. "Sugar and spice and everything nice."

Matt dove back in and Ollie nearly collapsed as his knees threatened to buckle with pleasure. Matt was a wizard with his tongue and knew just how to drive Ollie wild. He alternated between lapping and praising Ollie's hole, mostly in Italian, and then switched to gentle circles.

Ollie moaned when Matt's tongue stopped teasing and delved inside him. He lowered his chest to the desk and pressed his hips back chasing the sensation. Ollie let his head sag forward as he took a deep breath.

"Patience," Matt murmured, and smacked Ollie's ass again.

"It feels so good, I can't help it and you know it."

Ollie opened his eyes when he felt Matt's hand wrap around his cock. He ducked his head and watched Matt's long, thick fingers stroke up and over the tip to gather the pre-cum that was pooling there.

"So needy. So wet for me," Matt said as he pulled his hand away.

Ollie looked over his shoulder. "Bloody hell," he moaned as Matt pushed his now slick finger inside his hole.

Matt's tongue swirled around his finger as he pumped it in and out. He added a second finger and swept them both over that sweet spot that made Ollie's legs quiver. Matt had known almost nothing about the internal workings of the male anatomy when they first got together but had made it his mission to find out just what drove Ollie wild.

Matt gripped Ollie's hip with his other hand and stood, pulling Ollie out of his euphoric state and trip down memory lane. Matt kissed his way up Ollie's back and with a nip on Ollie's naked shoulder, he stepped away.

Ollie whined at the sudden emptiness, which earned him another light smack on his bottom. He looked over his shoulder.

"I can't fuck you with my pants on, Oliver," Matt said with a smile and quickly shed his t-shirt and sweats. "Now, where was I?"

Matt's hard length nestled between Ollie's cheeks as Matt wrapped his arms around Ollie's waist. Matt rutted against his lower back with a moan and some more huskily murmured Italian. He nibbled on Ollie's ear and tweaked a nipple between his fingertips as his breathing became urgent and strained. Ollie's cock jumped in response, and he wiggled his hips encouragingly.

"Stop teasing me, Lieutenant." Ollie turned his head, grabbed the back of Matt's neck and held him in place as he devoured Matt's mouth. Matt's hands roamed over Ollie's skin, touching every inch of his body as he sucked on Ollie's tongue and panted into Ollie's mouth. He felt Matt fumble on the desk for the lube and then heard the snap of the lid. A moment later Matt's cold, wet fingers were pressing back into him.

Matt sighed and rolled his hips, leaving a trail of pre-cum along Ollie's ass cheek. "You're so fucking tight. I love how this tiny little star takes my big dick. Like it was made for it. Made for me." Matt twisted and spread his fingers inside Ollie as he spoke.

"I'd really love it if you'd get said cock inside me," Ollie said with a moan. "I'm ready."

Matt nibbled along the side of Ollie's neck and pulled his hand away. Ollie bit back his disappointment at the loss of Matt's fingers again as he waited. His stomach fluttered wildly in anticipation as he heard the slick sound of Matt coating his cock with lube. He glanced back, unable to resist a glimpse of Matt's massive cock before it disappeared inside him. It was a work of art, perfectly formed with a fat mushroom head that was usually half-hidden by foreskin, and a long shaft that curved ever so slightly upward.

I truly can't believe that thing fits inside me, Ollie thought for the thousandth time. *It burns, but in the best way.*

Ollie craned his neck to watch as Matt spread him open with one hand and guided his cock into the space he'd created with his other. Ollie exhaled the breath he hadn't been aware he was holding and bore down as Matt eased in. Matt's eyes flicked up to catch Ollie's gaze and Ollie moaned at the passion he found reflecting back at him.

Matt turned his focus back to what he was doing with hooded lids. "That's it. Swallow my dick. Suck me in," Matt said and rubbed his thumb across Ollie's ass as he squeezed the flesh tight enough to turn his fingertips white.

Ollie raised up on his toes and let his head sag forward as Matt sank deeper. He was lost in the sensation of being stretched to the limit, as though it were his first time with Matt all over again. It wasn't always like this, sometimes it was hard and fast, both of them with their eye on the clock, and other times it was slow and lazy; comfortable. This was like new again, and Ollie felt everything Matt was doing in every cell of his body.

Ollie had lost track of the music several songs ago (as usual with Matt), but when Matt finally bottomed out, his hips nestled flush against Ollie's bottom and his hands firmly gripping Ollie's hips, the drum and bass beat caught his ear.

This is no ordinary love... Sade crooned through the speakers in the ceiling.

"I love this song," Ollie whispered to himself as Matt pulled out at Ollie's nod and then slid back in.

"I do too," Matt agreed and covered Ollie's back with his chest. His chest hair tickled Ollie's skin, waking up the nerves all over his body.

Ollie gasped in time with Matt's thrusts as they became more urgent. Matt shifted his grip from Ollie's hips to his shoulders as he leaned back with a grunt. Ollie spread his legs and arched his back as he sought the perfect angle of Matt's cock against his prostate.

"Jesus, Ollie. You feel like heaven."

Matt's rhythm was hypnotic and intense as he varied his pace with the music, finally settling his grip on Ollie's hips and squeezing to hold him in place. Ollie knew without looking just what Matt was focused on and gripped the edge of the desk as it jolted across the floor with each snap of Matt's hips. He was stuffed full of Matt and yet the pressure wasn't quite enough. Ollie braced himself on his elbows as he continued to chase the perfect angle.

"Touch me," Ollie breathed.

Matt hummed low, again like a growl, and ran his hands down Ollie's torso teasingly, before pulling out. Matt spun Ollie around and lifted him to perch on the edge of the desk so fast Ollie barely had time to complain. He gripped Ollie's thighs, Ollie's legs draped over his forearms, and slipped back in. Ollie threw his head back with a cry of delight as Matt's cock pounded against his prostate.

"I know this is what you wanted." Matt snapped his hips forward and Ollie's eyes rolled back in his head. "Just the right angle now, huh?" Matt asked with a smirk.

Ollie couldn't do anything but nod and moan as Matt pressed Ollie's knees into his chest and began thrusting in earnest. Not only was the angle perfect, but Matt was so deep Ollie swore he felt him hitting the underside of his heart. Ollie's hard cock was slapping and dripping on his stomach like a telegraph sending out an urgent code.

It was fucking urgent alright.

"You can't come yet, Ollie," Matt commanded, as though reading Ollie's mind.

"Fuuuck. I can't make any promises, Lieutenant. Not with you fucking me, like a god," Ollie moaned breathlessly, drawing out the 'o.'

Matt leaned forward and Ollie raised up, his stomach muscles tightening with the effort as he met Matt's mouth in a bruising kiss. Matt's hand gripped Ollie's throat while the other remained firmly around Ollie's thigh. Ollie relaxed back and Matt followed, his body trapping Ollie against the desk.

Matt's washboard abs rubbed against Ollie's cock, and Ollie felt his balls draw up as the pressure of Matt's thumb against his windpipe restricted his oxygen. Matt never squeezed too hard or for too long, so Ollie relaxed into the sensation. His mind floated on a wave of pleasure so intense he almost felt incapable of orgasming.

Almost.

He heard Matt as though from far away, and the ragged moan, the utter wrecked-sounding cadence of Matt's voice sent Ollie over the edge.

"Oh … god … Ollie," Matt groaned as his cock pulsed and filled Ollie so full, the cum spilled out of him and onto the floor with each thrust.

The rest of what Matt said was lost to the roar in Ollie's ears as he came with a blinding flash. Matt's grip on his throat eased at the same time his teeth sunk gently into the flesh where Ollie's shoulder met his neck. Matt cradled Ollie's head in his hands as he kissed every bit of skin on Ollie's face and then sighed into his mouth.

"I love you."

"I love you too," Ollie replied as his heartbeat continued to pound wildly in his chest. After a moment, of Matt catching his breath and cradling Ollie close to his chest, Ollie shifted when the pressure of something underneath him became too painful to ignore. He shifted his shoulders with a wince. "What the fuck is under me?"

Matt slid his hand under Ollie's back and with a chuckle pulled out a small dish of paperclips and a pen. "Whoops. You should've said something."

"I didn't notice until just now." Ollie laughed and held Matt's gaze. "Hard to notice anything when your tongue is in my mouth or when your cock is in my ass." Ollie quirked his eyebrow and looked down at his cum covered chest. Matt returned the grin and bent to lick the splatters off Ollie's skin. Ollie rested his head back on the desk and closed his eyes as Matt's tongue bathed him clean.

"You taste like a beach holiday," Matt declared when he was done, and his soft cock had slipped out of Ollie. "Stay put. I've got a towel here in my drawer."

Ollie laughed at the ceiling. Of course, Matt had a towel in his desk drawer. The man was prepared for everything. Ollie studied Matt as he swabbed gently between Ollie's legs. There was such a look of concentration on Matt's face, a look of soft reverence (one he always had after they'd made love) and it was in moments like these when Ollie could read Matt like an open book and could speak to him about almost anything.

Ollie considered asking about the plans for the weekend and opened his mouth to speak when the 'book' snapped shut and Matt clutched the towel in his fist as he held his hand out to Ollie to help him off the desk with a shuttered gaze. Matt nuzzled into Ollie's neck as he steadied him on his jelly legs and ghosted his lips up Ollie's neck, over his jaw and onto Ollie's mouth before pulling back.

"Thank you, princess. Now get your sexy ass to bed," Matt said softly and bent to gather their clothes.

"That was incredible," Ollie breathed as he watched Matt sort their clothes. "Are you coming to bed too?"

"I'll be up in a minute," Matt replied.

Ollie leaned into Matt as he took his clothes. He rubbed his face against Matt's five o'clock shadow and kissed his chiseled jawline. "Okay," Ollie replied, knowing full well he'd be fast asleep before Matt joined him.

3

The Boys are Back in Town

"I'M REALLY LOOKING FORWARD to the weekend," Naomi smiled and patted Ollie's thigh as he pulled out of her driveway. She had on a wide-brim sun hat and a billowy sundress as though summer wasn't officially about to end with the coming of Labor Day. "What's the plan?"

Ollie shifted through the gears and headed toward the highway. "I was thinking dinner at Mac's in Wellfleet tonight, then tomorrow I've booked us for yoga, massages, and all-around pampering at Eden's, where we'll eat lunch in between treatments." Ollie glanced at Naomi with a grin. "Something green and utterly too healthy for words. Then wherever you want for dinner on Saturday. And Sunday we'll have breakfast, do some yoga and then lay out on the deck or the beach, or we can go to the club and play tennis. How does that sound?"

"Sounds amazing." Naomi flopped back in her seat with a happy sigh. "I really need the break. Work has been so demanding."

"I hear that." Ollie nodded in agreement.

"Are we going to see Matt and his *bros*?" Naomi turned her head to look at Ollie.

"I'm not sure. He was a little vague. I get the feeling he wants to suss them out first before inviting us over." Ollie looked over his shoulder as he merged onto the highway and shifted through the gears to accelerate into the fast lane. "It's a guys' weekend, but I'm betting Matt would have felt better if Chuck had been able to be make an appearance."

"I talked to Finn yesterday. She's on Nantucket to help her dad close up the house and cottages. They do it every Labor Day weekend and she said she'd try to swing through before having to go back to Baltimore to teach."

"Oh, right." Ollie nodded. "I offered my assistance, but Bill said he had Chuck and his caretaking team. To be honest, I think he wanted the alone time with her. He misses her, and tells me every time I see him," Ollie said. "Besides, I'm not very good at things like that. Gardens and horses, yes. Manual labor and winterizing homes, not so much."

"Everyone has their strengths," Naomi said and squeezed Ollie's shoulder. "God knows I stay in my lane."

"And you own that lane like a boss," Ollie replied and took her hand to kiss her knuckles as he kept the other on the steering wheel. "I am in awe of your talent."

"Thank you, Ollie," Naomi said with a sigh. "Now I just need to find a straight guy who appreciates me and my work like you do."

Ollie let go of her hand and downshifted as the merging traffic from the lane drop caused a slowdown. He then accelerated a few moments later as the pressure wave smoothed and then was able to spare another glance at Naomi.

"What about Craig? Or Greg, was it? He seemed nice." Ollie tucked back into the fast lane and spared Naomi a glance.

Naomi sighed. "He turned out to be threatened by my career… and you. I told him you were my ex but that we were still close, and he couldn't deal with that."

"I'm sorry," Ollie said earnestly, suddenly full of remorse for what their ruse had put on her. "I don't want to stand in the way of you finding love. Bloody hell. I release you from your duties as my beard. Darling, your happiness means more to me than me having a fake girlfriend, and you don't have to say I'm an ex. The lie only matters on my end; I can just as easily say I never got over you if anyone asks why I'm single, which would be entirely true if I were straight."

Naomi made a frustrated sound. "Ollie! When you say things like that it just makes me love you more. Stop being so perfect.

"But really, me having you as my 'ex' weeds out the insecure men. Besides, I'd have to hide all our pictures, and if I never mentioned you, then I would never know who had the fragile ego. I will find my prince, and he will love you, or it's a deal breaker." She shrugged and leaned her head on his shoulder.

Ollie focused on the traffic in front of him as he thought about their relationship, and the unfair burden it put on her. How was she to be expected to live her own life, and find love, if she was tethered to him? He knew Matt had the same effect on Finn's love life, though Matt actively chased all the men away from her, but wasn't it unfair for them to ask this of Finn and Naomi?

Matt got to the beach house with a few hours to spare before the guys arrived. He checked on the food and beers he'd had arranged to be delivered by the local guy he'd found who ran a small caretaking company of sorts. Matt paid him a lot of money to check on things in the off-season and to run errands, and to do so without any questions or snooping, and he was worth every penny.

Matt then made sure that nothing of Ollie's was downstairs, though Matt kept the house so tidy there were very few of their personal items in the living spaces to begin with. He scooped up two of Ollie's gay romance books and grabbed the photo that Finn had taken of him and Ollie the previous summer, sitting side by side and shirtless on the gunwale of his boat, off the living room wall. He and Ollie weren't touching in the picture, though their pinkies nearly were, but with their matching necklaces (Matt's with the dime-sized moon pendant, and Ollie's with the tiny trident that matched Matt's tattoo) the image radiated an intimacy that he was sure Arturo wouldn't miss.

That man missed nothing.

Matt put the books and the photo in Ollie's home office overlooking Ollie's rose garden and locked the door.

I shouldn't have invited them, he worried.

Matt went back to the living room and hung the photo of his sisters and their families on his beach that he'd taken earlier that summer in the empty spot. He went upstairs to check the bedroom he shared with Ollie and saw evidence of Ollie everywhere. There was another romance book on his side table, hand lotion on the shelf below, and a pair of Ollie's pink suede, monogrammed slippers half sticking out from under the tall bed. He swept the items into the drawer under the shelf and moved Ollie's slippers to the large walk-in closet.

Matt stripped off his suit and went to the bathroom to turn on the shower. He put his clothes in the hampers, one for dry cleaning and one for laundry, and stepped into the glass and marble enclosure. There was even more evidence of Ollie in that space: his array of shampoos, conditioners, body wash, and lotions, and then there was the lube. The bottle was half empty, but Matt knew there were two more large ones under the sink from when Ollie went to Provincetown back in July with Naomi.

Matt scrubbed his hair and then his body as he remembered the stories Ollie had come back with from 'Bear Week.' According to Ollie, by way of the waiter at Ollie's favorite restaurant, Bear Week was the best week all summer and followed the 'worst' one, Circuit Week. Matt knew nothing about any of that, and really didn't care to know, as there was nothing about the LGBT community that he identified with. But Ollie had gone on and on, so Matt had half-listened and gleaned that one was the week of bitchy gays who 'tipped like shit,' and the other was the week of hugs for everyone and tips that actually paid some bills. Matt's ears had perked up at the 'hugs for everyone,' and he'd caught Ollie's sly smile, which earned Ollie a two-minute tickle session, followed by five minutes of bare ass spanks, and then a sixty-nine which left them both drained and breathless.

Matt came out of his trip down memory lane to find himself soaping his half-hard dick and shook his head as he pulled his hand away. There was no time for an orgasm. His buddies would be there in less than twenty minutes.

He quickly rinsed and dried, then dressed in jeans and a white button down before using a dab of Ollie's styling cream to arrange his hair in the messy style Ollie loved. He pulled on socks and went back downstairs, just as he heard tires crunching on the seashell driveway.

They're here.

Matt slipped on the driving mocs Ollie had given him for his birthday and opened the door. He stepped onto the porch as his buddies flung themselves out of Jules' truck.

"What the fuck, Kool Aid!" Joe declared in his loud voice. "This is a fucking palace!"

Matt grinned and stepped off the porch for bro hugs and teasing. Joe caught him first. He was tall, a few inches taller than Matt, and his lean body had filled out in the years since Matt had last seen him. Joe's auburn hair was trim, with a bit of grey at the temples, and his brown eyes darted around as he spoke.

"You've been holding out on us," Joe said with a good-natured grin.

Jules pushed Joe aside with a scoff. "I've been here a million times," he said convincingly. "Kam just begged me to never tell you." He winked at Matt and pulled him into a brief hug.

Jules was built like a brick shithouse, he'd always been the largest of their team, but he was significantly larger than he'd been in the service. He'd definitely put on at least fifty pounds, though it was all muscle. His bald head was shiny, just like he wore it in the service, but the trim black beard, that artfully framed the broad smile he had for Matt, was new.

Jules let go of Matt's hand and punched Joe's shoulder before turning to get the bags from the back of his truck. Joe rubbed his shoulder and grumbled as Arturo stepped forward with his arms spread.

"Kool Aid," he said with a smirk and dancing eyes.

"R2," Matt responded with wide arms of his own and slapped Arturo heartily on the back.

Matt stepped back and swept his eyes over Arturo. He hadn't changed except that his black hair was longer and swept over his forehead in a manner similar to how Ollie wore his, and that his physique had slimmed down to sinewy, toned muscle like a martial artist. His brown eyes were so dark they looked black, and he had a deep tan like he'd been spending quite a bit of time on the beach.

"You're looking good, old man. The playboy life suits you," Matt teased.

Arturo punched Matt's bicep lightly and narrowed his eyes. "Working for The Company is anything but living the playboy life."

Matt nodded at Arturo and took the bag Joe handed him. "I know, but you've clearly leaned into the cover with gusto."

Joe threw his head back and laughed the loud laugh Matt had missed. "He got you, R2. And I don't believe for a second that what you do is all that hard, mi *hombre*."

Matt laughed and joked with them as he showed them to their rooms and gave them a brief tour of the house and the view of the beach. He waited for them to get settled before asking what they wanted to do for the evening.

"Are there any clubs out here?" Joe turned from the view of the beach to face Matt.

"Not the kind you like, Paddy, no. But we've got a bar that has food, and dancing, and chicks that are out of college by a few years," Matt responded in a dry tone, remembering in a flash Joe's need to go out and be seen.

"Sweet!" Joe smacked Arturo on his chest with the back of his hand. "Let's get cleaned up and hit the town."

Fifteen minutes later they were piling into a rideshare headed for Jack's, a bar that was almost identical to the Beachcomber in Wellfleet but with a slightly older crowd and nowhere near a collapsing bluff. The outside bar was packed and inside was less so, but Matt noticed the band setting up and knew it wouldn't be long before the crowd migrated indoors.

Eyes followed them as they made their way inside. Even years later, the four of them stood out like sore thumbs with how they moved in sync. Perhaps each on their own could pass through public places without giving off a 'former military' vibe, but the four of them together definitely had no hope of flying under the radar.

"First round's on me," Arturo announced. "What's everyone having?"

Matt found a high-top with four barstools next to one of the open windows along the front while Arturo went to the bar with their drink orders. Matt sat and surveyed the space and noticed Jules and Joe doing the same. They all had scanned the corners and the room upon entering, by habit, but now they took their time sizing up the crowd.

All the college kids had long since left the Cape for school (not that they'd frequent Jack's if they were still on the Cape) and the crowd that remained were around Matt's age, with a few over-forty people sprinkled around. These were people taking advantage of the holiday weekend and the still vibrant bar scene that would eventually peter out by early October.

Arturo appeared with a tray full of pints and shots, and a broad grin on his face. Matt noticed the limes and shaker of salt and shook his head.

"Come on now, Lieutenant. Surely, you've made peace with the king of Mexico," Arturo crooned as he set down the tray and began lining up the shot glasses.

"No, R2. That bastard still pisses me off. I'm good with beer." Matt grabbed a pint and drank half the glass. "You bitches can fight over mine." He grinned at the group.

Jules swept the shot glass away from Joe's outstretched hand with a triumphant cackle. "I'm bigger than you and can hold my alcohol."

Matt laughed as Jules tossed back the first shot of tequila, sucked a lime, and then downed the second. "I'm gonna have to pay a cleaning fee again for the car ride home, aren't I, Downtown?"

"Fuck you, Kool Aid. That was food poisoning."

Matt threw his head back and laughed with the rest of the guys. It was the comment that broke the thin film of uncertainly that had been built up by years of distance. Matt felt in that moment that he and the guys were right back in the desert, right back doing drills and training and living in each other's space.

"Then how come none of us got sick?" Joe chimed in and then licked the salt off the side of his thumb and tossed back his tequila shot.

Jules sucked his teeth and grumbled into his beer. "It's why I don't drink brown liquor no more."

"Bygones," Arturo interrupted with a wave of his hand. "No brown booze for Downtown, no tequila for Kool Aid, and no puking from any-one tonight." He raised his shot glass and tossed it back with flourish.

"Solid plan, R2. But let's not forget about the ladies." Joe waggled his eyebrows. "Kam, turn and face the room so they can all get an eye-ful. I miss having you as my wingman." He shot a glance at Jules and then Arturo. "He's married and scary, and R2 likes to keep them all for himself."

"Now, now, bruh. I can't help that the ladies prefer Latino to Irish mutt." Arturo ran his hand through his hair with a smirk.

The two of them went back and forth trading barbs while Matt thought of Ollie. Most of Ollie's friends knew he was gay, maybe all of them did. Matt never asked Ollie if he had told his soccer friends or any of the people he played polo with. The fact that Ollie wouldn't care if anyone knew was something that still baffled Matt. He looked at his friends and then around the bar, catching more than a few women's eyes, and felt a flash of anxiety at the thought of his friends finding out he was in love with a man.

Head over heels in love with a man.

They would never look at me the same way, and I couldn't stomach that.

Ollie would probably tell him he was overreacting. That people don't care one way or the other, but he was wrong, and Matt would never budge on that.

"Kool Aid. Matt." Joe snapped his fingers in front of Matt's face. "There're two different groups of women looking our way and you've gone off to la la land. Pick one and summon them with your eyes while I flag down a waitress for more shots."

"I've got a girlfriend. I don't think she'd appreciate this." Matt raised his eyebrows.

"She doesn't need to know, and you don't have to do anything but get them over here for R2 and I." Joe looked at Jules and then back at Matt. "It's pathetic that you guys have taken yourselves off the market. Especially with all these beauties just waiting to be wooed."

"Wooed?" Jules deadpanned. "What are you, seventy?"

Joe rolled his eyes and turned in his seat to catch the server's eye.

Matt looked around to see which groups Joe was referring to. He saw what looked like a bachelorette party and instantly dismissed them.

No, thank you.

There was a group of twenty-somethings near where the band was setting up that he considered briefly, especially when two of the women who had been close talking with each other met his eye and smiled.

Hmm, maybe.

As he continued his scan of the bar, he noticed two attractive women standing near the bar. They were probably in their early thirties, and neither was wearing a wedding ring, not that that meant anything. If he gave them an inviting up nod, they would most definitely come to their table, and then he wouldn't be obligated to flirt with anyone, and neither would Jules.

"Not those two," Arturo leaned in. "They're waiting on dates."

"How do you know?"

"The blonde keeps checking her watch and the redhead just put on more lipstick."

Sure enough, a minute later the women turned with smiles as two guys wearing polo shirts and likely too much cologne, approached them.

Matt looked back at Arturo's grinning face. "You got lucky," he scoffed, while knowing that wasn't true.

"Not yet I haven't, but if you flash a smile with me at the ladies standing by the window at your six, I just might be later."

Two hours later, after watching the guys do more shots and eat their body weight in chicken wings, while he stuck to beer, Matt was making small talk with a corporate travel planner from somewhere he couldn't remember. Arturo had vanished with the blonde account manager in the mini-skirt, Joe was off dancing with the account manager's co-worker, and Jules was regaling the two remaining women with stories about his kids.

It was loud once the band started up, and the woman Matt was talking to kept leaning in close to be heard. She touched his arm every time she laughed and asked him probing questions. Matt kept his answers vague; he didn't need her to know who he really was. He told her he was self-employed and worked in security, but he was very direct and firm with his declaration of seeing someone. He didn't want there to be any doubt that he was not available.

She was pretty, and probably someone he would've slept with before Ollie, but Matt could barely remember what it was like to be attracted to women. She didn't have Ollie's broad shoulders, or his perfectly balanced mouth, or his long muscular legs. She didn't smell like sandalwood and expensive lotion and crisp autumn days. She didn't have a sense of humor that made his sides ache with laughter, or hair that made his fingers tingle with want to touch, or an accent and voice so melodic it made every word sound like a hymn. She certainly couldn't curl his toes in ecstasy with just her mouth. His heart wouldn't pound like a bass drum as he thrust into her over and over. Her moans wouldn't fill his ears and drive him to the brink every time like Ollie's did.

He felt his dick twitch with the thought of just how much he loved fucking Ollie, and brought his attention back to whatever it was that the woman (Sandra? Sarah?) was saying.

"And it was incredible," she finished with a smile.

"Sounds it," Matt replied and finished his beer.

Matt looked at his watch and saw it was after midnight. He met Jules' eye just as Jules was yawning and made a subtle head nod to the door. "What d'ya say, Downtown? If you guys wanna go fishing tomorrow, we better head out."

Jules stood and stretched. "I'll go check on the boys."

They said their goodbyes to the women and abandoned the table. Jules went in search of Joe and Arturo while Matt settled the bill. He waited near the entrance and opened his rideshare app. The band stopped for another break, or perhaps for the night, and the dance floor cleared, some heading to the bar and others for the door. Jules cleared a path through the crowd with ease and met Matt with a smile.

"Well, they're both… occupied at the moment," Jules said and followed Matt out the door.

Matt shook his head. "That didn't take long." Matt called up the group chat and typed in his address and that he'd leave the back door unlocked.

"It never does. They learned from the best." Jules punched Matt's shoulder lightly. "Meanwhile you and I are the old married men of the group. Me talking about my kids, and you zoning out while that chick draped herself on you. Were you daydreaming about that hot girlfriend of yours? Because you were completely oblivious to all the women drooling over you from everywhere in the place. Wholly unlike you." Jules laughed and followed Matt into the car that pulled up for them.

4

The Boys in the Boat

MATT UNLOCKED THE BACK DOOR to Finn's house with the key he'd slid under the doormat before he left for his dawn run. The house was silent; of course it was. Ollie never woke before nine o'clock on the weekends, and neither did Naomi.

Matt made his way through the kitchen to the guest suite off the living room where he knew Ollie was sleeping. It was the room they'd stayed in a handful of times before the renovations had been finished on their house next door. He slipped in silently, though Ollie slept soundly enough that he almost never stirred in his sleep, even when his alarm went off. Matt smiled when he saw Ollie stretched across the mattress, fully snuggled into Matt's side of the bed.

Matt stripped off his sweaty clothes and stroked his half-hard dick as he climbed into the bed behind Ollie. He lowered the sheet and admired Ollie's naked ass for a moment. It was smooth and white inside the tan lines from his tiny swim trunks. The white Speedo he wore on the boat that left nothing to the imagination and highlighted every inch of Ollie's glorious, uncut dick. Not to mention the perfect c-curve of Ollie's ass. There was no more perfect ass on the planet, and it was all for Matt.

Matt leaned forward and placed a kiss on the roundest bit of Ollie's ass, and then kissed his way down the curve to the top of Ollie's thigh. He inhaled through his nose and felt his dick fill as all the blood rushed to it in response to Ollie's scent. He'd obviously showered before bed, and the mix of his expensive bodywash and the bum balm he used, coupled with the undertone of Ollie's sweet muskiness made Matt's mouth water.

Ollie stirred in his sleep with a moan as Matt nudged one of Ollie's legs up and spread his cheeks with palms. Matt smiled at the sight of his tanned skin on Ollie's pale flesh and how perfectly Ollie's ass fit in his hands. Matt tapped gently on Ollie's pink starburst with his fingertip before following with his tongue. Ollie's hand landed on the top of Matt's head as he pressed back into Matt's face.

"Oh, Christ, Lieutenant," Ollie moaned as he looked over his shoulder with sleepy eyes. "That feels so fucking good. I love it when you wake me with your tongue."

Matt hummed in response, too busy giving Ollie's hole the attention it deserved to stop for conversation. He teased and lapped and probed with his tongue until the skin was soft, wet and relaxed and Ollie was humping the sheets while dithering unintelligibly. Matt slipped in a finger and then another before rolling Ollie over.

"That's quite a wet spot," Matt teased and wiped his mouth with the back of his hand as he came up on his elbows to look at Ollie when he shifted away from the damp circle that had been underneath him.

Ollie's dick was rock hard, and his hairless balls were pulled up in tight wrinkles. Ollie was close and Matt was eager to help him over the edge. He pulled himself up and straddled one of Ollie's legs as he took Ollie's rosy red dick in his mouth with a sigh.

"Oh, god. Fuck, your mouth is so warm." Ollie moaned again and lifted his hips as Matt took him to the back of his throat.

"Did you miss me last night?" Matt asked when he pulled off Ollie's dick with an audible pop.

Ollie groaned at the loss of Matt's mouth. "Tease. Yes, I missed you. Can we talk when you're done?" Ollie asked breathlessly and lifted his head to meet Matt's eyes.

"You're so beautiful all sleep tousled. And you smell so good." Matt emphasized the statement by pressing his face in the soft spot where Ollie's groin met his thigh and breathing deeply.

"Less talking, more sucking," Ollie said with a grin before slamming his head back into the pillow as Matt licked between his balls and then took them in his mouth one at a time.

Matt hummed with happiness before closing his eyes and focusing on the exquisite taste of Ollie's dick. He spread his hands over Ollie's hips as he took him deep, and humped Ollie's leg in search of friction. The harder Ollie's dick got, and the louder his moans echoed in the room, the more fervently Matt humped Ollie's leg.

Ollie's fingers gripped the sides of Matt's head and tightened in his short hair. "Oh, god. Just like that. Don't stop," he commanded and rolled his hips with each syllable.

Matt sucked and stroked in earnest, making sure he kept the same pace he knew would put Ollie over the edge. Sure enough, a moment later Ollie was shuddering and moaning and writhing under Matt's tongue. Matt swallowed the first burst and then sucked and filled his mouth until Ollie was done. He pulled off and straddled Ollie's body, pausing to admire the flush of Ollie's skin, his lust-drunk expression, before spitting some of Ollie's release into his hand and jerking himself over Ollie's abdomen.

Matt stared down into Ollie's eyes and then shifted his gaze over Ollie's body as his hand flew over his dick. The muscles of Ollie's abdomen were defined, but softer compared to the hard edges of his own. Ollie was firm and fit but had a sensuous layer that Matt's eyes feasted on. His orgasm barreled through him, and he cried out with the surge as he covered Ollie's torso with thick, white ropes of his release.

Matt rested back on his heels and caught his breath with a smile as he milked the last of his orgasm out over Ollie's balls. He stared at

Ollie, all flushed and blissed out looking, and felt a sense of rightness. A calm that only Ollie brought.

"Man, you look so good covered in my cum," Matt whispered against the swell in his chest.

Ollie ran two fingers through one of the splatters and sucked them into his mouth with a pleased sound. "Thank you for the spectacular wake up."

Matt leaned forward to kiss the loving smirk off Ollie's face. It was as if Ollie knew the depth of the feelings Matt was succumbing to and wanted to rescue him, or at least ease him through by making light. He met Ollie's tongue and then kissed his way across Ollie's jaw and then down the muscled column of Ollie's throat.

"I thought you guys were going fishing," Ollie said breathlessly, interrupting Matt's hickey-quest.

Matt lifted his head from Ollie's chest with a smacking sound. He looked down at the bruises he'd left on Ollie's flesh with a smug sensation in his belly.

"We are. But the guys are sleeping off their hangovers." Matt rolled off Ollie and swept up his t-shirt from the floor. He cleaned Ollie's chest and then himself with it. "I gotta get back and shower. Hopefully we'll get to the boat before ten."

Ollie stretched his lithe body and rolled back onto his stomach away from the wet spot. "Have fun," he murmured into his pillow. "Will I see you?"

Matt got off the bed and pulled on his underwear and shorts. He scanned his eyes over Ollie's body. "Maybe for drinks or a fire pit on the beach. I'll text you."

Ollie didn't need to say a word; Matt could sense his displeasure in every muscle of Ollie's body, but there was nothing he could (or would) do about it. Matt bent forward and kissed the heel of Ollie's foot before leaving the bedroom and the house, with his balled-up shirt.

The sun was up, but not hearty yet, as Matt made his way through the tree line. He left his shirt along with his sneakers on the back porch and headed for the outdoor shower on the beach side of the house. He rounded the side of the deck and nearly collapsed at the sound of a voice.

"Morning, Lieutenant."

Matt turned with a racing heart to face Arturo who was sitting on the sectional sofa with his feet up on the matching table. He was wearing a hoodie and sweats in the shade of the house.

"I didn't know you were out," Arturo added.

Matt caught his breath and swallowed, the taste of Ollie still rich on his tongue, the scent of his release still on his hands. "I went for a run."

Arturo eyed Matt's feet. "Barefoot?"

Matt shifted and then continued walking across the short grass between the deck and the walkway to the beach. "I left my shoes on the back porch, because I'm about to take a shower."

Arturo looked around and then back at Matt as he stood like he was going to follow Matt. "Where?"

"What is this? A CIA interrogation?" Matt asked with a grin to cover his nervousness. He was ever aware of Arturo's hyper-observation skills and wished he'd not only rinsed his mouth but also washed his hands. "The shower's on the side of the house, and you're welcome to use it when I'm done. There are towels in the changing stall. What the hell are you doing up so early anyway?" Matt added.

"My hangover wouldn't let me sleep."

"Ahh. I'm guessing Paddy and Downtown aren't faring much better. You'll have to wake them soon if you want to catch anything out there." Matt gestured toward the ocean with his chin and then kept walking.

Matt rounded the corner of the house and opened the door to a seven-foot-tall wooden enclosure attached to the house. He looked over his shoulder at Arturo who was standing on the edge of the deck and nodded at the sign hanging on the wood fencing that said '$1 to shower, $5 to watch.' "I charge spooks extra. In case you were planning on watching."

Matt wondered at Arturo's curiosity and hoped he had remained downwind of him.

Arturo laughed. "No thanks. I've seen enough of your naked body to last me a lifetime, and none of it was willingly. Just hurry up so you can make some coffee. I couldn't figure out how to work that thing you call a coffee maker."

"Roger," Matt nodded and let the door swing closed behind him.

Matt ordered breakfast burritos from the shop he went to when Ollie wasn't around to make breakfast and called ahead to the Truro yacht club to have them stock some coolers with food and drinks for him to grab from the clubhouse. Arturo roused the guys who shuffled down the stairs like wraiths, holding their heads.

"Fuck," Joe cursed as he missed the bottom step. "Why the fuck did you guys let me drink so much?"

Matt suppressed a grin and handed Joe a travel mug of coffee from Ollie's (extravagant) coffee maker. He handed one to Jules who was already wearing his Oakley sunglasses and a stoic expression that might have fooled anyone who'd never seen him hungover before.

"You lightweights are keeping us from catching anything decent out on the high seas. So, suck it up, buttercups. And get your asses in the car. I got hangover cures," Matt held up the bag of burritos that had been delivered, "and some fresh air waiting if you can keep from hurling."

Jules tossed his truck keys to Matt with a grunt and swept the bulging paper bag from Matt's grip. "Not a scratch, Lieutenant." He said in a stern tone.

Matt snorted. "I busted that Humvee out of Darfur under heavy fire without so much as a bug on the windshield. So shut your pie-hole, Downtown."

Twenty minutes later Matt had his fifty-foot Sunseeker Predator docked at the pier and the guys were loading the fishing gear from the back of Jules' truck onboard. Matt set the drink cooler down against the outside of the sliding glass cabin door and carried the food cooler down to the kitchen. He wished, not for the first time, that Ollie was there to oversee the hospitality side of this excursion as he always made everything better, in every way. Ollie was the perfect *Yang* to Matt's *Yin* and while Matt craved him in that moment, he knew he needed to keep Ollie and his perfection away from this part of his life.

Ollie would never understand.

Matt steered his boat out past the tip of the Cape and headed for prime fishing ground. It was highly unlikely that they'd catch anything this late, but the guys wanted to fish, and ninety-five percent of fishing was enjoying the silence and monotony anyway. He'd made sure that the food and beverage stocked by the yacht club included sports drinks with electrolytes and strong coffee so, somewhere out in Nantucket Sound the guys came to life and began their ribbing of each other.

It was hot under the rising sun and when Matt cut the engine out of sight of land, while the guys gathered the fishing poles, he reached behind his head and pulled off his t-shirt to reveal a long-sleeved wetsuit top. He had on blue board shorts that were decorated with great whites, instead of his usual tight trunks, because he'd seen how the guys had foregone the spandex compression-style shorts they'd worn in training for the long, bro-suits that most American men wore.

Matt hoisted himself up onto the gunwale of his boat and waved off his friends' complaints.

"I'm not gonna disturb the fish. There aren't any, it's nearly noon." Matt twisted his mouth and then dove into the swells.

The water was bone-shatteringly cold but Matt welcomed it. He'd always felt at peace in the depths, whether the water was clear and cold, or murky and warm, it didn't matter. He was like a babe in utero, even in a pool, and he needed it daily.

Matt surfaced and glanced at the boat, catching Arturo's eye before submerging again and swimming under the hull. As he suspected, there didn't seem to be any fish for miles, but Matt knew the guys would still have fun whether they caught anything or not.

There was a splash in front of him as he emerged from under the boat. It was too big of a splash to be anyone other than Jules and Matt surfaced to a shout that ended on a groan.

"Fuck it's cold," Jules griped.

"That's why I've got this on." Matt lifted his wetsuit covered arm. "It's just shy of seventy degrees, and even with all that padding you've put on since the service, you risk hypothermia." Matt pulled himself out of the water and onto the back platform of the boat in one fluid motion.

"Fuck you, Kool Aid. I'm not fat." Jules swam to the side and joined Matt.

Matt handed him a towel with a grin. "Yeah, yeah. You're just big-boned. I know." Matt unzipped his top and draped it over the chair on the deck.

"When did you start wearing jewelry?" Arturo asked with a nod at Matt's necklace. He was leaning against the gunwale and putting bait on his hook. "I thought you hated it."

Matt touched the moon pendant that stuck wetly to the hollow of his throat. He wished he'd remembered to take it off, especially since Arturo was remembering how Matt used to mock Joe for the gold crucifix he wore. In Matt's defense that crucifix was pretty gaudy and begged for mockery.

"What changed your mind?" Arturo prodded. "And what is it, a poker chip?"

"My, uh, girlfriend gave it to me." Matt let go of the pendant and ran his hands back and forth over his head to release the water. "It's the moon."

"That seems a bit too romantic for you, Kool Aid," Joe teased. "Sounds like you've gone soft. You and Downtown."

"Hey now, there's nothing wrong with romance," Jules chided and draped the towel around his neck. "With the right person. And you've seen the pictures of Kam's girl back at the house. I'd lock that down too." He grinned and tapped Matt's bicep with his fist.

Matt had never been one for romance, and clearly the guys remembered that, or at least Arturo did. He'd never met anyone who brought that out in him until Ollie, and everything about Ollie made Matt want to do special things for him, secretly of course. He'd bought him a Rolex, a condo, and a Maserati. He would never deny Ollie anything he asked for.

Joe handed Matt a fishing rod with a smile, interrupting Matt's musings. "You got it bad, dude," he said with a smirk and headed for the front of the boat with his gear. "Now let's focus and catch us some fish! I gotta a good feeling," he called over his shoulder.

Ollie followed Naomi out of the spa and blinked at the bright afternoon sun. "Christ, I feel like we were in there for days. And I mean that in the best of ways," Ollie added as he draped his arm over Naomi's shoulder and pulled her against his body.

"Don't let go of me. My legs are noodles." Naomi leaned into him.

"Mine too. Perhaps we should roll to the car."

Naomi laughed. "I'm just glad it's a short ride back to the house. I'm ready for a nap."

"Me too."

Ollie unlocked the car and looked at his watch. It was just after three o'clock and he wondered where Matt and his Bro-Team-Six were. He hadn't heard anything from him, but he hadn't really expected to. When Matt mentioned drinks later, it didn't seem like he was serious.

Ollie put on his Ray Bans and started the car. "Nap for an hour and then showers and dinner at Mac's?"

"Solid plan, Oliver." Naomi held her fist up for a bump and then adjusted the volume on the radio. "I love this song."

Naomi bopped along with Tove Lo while he followed Route 6 back to Finn's place. He almost turned into his own driveway out of habit but continued driving past and pulled down Finn's long driveway. He followed Naomi into the house and kicked off his shoes. She made for the stairs as he ducked into the first-floor suite. He'd just closed the bedroom door when his phone buzzed in his pocket.

> Come over for
> happy hour we
> got a tuna

The next text that came through was a picture of a massive man holding a massive fish.

Sure. What time?

The text bubble appeared and hovered for a while before two texts came through in succession.

5

I got avocados, and those
wonton chips you like.

Ollie sighed at the implication that Matt wanted Ollie to make his favorite appetizer. At least he wasn't expecting dinner. To be honest he was pretty excited to get to work with fresh tuna. He was also a little more than curious about Matt's friends.

See you then
I love you

I love you too.

5

It All Makes Sense

OLLIE AND NAOMI made their way on the path through the tree line between Finn's house and the house he shared with Matt a little after five PM. They'd both showered and changed, Naomi in capri pants and a Stella McCartney top with a sweater over her shoulders, and Ollie in a pair of jeans and a pink button down with the top two buttons undone.

"Jesus Christ," Ollie exclaimed as he laid eyes on the biggest pickup truck he'd ever seen.

It was a black four-door truck with tinted windows and a company logo on the side that looked like exploding dynamite. The rims and grill were polished chrome, and Ollie couldn't help but notice a *Punisher* decal on the tailgate opposite another decal that matched the Navy SEAL tattoo on Matt's bicep as he passed. There was a running board under the passenger door to assist entry up and into the cavernous depths and presumably a matching one on the other side.

"Do you think he's compensating for something? Or is all this, in fact, necessary?" Ollie waved his hand up and down as they continued past the behemoth.

"Experience would say the former," Naomi began with a grin. "But if he's in construction, or whatever that logo means, then chances are he needs it."

Ollie made a thoughtful sound and reached for the back doorknob, before catching himself.

"Fuck it. I'm not knocking on my own door," Ollie declared with an eye roll and turned the knob.

Naomi rubbed his back with a laugh. "No, you definitely shouldn't."

They stepped into a mudroom that led to a wide hallway as Matt appeared in the entry to the main living space.

"Hey, Naomi, Ollie." Matt kissed Naomi's cheek and gave Ollie a soft look.

An almost apologetic look, if Matt were the sort to apologize for anything.

Which he wasn't.

"Thanks for coming," Matt said quietly, and then louder, "come in and meet the guys and check out the tuna. Joe dressed it on the boat, so it's already in pieces."

Matt turned and headed past Ollie's home office into the main part of the house. Ollie resisted the urge to test the knob, knowing it would be locked, because Matt always locked that door when his sisters and their families came to stay. He often wondered what Matt told them about that locked door. He made a mental note to drop a hint that it was an S&M dungeon the next time he was invited for Thanksgiving.

Ollie took Naomi's hand and laced their fingers together with a squeeze as they followed Matt. When they reached the kitchen Ollie gazed at what he loved most about the house: the incredible view of Cape Cod Bay from the giant main room. The far wall was almost entirely glass, from floor to twelve-foot ceiling and looked over a deck that spanned the width of the house, with sand dunes and grasses between the house and the beach.

When he drew his eye away from the view, he scanned the men sitting in his living room. The first thing that struck him was their age: two were solidly in their forties, while the third could've been late twenties or mid-thirties. The second thing that struck him was how alert they all seemed in their relaxed state. Three pairs of eyes homed in on Ollie and then shifted to Naomi, where they lingered.

One of the forty-somethings had dark red hair and two full sleeves of tattoos, one of which was the familiar anchor, gun, trident and eagle of the Navy SEALs that Matt also had. He was moderately attractive with a longish nose and was wearing a loose-fitting tank top and dark blue sweatpants with the word Navy written in gold down one leg. The other forty-year-old had a shaved head and a trident like Matt's tattooed on his forearm. He was wearing a tight t-shirt (Ollie imagined any t-shirt would be tight on that man) and baggy gym shorts.

Ollie pulled Naomi in under his arm as Matt made the introductions, using their given names. The guys put their beers down and stood to shake hands. They were all taller than Ollie, who at just over six feet was not short, but these men made him feel small, particularly Jules, who was larger and broader than Ollie expected for a SEAL.

Ollie was thankful for Naomi, feeling as if he'd been there meeting these men without her, he would've stuttered and stammered his way into oblivion, which was wholly unlike him. She was a rock by his side, and made the small talk Ollie was suddenly incapable of. Being in a room with them made Ollie intensely aware of Matt's military service in a way that had never felt so real or dangerous.

"Do you guys want something to drink?" Matt interjected as he looked between Ollie and Naomi.

Ollie shifted his gaze to Matt with a bit of relief. "Are you making cocktails? Because I'd love a margarita," Ollie replied as he found his voice. Matt knew how to make only one cocktail, and it was one Ollie didn't drink.

Matt narrowed his eyes and looked at Ollie's tickle spots meaningfully. Ollie pressed his lips together to keep from smirking.

"You have tequila in the house, Kool Aid?" Arturo interrupted in a tone that sounded mocking.

Ollie turned to look at the man Matt referred to as R2D2. Arturo was all dark eyes and dark hair and exuded an aura of danger like a villain from a movie. He wasn't as broad as Matt, but he managed to stretch the confines of his t-shirt. Arturo shifted his gaze from Matt to Ollie, as though he felt Ollie's eyes on him and Ollie's initial instinct was to hide.

"I brought it, the last time I was here," Ollie replied, and it wasn't a lie, he really had brought the Patron earlier in August. "I'll make margaritas for anyone who wants one."

"Let's do some shots," Joe said emphatically. "You got any shot glasses, Lieutenant?"

It was weird hearing someone else call Matt that, and Ollie was certain he didn't like it. Which was ridiculous considering that was Matt's rank and what everyone called him in the service. Ollie watched the guys follow Matt over to the bar where they definitely did not keep the shot glasses.

Matt opened the cabinets and looked inside, moving around the bottles and jars of olives and Luxardo cherries in a fruitless search.

Ollie looked at Naomi. "They're not in there, and I know he'll never find them because we haven't used them yet."

"I got the lid to the shaker, which is an ounce." Matt held up the stainless cap and shot Ollie a helpless look.

"They're over here in your, like, fancy cabinet." Ollie crossed to the art deco chest under the abstract painting he'd bought in Provincetown the summer before. "Chuck and I did shots the last time I visited." Ollie lied.

He pulled out a small silver tray with six crystal shot glasses and put it on top of the cabinet. Ollie stepped back as Joe took charge.

"Jesus, your girl has fancy taste," Joe teased Matt as he opened the Patron and started filling the glasses. "You two want a shot?" he asked Ollie and Naomi over his shoulder.

Ollie met Matt's eye. The tray had been Ollie's grandmother's, and the glasses were a birthday gift to Ollie from Matt. Ollie turned away after telling Joe no thanks and went to find the limes in the kitchen.

Matt looked up as Ollie and Naomi came into the living area with two large plates of minced tuna on top of guacamole surrounded by wonton chips. Ollie had decided to busy himself (and hide in the kitchen) while eavesdropping on Matt and his friends. Ollie put one down on the end of the coffee table in front of Matt and Arturo as Naomi put the other on the table between Jules and Joe and then they sat down at the other end of the sectional from Matt and Arturo and looked around.

"Sláinte," Ollie said and raised his glass. "Now, tell me where you're all from and what you do." He looked expectantly at Arturo who was to his immediate left.

Arturo shoveled a heaping chip into his mouth, just as Matt did the same, and chewed. "This is fucking good," he complimented Naomi (assuming, erroneously, that she made the dip) after he swallowed his bite. "I'm from Texas, but I'm currently living in Mexico City. I work for the State Department," Arturo replied and looked at Joe.

"I'm from Brooklyn and live in Jersey. I work in corporate relocation," Joe replied and took a handful of chips from the plate.

"This is fucking good," Jules agreed as he leaned forward and swept another chip through the dip. "I'm from Birmingham and live in Virginia. I own a demolition company."

"Downtown has always had a thing for blowing shit up," Arturo smiled. "Buildings, caves, toilets."

"Fuck you, R2." Jules threw a chip which bounced off Arturo's shoulder and into Matt's lap. "I had nothing to do with that latrine."

Matt laughed along with Joe and Arturo as Jules shifted his gaze back to Ollie. "Kool Aid told us you're his GC, and what do you do?" Jules looked at Naomi.

"I'm an interior designer. I did this house," Naomi replied and gestured around the room with a smile.

The guys looked around appreciatively then made a few jokes about Matt's lack of taste.

"Where are you guys from?" Arturo asked once the teasing died down.

"London."

"Southern California," Naomi replied and sipped her margarita.

"How'd you two meet?" Arturo asked.

"Through his girlfriend." Ollie nodded at Matt. He'd called Finn that more than once over the years, but it didn't mean he liked the feel of it on his tongue.

"She and I were roommates in college," Naomi explained. "He needed an interior designer for his condo when he moved to Boston, and we just totally clicked." She squeezed Ollie's knee with a smile.

Matt was thankful again that he'd enlisted Naomi to be Ollie's 'beard.' She took to the role beautifully, and wasn't nearly as bothered by the ruse as Ollie was. Matt could tell Ollie was less than pleased with the charade. He had noticed the clench in Ollie's jaw when Joe made his remarks about the glassware, and how it pained him to pretend as though they, and everything else in the house, weren't his. Matt remembered how proud Ollie had been when he'd brought home that mirrored cabinet with large brass handles from an estate sale on the North Shore, and he really should've remembered what Ollie had put inside.

Matt was pulled back into the conversation with a comment about his boat, and the chatter turned to discussions about yachts and how they compared to the boats they typically used on missions. Matt noticed Ollie perk up a bit; he was always eager to hear about Matt's time in the service, though Matt was hesitant to talk about it much. When Jules started reminiscing about a non-classified mission that had been one of their more harrowing ones, Matt wanted to change the subject.

"We don't need to bore them with your shenanigans, Downtown. What did you guys do today while we were out on the high seas?" Matt asked Naomi and Ollie.

"It was spa day, at Jezebel's," Naomi replied. "We did some yoga, had a couple's massage," Naomi rubbed her hand on Ollie's thigh, "and then I had a seaweed wrap. What did you do when I was in there?"

"Facial," Ollie replied.

"Right. Then we had a ridiculously healthy lunch followed by mani-pedis and then came home."

There was a pause and Matt looked at his friends sizing Ollie up in a way that made him feel defensive. Ollie looked amazing, his skin was glowing and his hands looked so soft he couldn't wait to feel them on his body. From Ollie's expression, Matt doubted that would be happening anytime soon.

"*Spa day?*" Joe looked at Jules and then back at Ollie. "Boy, you are whipped. That sounds super gay."

"It's actually quite relaxing, and I highly recommend it," Ollie replied coolly. "Especially the pedicure. You've never had one? I bet your feet are nasty." He raised his eyebrows in a challenging way that was so unlike him.

"Ooh, damn. That's some shade, but he's not wrong, Paddy. The stench of your feet could clear a room faster than our team on a mission." Jules said with a smack to Joe's shoulder.

Matt appreciated how quick Jules always was to diffuse a situation. Which was ironic considering his specialty in the service and what he did for a living now.

"I get pedicures," Matt chimed in. Ollie was clearly pissed, and while Matt couldn't rub the back of Ollie's neck or admit to these guys that he also got facials, he could offer up some support. "Feet are gross if you don't take care of them."

Matt never got polish with his pedicures, but sometimes Ollie did. He wondered if Ollie had this time and suddenly wanted to see and then suck on his toes. He cleared his throat and finished his beer.

"Speaking of gay," Arturo leaned forward to swipe a chip through the last of the tuna dip, "did you hear about Dallas? He fucking married a dude."

"What?" Jules and Joe said in near unison.

"Yeah. I bumped into Dallas' former CO who said Dallas came out when he retired and married some guy he went to high school with."

"That's fucked up. So, he was a fag at BUDs?" Joe crossed his legs with a shudder. "I showered next to him all the time. He was probably checking me out."

"Dude, you have no ass whatsoever, I promise he wasn't checking you out." Jules laughed.

Joe punched Jules' shoulder and then chugged the rest of his beer. "Whatever, I just can't believe it. Dude sucks dick. That's disgusting."

There was a beat of silence and Matt didn't dare look at Ollie as he felt his cheeks flush.

Arturo shifted on the sofa next to Matt as he looked at the nearly empty plate on the coffee table and then at Matt. "What time is dinner coming, Kam?"

Matt looked at his watch, his relief palpable at the change of topic. "In a half an hour."

He risked a glance at Ollie who was clutching Naomi's hand and staring at the floor with a slight frown. Matt was sure Ollie's mind was racing but he really hoped Ollie was realizing just why they could never be open about their relationship.

"What's Cam, and Kool Aid?" Ollie asked after a noticeably rough swallow.

Arturo's elbow caught Matt under his ribcage, and he laughed as Matt grunted and shoved him away.

"Kam is short for Kool Aid Man," Joe said and clapped Jules on the shoulder. "We were doing a training exercise, between missions, and Downtown thought it'd be funny to lace his explosives with dye, like those exploding packs banks put in with cash in a robbery." He took his hand away and looked at Ollie. "He blew out a wall knowing Matt would be the first one through and he got covered in red stain. Looked like the Kool Aid Man, and it took, what? A week to get the dye out of your skin?" Joe laughed at Matt.

"More like two days, but have your fun," Matt scoffed.

"The Kool Aid Man?" Ollie looked at Naomi and then scanned his eyes across the other men in the room. "Who?"

Arturo pulled his phone out of his back pocket and swiped in. A moment later he found what he was looking for and turned the phone toward Ollie. "This is the Kool Aid Man."

There was a loud pop from Arturo's phone and then a blast of red-colored debris which Matt, in full gear (camouflage, tactical vest, helmet, protective eyewear, and some sort of weapon) came bursting through.

Ollie heard tinny laughter as video-Matt shook his head and wiped the red haze from his glasses with a gloved hand. The image shook and then the video ended with a shout from Matt as he stormed toward the camera.

"I told you to delete that," Matt said as he grabbed for Arturo's hand.

Arturo was faster than Matt and held it out of reach. "No way, Lieutenant. Whenever I'm feeling down, this video perks me right back up." He laughed along with Jules and Joe.

It was embarrassing and Matt didn't want Ollie to see it. He'd been pissed at the prank, but not enough to sanction any of them. They'd done it because it had been his birthday; he was just glad it didn't have glitter in it. He found out later that was only because Jules hadn't been able to get his hands on any.

"It wasn't so bad, and certainly didn't deter the ladies that night, if I recall," Joe said and then stuffed a laden chip in his mouth. "Was it two or three that night?" he added with a grin.

"No, they weren't deterred at all," Jules agreed and held up his glass with a wink at Matt.

Matt returned the gesture with a smirk for the guys' sake and didn't dare look in Ollie's direction.

Ollie put his half empty glass on the coffee table and stood. He pulled Naomi to her feet and glanced around the room. "It was nice meeting you all. We've got a dinner reservation to get to." He looked at Matt. "Thanks for having us. I'll see you at work."

Fuck.

Ollie was pissed and Matt supposed he couldn't blame him. He stood as everyone shook hands and said goodbye. He watched Ollie leave as Arturo grabbed another round of beers.

"She was hot," Joe remarked as they all took their seats. "But a fucking spa day? A facial? I don't care how good the pussy is, that's just too fucking gay."

Matt bit his cheek as his stomach clenched. He loved when Ollie had spa day, because he came back all smooth and relaxed and smelling like heaven. He wanted to say something in defense, but at that moment the doorbell rang.

"Dinner's here," Matt declared as he stood. He let the caterers in and showed them where to set up the clambake.

They ate on the deck and stayed out drinking until the caterers left and the stars came out. After several yawns from each of them Matt called it a night and herded everyone inside and locked the slider behind him.

"Dutch, dim the windows," Matt said over the chatter of his friends.

The wall of windows facing the beach frosted instantly and Matt turned back to see his friends all staring.

"What the hell just happened?" Joe gestured with his empty beer bottle at the glass. "And *Dutch*? What happened to Alexa?"

"Yeah, Kool Aid. You let that spy shit in your house?" Arturo asked with his eyebrows raised.

Matt faced them with a grin. "I frost the glass for privacy at night. It's a private beach but people still stroll by. And *Dutch* is one of the greatest characters Arnold ever played." He looked at Arturo. "Of course I haven't let any kind of shit into my house, R2. I work in cybersecurity, the firewall on this house is twelve feet thick. I have the best and the brightest minds working for me. Dutch is in-house only, and the Wi-Fi is bounced all around the world."

Arturo raised his beer and tapped it against Matt's with a smile. "It's good to be here with you, Lieutenant."

6

Not on my Watch

OLLIE WAS QUIET over dinner, and happy to let Naomi lead the conversation. They had discussed Matt's friends at length in the car and then as they waited for their food. On the one hand Ollie was furious with the homophobia he'd been subjected to, and on the other he completely understood Matt's determination to stay in the closet—not that he agreed with it—just that he could understand why Matt felt the need to hide.

"It's so fucked up that people are still so consumed with who other people love. Like, how does it affect them in any way what that guy Dallas does with his own life?" Ollie scowled. "Or Matt for that matter."

"I know. And the worst part is, most of the people who think that way, also scream the loudest about freedom." Naomi took a bite of her salad. "I wish you had let me say something."

"It wouldn't have done any good, and it wasn't worth getting into it with him. They'll be gone tomorrow, god willing."

"I know." Naomi sighed. "I'm not sure Matt could ever come out to those guys, but would he have to? You said yourself that he hasn't seen them in years."

"Whether he sees them or not is not the point," Ollie replied dejectedly. "It just cements in my mind that he'll never be able to, but I'm okay with that. I have to be," Ollie added vehemently, mostly for his own benefit. "Plenty of celebrities are gay in private, have secret relationships, we're no different. And the fact that the people who matter the most to us know," Ollie covered Naomi's hand with his own and squeezed, "makes it all okay. I don't need the world to know my business. It's not like I went around telling everyone before I met Matt."

Naomi turned her hand in his to lace their fingers together. "I get it, and we all love you."

"I love you too," Ollie replied and pulled his hand away as their waiter appeared with their entrees.

* * *

Ollie and Naomi grabbed a light breakfast before a class at Ollie's favorite yoga studio on the outer Cape. The instructor greeted him by name and Ollie reintroduced him to Naomi as they set up their mats at the front of the room. It was a full class with a few familiar faces, including a group of guys Ollie knew ventured in from Provincetown. They were never shy about ogling him but were always polite and friendly in conversation.

Ollie tuned out the people around him and focused on bending and stretching his body, the instructor's voice a soothing background hum as he guided the class. Ollie's mind wandered to Matt as he transitioned seamlessly through the sun salutations. Matt hadn't come to see him that morning, but he had texted a Matt-version-of-an-apology for the way his friends had behaved.

> I wish you could've stayed.
> They're idiots, and are
> leaving tomorrow.
> I love you.

Ollie had replied with two heart emojis and an 'xo.' It wasn't worth asking for more. He knew Matt had deep rooted issues with apologizing. Something about it being a sign of weakness and a belief his dad nearly beat in to him as a kid. Ollie knew how to read between the lines at this point in their relationship and pushed past any lingering expectations.

They moved to the floor portion of Ashtanga and Ollie lifted his feet off the ground into boat pose. The movements became strenuous, and thoughts of Matt flew from his brain as he turned his attention to breathing and controlling his muscles. The hour passed quickly, and Ollie wiped the sweat from his brow with his soaked towel when they were done.

He turned his head with a grin at Naomi's groan. She rolled onto her back and sighed heavily.

"I hated every minute of that, but in five minutes I'm gonna be so glad I did it." She laughed. "No, make that ten."

Ollie came to his knees and rested on his haunches next to her as the people around them chatted or silently rolled up their mats. "We have definitely earned our chill time on the beach."

Ollie helped her to her feet and returned their blocks to the shelf. He chatted briefly with the instructor and nodded goodbye to the guys as they passed, while Naomi rolled up their mats. Ollie promised to return the next time he was in town before following Naomi out the door.

After showers and a snack, Ollie and Naomi slathered each other with sunscreen and laid on Finn's cushioned lounge chairs on the deck. Ollie was fully dozing when a wet nose snuffled under his arm with a happy woof. He pulled himself up onto his elbows and stared into the happy and alert eyes of a black German Shepherd.

"Jayne!" Ollie exclaimed and then looked around for Finn. He rubbed the dog behind her ears and dodged her tongue as Naomi sat up on the lounger next to him.

"Hey, guys," Finn said with a smile as she came around the side of the house.

Ollie stood and scanned his eyes over Finn as she came up on the deck. She had her honey blonde hair tied back in a loose bun and was wearing a white sundress. Her beauty was the same type of effortless as Naomi's but with an added magnetism that was indescribable. People at Oxford had always remarked on how much he and Finn looked alike. In fact, that was how they first met, when mutual friends introduced them at a party, declaring them separated at birth.

"Hey, Chuck." Ollie pulled her into a hug. "I thought you were on Nantucket for the holiday."

Finn hugged Naomi and then looked at Ollie. "I wanted to see you guys before I had to zip back to Baltimore, and I couldn't pass up the opportunity to meet Matt's Navy buddies. I only met two at the Navy ball back in 2012, and I don't think it was any of the guys here this weekend."

"I can't say you're missing anything," Ollie said in a dry tone. "Except maybe some homophobia."

Finn held Ollie's gaze with a sympathetic expression and wrinkled her nose. "Really? Not directed at you I hope."

"No, thankfully. To be honest it was really only one of them that was truly horrible, but they didn't stop him, not even Matt." Ollie added with a shrug.

Finn looked away. "Well, not that I agree, but of course he wouldn't say anything." Finn brought her gaze back to Ollie. "It's different with them. You see that don't you?" She glanced briefly at Naomi and then sighed. "I'm sorry, Ollie. You put up with so much." She rubbed his arm and kissed his shoulder before brightening and stepping back. "I bought a shit ton of food and told Matt to bring the guys over for lunch. They're on their way."

Ollie looked at Naomi and raised his eyebrows when she met his eyes. Just then the sound of male voices came from inside the house. The slider opened and Matt appeared, his face beaming.

"Chuckleberry!" He exclaimed and wrapped Finn up in a tight hug. He kissed her and turned to his friends who had spilled out of the house and onto the deck behind him. "Chuck, this is Arturo, Jules, and Joe."

Ollie felt exposed in his tight blue trunks and looked around for his t shirt as Naomi swept her cover-up over her bikini. He remembered that he took his shirt off inside at the same time he met Arturo's dark eyes. Arturo dropped his gaze to Ollie's throat and then at the hickeys on his chest before flicking a speculative glance at Naomi. Ollie fought the protective urge to cover his trident pendant and his chest.

Ollie broke eye contact in time to catch Joe sizing him up, his eyes scanning from the hairband Ollie was wearing to keep his hair off his face, to the expanse of his hairless chest. There was a quirk to one of Joe's brows as he took in Ollie's swim trunks and Ollie bristled defensively. He wanted to say something about Europeans being more evolved, but the introductions were still being made, and he didn't want to draw any more attention to himself.

Matt seemed to be studiously ignoring him, so Ollie used the distraction as a chance to slip inside the house. He hadn't expected to see any of them before they left and as such the t-shirt he had tossed onto the chair by the door was one of Matt's Navy ones. The angry side of him wanted to put it on anyway, but the rational side implored him not to, so he swiped it off the chair and made for his bedroom to get a different one. There were platters of food and an assortment of drinks covering the large kitchen island and Ollie hurried to find a shirt so he could help set everything up.

Ollie was coming out of the bedroom as everyone came in from the deck, led by Jayne who bounded over to him. It was cooler inside with the air conditioning, so Ollie had pulled on a pair of grey sweats along with his Prada t-shirt. Arturo's gaze swept the room and the people in it with shrewd eyes that took everything in. Ollie was glad the trident on his necklace was now hidden as he began unwrapping and unpackaging the food Finn had brought.

"Is that your Maserati in the driveway?" Jules asked Ollie with a nod toward the back of the house.

"Uh, yeah," Ollie replied with a smile. Jules was big and intimidating but had a kindness about him that the other two didn't.

"It's a sweet ride. Is it a 2018?"

"Yes. I got it last winter." Ollie left out that Matt had been the one to give it to him for Christmas. "The fob is on a hook by the door if you want to look inside. I don't know if you'll fit," Ollie added with a chuckle.

Joe had drifted over to listen and clapped his hand on Jules's shoulder with a laugh. "I'll sit behind the wheel and let you know how it feels, DT." He flicked a glance at Ollie. "Is it okay if I start her up? I won't go anywhere."

"Absolutely do NOT let him drive your car," Jules warned.

"Hey now," Joe replied defensively.

"What's this about Joe driving?" Matt turned from chatting with Finn and Arturo. He had the barest hint of a mocking expression on his handsome face.

Joe scoffed exasperatedly and slapped his hands against his thighs. "You fuckers."

"Excuse me? How is your shitty driving our fault?" Jules asked with a smirk.

Ollie bounced his gaze between the three of them as they bantered back and forth. It was clear this was a long running joke.

"None of those accidents were my fault!" Joe exclaimed.

"You backed into the only rock outcropping for miles," Matt said incredulously. "We were in the flats; it was like a Walmart parking lot."

"Jules's big head was in my way. I couldn't see."

"What about when you scraped the entire side of the captain's transport. He nearly threw you out of the Navy," Jules interjected.

"His driver had parked crooked. Totally over the line and in the way." Joe scowled and picked a mini quiche off the tray Ollie had unwrapped and popped it in his mouth.

"I told you to go around; there wasn't enough room," Matt shrugged. "You defied an order; I should've let the captain toss you."

"How about when you nearly flipped the Humvee on our way out of—" Jules looked at Ollie and then back at Joe. "You overcorrected."

"Pfft. The wheels never left the ground," Joe replied.

"You shouldn't even have been driving. I had already revoked your privilege at that point." Matt crossed his arms and raised his eyebrows.

"Petty Officer High Horse would never have been able to get us out of there."

"I forgot about him," Arturo chimed in. Whatever conversation he'd been having with Finn and Naomi had come to halt with the playful arguing happening behind them. "He was a better driver than you, Paddy."

"In light of recent facts, I'm going to have to rescind my offer of the key fob," Ollie interjected in a light tone when the opportunity arose. "Maybe we should just eat instead," he added once all the dishes were uncovered.

Finn brought out plates and cutlery as Matt picked up a sandwich quarter and popped it in his mouth.

"Come on, I'll show you the car. I did all the research, I could tell you more about it than Oliver can," Matt added with a wink at Ollie.

Ollie watched the guys follow Matt out of the kitchen as Matt explained to them that Ollie had wanted a high-performance car but didn't know anything about them. It sounded like Paddy said something derogatory about the British, but Ollie couldn't be sure. Ollie looked at Naomi and rolled his eyes.

After lunch, during which they talked about everything from Nantucket to how Finn and Ollie had met at Oxford and then how Ollie had come to work for Matt, Matt's buddies began grumbling about going back to Sandwich and then how returning to work was going to be rough. Matt could tell Ollie was counting the minutes until their taillights disappeared down the driveway, and Matt couldn't blame him. It was great to see the guys, but having them in his space, especially with Olie there, was even more stressful than being behind enemy lines.

"You drive a top-of-the-line Porsche, he's got a fully loaded Maserati." Joe nodded at Ollie. "Your company must be making bank. You hiring?" he asked with a grin that seemed like he was only half kidding.

"No," Ollie replied tersely before Matt could even open his mouth. When Ollie looked his way, Matt saw the hardness in his gaze.

"Seriously?" Joe looked at Matt.

Matt was about to respond when Ollie cut in. The expression on Ollie's face was the one he wore in tough negotiations, and Matt braced himself.

"Seriously. We rarely have openings, and only when we're expanding into new territory. SharkFinn pays double the industry standard, sometimes more, at every level from interns to our C-suite. Our benefits package is head and shoulders above any other American company. Our healthcare is fully funded by us, there are no co-pays, and no denied claims. I designed it that way so our American employees can have the same level of coverage their European counterparts enjoy."

Ollie took a breath. It seemed like he was just getting started, and Matt wondered if he should step in to cool things down. He then remembered that cutting Ollie off mid-tirade would only earn him his ire and possibly a week of celibacy, so Matt kept his mouth shut.

"We also offer fourteen weeks paid maternity and six weeks paid paternity leave, generous vacation time, and every one of our offices across the globe has daily catered lunch. We have profit sharing and bonuses for targets met, also at every level.

"And finally, but most importantly, SharkFinn has a zero-tolerance anti-bigotry policy that employees are required to sign acknowledgement of. Any racist, sexist, or homophobic comment, intentional or in jest, can and will be grounds for termination." Ollie held Joe's slightly stunned gaze. "Your comments yesterday automatically disqualify you for consideration of employment. Even if *Kool Aid* here were to try to let you apply, you would be denied." Ollie sat back in his chair with a glance at Matt.

Matt looked at Joe, who was staring at Ollie with a look that bordered on hostile. Joe flicked a glance at Matt.

"How the fuck do you make any money?"

Matt opened his mouth to respond but Ollie beat him to it.

"SharkFinn is one of the most profitable companies in the industry, if not in general, and it's privately held. We don't have greedy shareholders dictating policy to us and draining our coffers. Contrary to what most corporations would have you believe, paying your employees well, providing them with tremendous benefits and such, doesn't negatively affect your profitability; quite the opposite in fact. It will mean your CEO to worker pay ratio is far more equitable, but we," he gestured between himself and Matt, "still manage to make more than enough."

Joe studied Ollie and raised his eyebrows. "*We?* Is it your company too?"

A look of calm came over Ollie's face. The expression Matt knew covered an inner storm. "I own a share." He flicked a glance at Finn. "But I'm also one of those extremely well-compensated employees and SharkFinn is a collective that we take pride in. Yet another reason why we have a zero-tolerance policy for bad behavior. There's just no place for it."

Matt looked at Finn who was looking at Naomi with wide eyes. He opened his mouth to say something, anything, when Jules barked out a laugh.

"Shit, Paddy. Good thing you didn't spend any time updating your resume." Jules looked at Arturo and pushed his chair back from the table. "We gotta fly. I told Gina we'd be back with the tuna for dinner."

Arturo and Joe stood, Joe with a stiffness in his shoulders that Matt knew all too well. The guys were gonna have a lot to discuss in the car ride back to the Upper Cape. Ollie might have come down a bit too hard on Joe, but Matt knew it was because he'd held his tongue the day before and Joe's comments about Dallas had had time to fester overnight.

They said their goodbyes and Matt walked the guys back to his house, knowing he'd get an earful from Ollie when they were alone.

7

Ten out of Ten

MATT GAVE UP waiting for Ollie to come back to their house an hour after his buddies left and made his way back to Finn's on the path through the tree line he had the landscapers cut in between his and Finn's property. He let himself in and took a breath before entering the living space to find Ollie, Naomi and Finn sitting on the couches facing the ocean. Ollie looked at him with his eyebrows raised and held his gaze until he sat beside him.

"Do I even have to guess what you guys have been discussing?" Matt asked as he laid his hand on Ollie's thigh.

He couldn't help but squeeze Ollie's leg as Ollie flexed his thigh under Matt's grip. He refrained from stroking any higher up as he would have if they were alone and looked at Finn expectantly.

"They were… interesting." Finn quirked her eyebrow and glanced at Ollie and Naomi before looking back at Matt. "I remember Jules from the Navy ball back in 2012, he's still so great by the way. But the other two…." Finn furrowed her brow. "I have to agree with Ollie and Naomi, Joe is kind of a dick, and Arturo, well, he's unnerving. What does he do again?"

"Officially, he works for the State Department. In actuality, he works for the CIA."

"Oh, that makes perfect sense," Ollie exclaimed. "He creeped me out; felt like he was staring into my soul while simultaneously searching for my weak spots."

Matt poked Ollie in his side. "They're right here," he said with a grin as Ollie jerked away automatically. "He would've found them in a heartbeat if he were really looking."

"You're a sadist," Ollie said under his breath. "Anyway, I'm glad they're gone. What's the plan for the afternoon?"

"I'm headed to the pool for a swim, barely got in the water yesterday, and then I'm hoping you'll work your magic on the rest of the tuna I kept."

"Don't you have a fridge full of leftovers?"

"There wasn't much left, and I sent it with the guys."

Ollie looked at Finn and then Naomi. "What do you ladies feel like doing? Either of you want to play tennis?"

"I've gotta walk Jayne, and then I have to update my media for this week's classes. There are a couple of slides I need to redo," Finn replied and stretched in her chair. "A discovery south of Baghdad turned up some very interesting artifacts, though a lot of it was rubble."

"What discovery?" Naomi asked.

Finn lit up. "A group of archaeologists found a demolished temple in an area well outside the site of ancient Babylon. It was beyond the military base the US built after the invasion in 2003, so it wasn't the US who damaged it, like they did with the rest of the site." Finn shot Matt an irritated glance.

"Hey, don't look at me. That was before my time." He held up his hands.

"Anyway," Finn continued, "they're pretty sure the damage was a casualty of the Second World War. I remember Ned, you know, my mentor at Oxford," Finn reminded Naomi who nodded, "talking about the battles that took place there. His father, the previous Lord Archer, was in the war and spent time in the region."

"That's awful that it was destroyed," Naomi shook her head. "War is so senseless."

"Sometimes it's the only option," Matt interjected. "When diplomacy fails."

"No matter what governments, especially the US *government*, say, war is fought for two reasons, and two reasons only: religion, and greed. There's usually little to no diplomacy tried first." Ollie stated with a shrug.

"No. War is often fought to defend freedom and democracy." Matt frowned.

Ollie shook his head and turned on the couch to face Matt. "I truly don't want to have this argument with you, because I know you served your country with pride, and you looked bloody hot doing it, but that's a bullshit argument, especially when you look at the Middle East and South America. There's no democracy being defended. In fact, the US were in support of authoritarian governments, and directly against any government for and by the people. This goes for the British government too. They're all about protecting their economic interests."

Matt stared at Ollie. He wasn't entirely wrong, but he wasn't entirely right either. He wondered how he could defend the actions without giving anything away. "What about World War two?" He gestured at Finn, hoping for some commiseration. "That was to stop Hitler. Stop the spread of fascism, stop the killing of innocent people."

"Yes, but the war was started because of greed: Hitler wanted more resources, more power, and people fought against him to protect their interests first, and their people second."

"Okay, I hear your argument, Oliver. But I have been privy to intelligence briefings, I've seen things firsthand, and I don't want to have this discussion. I can't." Matt stood, signaling an end to the conversation. He held his hand out to pull Ollie up. "I'm going for a swim, and I'll be back by five or so."

Matt nodded goodbye to Finn and Naomi and led Ollie to the back door. He turned to take Ollie in his arms and dipped his face into the warmth of Ollie's neck. He breathed deeply through his nose and inhaled Ollie's scent before ghosting his lips up Ollie's faintly stubbled jaw. "I don't want to argue. I missed you."

Ollie ran his hands up Matt's bare arms and then threaded his fingers into Matt's short hair. "I missed you too. But I'm still a little irritated by your friends. This won't become an annual thing, I hope. And promise me you won't consider hiring them."

"I promise," Matt swore, and he meant it. "I keep distance from everyone at work, you know. But I served with these guys, there's no barrier. I could never retroactively put one in place. They put their lives on the line for me, and I for them, and that's something I could never walk back." Matt ran his fingers through Ollie's soft hair. "You matter more to me than any of them. Even if they begged me for a job, I would always say no. I love you, Oliver Turner."

Ollie's body melted against Matt's and Matt gripped him tightly with a sigh. He ran his hands down Ollie's back and settled them on Ollie's hips where they fit like a puzzle piece.

"I love you too…Kool Aid," Ollie murmured against Matt's neck.

Matt dug his fingers into Ollie's sides and laughed at the resulting pleas and squirms. He pinned Ollie against the wall and stilled his hands. "I'm gonna swim, and then I'll be back for dinner, and after that I'm gonna love every inch of your body. So, use the shower attachment." Matt shrugged his eyebrows before leaning in and capturing Ollie's soft lips between his own.

Matt came back from swimming smelling like chlorine and expecting Ollie to be pliant. To be clear, Ollie wanted to be anything but, however, he did use the shower attachment and smoothed on the bum balm Matt loved. It wasn't Matt's fault the men he served with were homophobes; it also wasn't Matt's fault that he had internalized homophobia. It was, however, Matt's fault that he hadn't done anything to overcome it, or at the bare minimum acknowledge that he had it.

Matt leaned over Ollie on the couch in their living room and kissed him with the barest hint of tongue before pulling back and looking around. "Is Naomi here?"

"No, she's next door with Chuck, lamenting men. I can't say I disagree with them."

Matt smirked and sat next to Ollie. "Come on, Ollie. Not all men."

"Holy shit, you're not really pulling that for real right now?"

"What?"

Matt looked genuinely perplexed, and Ollie bit his tongue. "Of course, not all men." He sighed and put his phone down.

Matt smiled that irresistible smile of his and pulled Ollie astride his lap. He ran his hands up Ollie's thighs and around to cup his ass in his large hands. He squeezed each cheek tightly as he tilted his face up to Ollie's for a kiss. Ollie settled deeper into Matt's lap and kissed Matt's waiting mouth. He tasted faintly of the mints he favored, and his hair was still damp from the pool or the shower.

Matt pulled his mouth away and trailed kisses down Ollie's neck as he slid his hands up the back of Ollie's shirt. "Your skin is so soft," Matt said against Ollie's collarbone before lifting Ollie's shirt up and over his head. "Tell me about spa day." He licked Ollie's nipple and wrapped his arms around Ollie's waist. "I'm a little disappointed you didn't paint your toenails."

Ollie let his head fall back as Matt's lips grazed all his sensitive spots. "That guy you like, Brock, with the hands that find and decimate any knot, did my massage and used that super hydrating lotion." Ollie hummed as Matt slipped one hand down the back of his shorts. "He asked me about my upcoming polo match." Ollie gasped lightly at Matt's finger tapping against his hole and then rolled his hips. "Which reminded me to remind you that I've got the last Chukker Cup of the season on the thirtieth of this month."

Matt pressed his dry finger into the first knuckle which made Ollie gasp again. "It's in my calendar, princess." He kissed Ollie's collarbone and nuzzled into his chest as his finger made itself known in Ollie's ass. "As your sponsor, of course I will be there to see my team win."

"Dutch, the windows, please," Ollie said to the ceiling and sank into Matt's embrace as the glass behind him frosted.

—

8

—

Centaurs at Play

"YOU FEELING AS GOOD as I am about this match?" Bill asked Ollie as they got out of Bill's vintage Jaguar behind the stables at Sentry Club in Dover. The breeze lifted the salt and pepper strands of his hair, and he ran his fingers through the short length to neaten them.

Ollie smiled at Finn's father and skimmed his eyes over his fit frame. Bill was dressed in the same gear as Ollie: a teal polo shirt with the SharkFinn logo, and white breeches with brown riding boots, and he looked far younger than his age. His blue eyes were hidden behind his Ray Bans, but Ollie knew the flash of excitement they held.

"Oh, we're gonna kill them." Ollie nodded in response. "We've got Lucas again, and Sharon's been on fire this season. There's no way we won't win."

Bill smiled and led the way to the stalls where their polo ponies had been housed for them by their grooms, Xander and Kip. Ollie greeted each of his horses with pats and smiles and promises of treats when the match was done. He spent extra time with his two favorite horses, Tragic Hero and Last Resort. They were both liver chestnut mares and were distinguishable by their markings (and personality). Tragic Hero had a white flame between her ears and was about the cheekiest horse Ollie had ever ridden, and Last Resort had white cuffs around her back hooves and no patience for grey horses, or maybe she just didn't care for Bill's mare, Lady Catherine.

Ollie grabbed a hoof pick from the grooming kit and began checking each horse's hooves, though he knew Kip had already cleaned them. It was as much a ritual as it was a superstition.

"Hey, naughty girl," Ollie laughed and shifted as Tragic Hero untucked his shirt from his pants and nibbled the bare skin of his back with her lips. He straightened and rubbed her neck as she nuzzled him. "I know you're mad I got nothing in my back pockets, but I promise after the match I'll give you some carrots."

He tossed the pick back into the box and led Tragic Hero out where the others had gathered. Ollie shook hands with Sharon and Lucas, who pulled him into a one-armed hug.

"I'm glad to be back on your team." He looked at Bill and Sharon and then back at Ollie. "We will win again, yes?" Lucas added in his smooth accent with a grin.

"We've had a great season," Ollie gestured at Sharon and Bill, "so with you joining us, I don't see how we can lose," Ollie replied with a matching grin.

Lucas was a handsome, incredibly talented, Argentine on the professional circuit, and Ollie had a hard time keeping his inner fanboy in check the first time he'd played with him. He was a few inches shorter than Ollie, with a sinewy build, and had a full head of wavy jet-black hair, and whisky-colored eyes. More than one media outlet had compared Lucas's looks and skills to the Argentine player known as 'the David Beckham of polo,' and Ollie agreed. That player was a legend, but Lucas was close on his heels and Ollie had learned a lot from playing with him and truly looked forward to learning more.

"You make your calls for plays when you see them, as will I," Lucas said. "I remember your advice, coach," he added with a wink.

Ollie felt himself blush. As number three, Ollie was the *de facto* captain of the team, and the previous time he'd played with Lucas he couldn't help but guide the team with his usual chatter, only to realize belatedly he was giving orders to a pro. Lucas had been as gracious then as he was being now, and Ollie mounted his horse with a smile. They walked their horses in a loose formation onto the field and Ollie took a moment to look around.

The Sentry Club of Dover was built by an anglophile in the 1980s and modeled after Guards polo club in Windsor, UK. There were stands behind a white picket fence on one side of the field near the clubhouse, which made Ollie feel like he was back in England, but the opposite side, was distinctly American. On that side, between the fields and the tree line were a row of cars and dedicated spots that people paid a lot of money to reserve season after season. Behind the low boards that ran along the edge of the playing field, next to a three-foot-high granite post, with 'Hawthorn' engraved up the side, were Ollie's parents with Matt and Naomi in Bill's spot. That post was one of several, identical, evenly spaced posts engraved with names that dotted the sideline.

The final tournament of the season was also the annual tailgating competition for Bill's side of the field, and this year's theme was Fall Harvest. Like most of the groups gathered along the boards, Bill's spot was fully decked out. Matt, and Ollie's father, David, had set up a ten-by-ten white canopy under which was an oriental rug spread on the grass, and two tables draped in fall-colored fabrics. There were two heated tureens (that Ollie knew held lobster bisque and chili), charcuterie boards, platters of sandwiches, baskets of cookies and muffins, and an assortment of beverages.

Bill's spot was decked out like a magazine spread, and Ollie knew that Naomi was responsible for the decorations. There were several large floral arrangements, both on the tables and in pots on either side of the tent poles and she'd clearly had Matt string flower garlands around the perimeter of the canopy (he was the only one tall enough to reach). From Ollie's vantage point astride Tragic Hero, he could see the china, silverware, and crystal glasses that had been set out for them and any of the surrounding spectators who came for a chat, and he smiled at the fanciness.

After surveying the setup, Ollie's eyes went to Matt like a magnet. He was in a tan linen suit with a dark blue shirt, open at the throat, and had on the Ray Bans that made him look like a model. He was sitting in a relaxed pose next to a similarly dressed David (though David's suit was grey) with a bottle of beer in one hand and a half-eaten sandwich in the other and was chewing a big bite while listening to something David was saying. The bulge in Matt's cheek was almost as big as the one Matt had in his pants twenty-four seven, because even when Little Matt was dormant, he was unmistakable. He couldn't help his smile at the thought of Little Matt in any state and forced himself to think of other things as he shifted in his saddle.

As Bill greeted the other team's number one, Ollie's gaze shifted to his mother who was wearing the same brown and white polka dot dress she wore to his and Matt's commitment ceremony back in 2016, but with a chunky-knit cardigan to ward off the cool autumn air. She was standing off to the side of the tent chatting with the Bakers, who occupied the spot next to Bill's. She and David had gotten to know them from the other times they been to watch Ollie play and had become somewhat friends. Ollie smiled to himself with how seamlessly his parents had adjusted to visiting him in America, a country his mother had never wanted him to move to.

Ollie waved his raised mallet to them in greeting when the announcer's voice made the spectators all turn toward the field. Matt raised his beer in salute and Ollie knew it was accompanied by a wink behind his shades. His heart swelled in his chest, and he beamed in response before blowing a kiss to Naomi and turning his attention back to the woman at the podium announcing their names and those of the third men: the umpires.

With the horn the match began, and Ollie lost sense of anything around him except for the little white ball and the crush of the game. He was fully focused on the mallet in a tight grip in one gloved hand, and the leather reins in his other, on the solid muscle of the beast between his legs, and the sound of voices calling out around him. The first three chukkers passed in the blink of an eye. Each seven-and-a-half-minute long period was like putting the horses through three Kentucky Derbies, and it wasn't just the horses who felt the fatigue. They were all drenched in sweat after a very successful first half. Ollie had called as many, if not more, plays as Lucas and as a result their team was ahead by four points.

The half time show was a mix of showing off the hunting hounds (who no longer hunted real foxes), and the traditional divot stomp from the crowd. Other matches that summer saw vintage cars on the field at halftime, including Bill's 1963 Jag, or Finn's 1967 split window Stingray, when it was in town, or had a mini match with young players for the halftime show. Just like the Superbowl, the crowd would be entertained while the players used the time to rehydrate and discuss strategy.

It was with a sigh of relief that Ollie took the helmet off his sweaty head and dried his brow with the back of his forearm. He found an elastic hairband in his satchel by the barn and slid it over his hair as he rejoined the group. He'd grabbed a few water bottles from their cooler and passed them around as they discussed weaknesses in the other team. Ollie offered up suggestions for plays and encouraged the others to do the same.

Halftime always flew by and soon enough he was astride Last Resort while Bill made sure to be on any horse other than Lady Catherine. The stands were full, and the cheers were raucous as the play began again. Each chukker was more intense than the one before as the teams battled for yet another point. After scoring two more goals, and the opposing team sneaking one in on them, Ollie managed a long drive of the ball in the final chukker toward Lucas before turning away from the line and covering the other team's number four. It was a crush of ponies and dodging mallets (or being hooked by one) when Lucas freed the ball from the melee and headed for the goal. The crack of the mallet hitting the ball was a sharp sound that rose above the chuffing of the horses and the heavy breathing of the players.

Ollie let out a shout of excitement and rode up alongside Lucas for a fist bump. He did the same with Bill and Sharon and turned to look at the sidelines where Matt and Naomi were on their feet cheering along with Ollie's parents. Lucas's goal brought their score up to eleven, which was a record for the season; what made it all the more momentous was that five of those goals had been made by Ollie.

Ollie's handicap as a player in high school had always been a solid four before he gave it up to focus on football, but now he felt like he was hitting his stride. Handicaps of five and above were considered skilled enough to play pro, in fact, Lucas's handicap was seven, which put him in a very elite league, and Ollie wondered briefly what his own handicap would be now if he'd never taken the long break he had.

The sound of the announcer and the whistle brought him out of his musings back to the game and he promptly lost himself in the endless chase of that little white ball. Playing pro was not an option, nor a true interest, so Ollie just focused on the game at hand.

Matt was feeling the three glasses of whisky he'd consumed while catching up with Ollie's dad and chatting with all the familiar faces up and down the line of named spaces. He mingled with ease, because he'd been surrounded by people like this his whole life. He'd grown up in one of the poshest towns in Massachusetts, though his family were solidly working-class, and was best friends with someone whose ancestors were among the original one percent in America, but he'd never thought he'd become a fan of their most elite sport. In fact, he knew nothing about polo other than Finn's father had played it for years until her mother, Diana, had put an end to it with worry about injury.

Matt winced with the memory of Finn's mother. A woman who moved through life with a force that Finn had definitely inherited. A woman, who despite being born into a privileged life few could comprehend, had a depth of empathy and understanding that set her apart from her ilk. Matt watched Bill as he took possession of the ball and turned his horse away from the cluster and hammered the ball toward the goal. If only Diana had worried more about her safety with the sport that had been her undoing and not about Bill on a horse.

Matt shook his head away from the maudlin thoughts and downed the last of his whisky. He was not going to get lost in contemplation about hindsight, and foresight and jinxing shit. All that mattered was the moment he was in, and any other thoughts he had about destiny were just justification as to why he never got drunk.

He swapped his glass for a bottle of water and turned his attention to the field, or rather, Ollie on the field and his fit body astride that brown horse of his. Matt knew the horse was one of Ollie's favorites, but he couldn't remember its name, despite how many times Ollie said this one with the white on its face was so and so, and the one with the white feet was such and such. All horses looked the same to Matt, unless they were different colors, and it seemed as though Ollie's were all brown.

All Matt cared about was how hot Ollie looked astride any horse and damn, did he look fucking hot. Even from a distance he could see the sweat running down the column of Ollie's corded throat and into the collar of his shirt as he rode up and down the field with that utter concentration of his. His honey blond hair was plastered to his neck beneath the bottom of his helmet and his cheeks were flushed with excitement. Matt felt a surge of pride and possessiveness.

Mine.

Ollie was so beautiful. The most beautiful man Matt had ever seen, and Matt couldn't keep his eyes off him. The sweat Ollie had worked up made his shirt cling to his broad shoulders and his muscular torso in the most delectable way, and Matt couldn't wait to get Ollie alone later. Whenever Ollie won one of his little games, he came home so high, so horny, that Matt got horny right along with him. Matt hoped Ollie didn't wash away all of the sweat in his shower after the game and ran his tongue over his bottom lip at the thought before catching himself.

He shook his head and resisted the need to adjust himself in his pants. He looked around to cool off instead. Ollie's parents were chatting with a group of bystanders with one eye on the field, and Naomi was snapping pictures of players with her fancy, long-lensed camera. He knew she was focused on Ollie, because who wasn't? In Matt's opinion Ollie was the best player on the field, even better than that smug Argentine who stared a little too long at Ollie. Ollie of course denied that the guy was smug or into him, but whether or not Matt was right or wrong in his opinion on those matters, was irrelevant. He didn't like the guy.

The bell rang, signaling the end of the tournament, and the announcer called out the final score. The crowd cheered as the players rode around each other in circles and then lined up to shake hands from astride their ponies. Matt stood and snatched a ham and swiss on a slider roll and another bottle of water from the table behind his chair. He ate the sandwich in two bites and chugged the water as he watched Ollie break away from the group and ride over to them. Was it a trot? A canter? A gallop? Matt didn't know or really care. All that mattered was Ollie was headed his way.

Ollie had a broad smile on his handsome face and his polo mallet in his hands across his lap. The veins in his arms stood out prominently from exertion and his thighs flexed as he controlled his horse without using the reins. Or was it pony? Right, they were called ponies but were actually horses; that was a detail he *did* remember.

Ollie's horse magically came to a stop in front of the low boards that ran along the side of the field. Matt was now eye-level with Ollie's crotch, and he had to drag his eyes away. He looked up and saw the smirk on Ollie's face. Ollie leaned back slightly, as if to give Matt a better view and his damp shirt molded to the ridges of his abdomen in an almost pornographic way.

"Ollie!" Naomi cried happily from beside him, jarring Matt back to reality. "You were amazing out there! Wait until you see the pics I took. I got some really great ones of you and of Bill."

Naomi handed Ollie a small towel, which he took gratefully, and then patted the neck of Ollie's horse while Ollie wiped his face. He leaned down and kissed Naomi lightly on the lips but kept his eyes locked on Matt. Ollie's parents joined them and Ollie broke eye contact.

"Thank you, darling," Ollie said to Naomi as he straightened in the saddle and then greeted his parents. "Just wanted to come say hi and tell you to save some food for me." He looked pointedly at Matt when he said that last bit and Matt grinned.

Ollie's mother grabbed a slider, wrapped it in a napkin and handed it to Ollie. "I think Matt's had about forty of these," she said with a grin. "Best take it now before they're all gone." She shot Matt a soft look.

"It was more like twenty, but you make them taste so good," Matt said with a shrug. "And now I don't need dinner."

Ollie barked out a laugh and rolled his eyes.

Matt raised his eyebrows wiggled his fingers by his sides.

Ollie snorted. "Anyway, I've got to get Last Resort to Kip for cool down, and then we've got the trophy ceremony and whatnot."

With a head nod at the group, and wave to the Bakers, Ollie turned his horse and rode back across the field.

PART TWO

LOVE IS BLINDNESS

—

9

—

Stranger Things

Late October 2018

"HAVE YOU HEARD FROM CHUCK?" Ollie asked over lunch at a restaurant near their offices on the harbor.

"No. But she's heading into midterms now, so I'm not expecting to." Matt popped a shrimp into his mouth. "I have to be in DC the week after next and will be staying in my room at her place. You wanna come?" He raised his eyebrows.

"I wish I could. But my schedule for the next six weeks is fully booked," Ollie replied with a sigh. He loved Finn's neighborhood and all the restaurants nearby.

He was about to suggest visiting her before Thanksgiving when Matt's phone buzzed in his suit pocket.

He looked at the screen and grinned at Ollie. "Speak of the devil." He swiped into his phone. "Chuckleberry Finn! Were your ears ringing? We were just talking about you."

Ollie listened to Matt exchange pleasantries and then tuned out the conversation as he took another bite of his salad.

* * *

Kodi, Bill's black Labrador, woofed once as Matt came through the side door of Bill's house followed by Ollie.

"Hellooo," Matt called as they came into the kitchen and paused to lavish attention on Bill's exuberant dog.

Bill appeared in the hallway from the front of the house with a big smile on his handsome face. He was dressed in navy blue khakis and a tailored button-down that highlighted his fit frame. His hair was damp from a shower and the waves of his brown and silver hair were as relaxed as he looked.

"Matt, Ollie. Great to see you." He hugged them both and then looked at the bag Ollie was holding.

"I brought you some tennis balls for our next match. The non-cheaty kind," Ollie added with a grin as he handed the bag to Bill.

Bill laughed and put the bag down on the kitchen island after peeking inside. "Still sore over your loss then, huh?"

Ollie snickered. "I would tease you about the age of the *balls* you brought and their bounce, but Matt here," Ollie angled his head, "would have a coronary. So, I'll save the trash talk for the court."

Bill threw his head back with a loud laugh and slapped Ollie's chest with the back of his hand. "I look forward to it, Oliver."

"Yeah, I definitely don't want to hear it." Matt walked past them with a look of discomfort on his face that made Ollie chuckle.

If only Matt knew the conversations he and Bill would have over their many outings, he would be mortified. Between tennis, polo, and meals after, Ollie and Bill had spent a lot of time together where Ollie discovered just how wicked Bill's sense of humor truly was. Ollie exchanged a grin with Bill and took off his coat.

"Something smells amazing. Dierdre working her magic again I see," Matt continued on, oblivious of Ollie and Bill's silent exchange.

"Yup. She pulled out all the stops when she heard you were coming." Bill smiled at Matt and crossed to the built-in bar between the kitchen and the dining room. "What can I get you boys to drink?"

"Please tell Dierdre I loved dinner," Matt said and pushed his plate away after having thirds. "Ollie feeds me like a king, but there's nothing like comfort food to remind you of your youth." Matt smiled at Bill and squeezed Ollie's forearm briefly.

Ollie pressed his knee against Matt's under the table in response and Matt returned the gesture before turning his attention back to Finn's dad.

"I'll let Dee know. Now, what's this errand that Finley's got you here for?" Bill asked as he sat back and crossed his arms, his light blue eyes flicking back and forth between their faces.

Ollie shrugged. "Don't look at me. I'm just as in the dark as you are."

Matt put his elbows on the table. "She wants a crate that her mentor, Lord Archer, left to her when he died and said it's in your basement. Knowing Ned, it's probably got a mummy in it or something equally ancient and grim." Matt grinned. "If you've been haunted since it arrived, I'm sure you'll be happy to see it go."

Bill laughed. "I think you're probably right. I can't imagine that it would be anything but a box of dusty relics." He looked at Ollie. "Did you know Ned?"

"I knew of him at uni; nearly everyone did. And I went to his house in Oxford for dinner with Finn a couple of times. He was brilliant, and odd, though I suppose most people as intelligent as he was, are pretty odd.

"His death was pretty sudden, and I know Finn took it hard," Ollie added.

"Was it a heart attack? I forget."

"Pancreatic cancer," Matt replied. "Same as my dad."

"Ah, right." Bill nodded and then looked around with a sigh. "We playing squash anytime soon? Or tennis? Doesn't matter to me. I miss you now that the horses are in Aiken." Bill changed the subject with a glance at Ollie.

"I'd love to hit the squash court. Am I going to need to buy new balls for that as well?" Ollie smirked.

"Ollie, I didn't cheat. You just can't keep up." Bill winked.

Ollie tilted his head and narrowed his eyes. "Challenge accepted. Let's get something on the books."

"How about while Matt's in DC? We can play squash at the club, or tennis at B&T. You decide."

Matt finished his wine with a smile as he listened to them banter back and forth. He was so thankful that Bill and Ollie had hit it off as incredibly well as they had, especially considering their rocky start. It seemed like a lifetime ago that Bill had caught them coming out of his hall closet on New Year's Eve, sparking off a chain of events Matt never wanted to think about again. It had taken him a bit of time to get over his nerves around Bill but the fact that Bill and Ollie were even closer than he himself and Bill were had helped immensely.

"Yes, let's do both," Ollie beamed with a nod at Matt, bringing Matt back into the conversation. "He leaves on the twenty-fifth. I have a football match Saturday morning but am free Sunday."

"Let's play tennis this weekend and squash on the twenty-fifth. I'll email you." Bill stood. "Now, let's go see what Finley needs you to retrieve."

They followed Bill to the storage room at the far end of his large basement and waited for him to turn on the light.

Matt surveyed the tidy and well-organized space and saw a wooden crate that was slightly larger and taller than a steamer trunk under a stack of boxes. He and Ollie made quick work uncovering it with Bill's help and then hefted it between them.

"Christ! What's in this thing?" Ollie grunted as he shifted his hands underneath to get a better grip.

"I don't know, but I'm guessing something bigger than a mummy. It's probably filled with stone tablets from Mesopotamia that are some very dead person's shopping list," Matt said as he surreptitiously admired how Ollie's biceps flexed pleasingly with the effort.

Ollie blew a strand of hair out of his eye as he stopped to admire Matt's muscles as well. Matt quirked his eyebrow and flexed his pecs, the twitching under his shirt drawing Ollie's gaze.

Bill cleared his throat, and with a grin that made Matt flush at being caught, led them to the door out of the basement. Matt and Ollie trailed him around the side of the house to the driveway where they hefted the cumbersome package into the back of their Range Rover.

* * *

Ollie arrived at the dark and empty brownstone after an afternoon of squash and then dinner at the Oak Bar with Bill. He dropped his gym bag by the stairs and took the paperwork for the upcoming board meeting Bill had given him to Matt's home office. He switched on the light and looked around Matt's space, noticing how everything was 'just so' and perfectly aligned.

Ollie forced his feet to move. He was always a bit hesitant to step into Matt's sanctuary when he wasn't home for fear of inadvertently disturbing something. He put the papers in front of the keyboard on Matt's desk and turned to leave. A cardboard box behind the door caught his eye.

It wasn't like Matt to leave packages unopened or tucked in a corner, so Ollie couldn't resist the curiosity. He leaned over and peered at what was written on top.

BOAT

Matt's neat and authoritative handwriting was unmistakable. Ollie shifted his glance down the hall as his heart suddenly picked up pace at the thought of being caught snooping (which was ridiculous because Matt wasn't due home until the following evening) and then looked back at the box. The flaps were woven over each other to stay shut, so it wasn't like he had to cut any tape to see inside, but he still looked at them for what felt like an eternity before pulling them open. Ollie wasn't sure why he cared or what spurred his curiosity as he peered inside.

There was a bottle of scotch, a small sealed box with the picture of a compass printed on the outside, a medium-sized bottle of lube (such *a perv, Lieutenant*), a book by Tom Clancy, and a laptop standing on its side. Ollie frowned lightly and pulled the laptop carefully from the box, knowing that Matt would know if something wasn't put back exactly how he left it. He felt the blood drain from his face when he saw the Liverpool F.C. sticker. Ollie hated the Liverpool team, but he knew quite well who had loved them.

Ollie opened the laptop as if someone else was controlling his movements and turned it on. He tried a few passwords. First, ones he thought Andy would use, and then tried a couple that Matt would, before being locked out. He held the power button down until the screen went blank and put the laptop back exactly how he found it, careful to layer the flaps precisely as they'd been.

Ollie left the room in a daze, barely remembering to turn off the light, and had gone through his bedtime routine on autopilot. He thought about his ex, Andy, and all that Andy had done the previous year, from the blackmail to Andy's stalking him and Matt outside their townhouse. Andy was still missing, presumed dead, and the person the police thought was responsible was in jail awaiting trial.

Ollie laid awake in bed for a long time, wondering how and why Matt had Andy's laptop. The news reports said that Andy's apartment had been broken into the month before he disappeared. Ollie knew that break-in happened not long after he and Matt had dinner with Bill at a restaurant where Andy was waiting tables.

Could Matt have been the one who broke in? Or did he pay someone to do it? How else could it be that Matt had Andy's laptop?

What did Matt want with the laptop? And why was it headed to Matt's boat?

Ollie finally fell asleep telling himself the how or why didn't matter when he could never ask Matt about it.

10

No Turning Back

OLLIE PICKED MATT up from his hangar at Hanscom Field, exiting the driver's seat so Matt could drive them home. He had pushed all his questions about the laptop deep into the recesses of his brain and locked them away. Matt had nothing to do with Andy's disappearance and that was all that mattered.

"I missed you. How was Chuck?" Ollie asked after an exchanged glance and a lingering handshake. "What was in the crate?"

"I missed you too, babe, and as far as the contents of the crate…." Matt shook his head. "Some crazy shit," he answered as he adjusted driver seat slightly for his longer legs. "There was a box covered in some weird-ass symbols, and two big clay jars. Chuck said they were like the ones that Egyptians would use for the mummy's organs, but bigger, and with plain lids." Matt shuddered slightly with a glance at Ollie and merged onto the highway. "You know I always teased Chuck about her work with Ned, but I got serious heebie jeebies from the whole thing."

Ollie raised his eyebrows. "Wow. What do you mean, you think it's seriously haunted or something?"

Matt quirked his mouth. "Ollie, you know I live in the tangible, rational world. But I have to admit, I was unnerved." He shrugged. "So, I'll need you to comfort me when we get home." He grinned salaciously.

Ollie snorted. "Of course." He looked out the window. "Why did she need it? Did she say?"

"You're not going to believe this, but she said the FBI has her translating some ancient text and she needed this to help her."

Ollie laughed and looked back at Matt waiting for a smile that never came. "The FBI? What? You're making that up to tease me. That's preposterous."

"I swear, Ollie, but she was cagey as fuck when I asked her about it." He shrugged and sped into the fast lane. "She's coming home for Thanksgiving, and I plan on grilling her when she does."

* * *

Matt and Ollie pulled up to his mother's house in Wellesley just after noon, for Thanksgiving dinner with his sisters and their families. The small, Cape-style house was nearly bursting at the seams with people, but somehow managed to fit everyone, with the adults in the dining room and the six children, ranging in age from twelve to four years old, around the table in the kitchen. All four of Matt's sisters were there, along with three brothers in law, one of whom, Patrick, had Ollie deep in conversation about football shortly after greetings had been exchanged.

Ollie had accompanied Matt to Thanksgiving twice before, and each time it had been under the guise of Ollie not having other plans. This year the excuse was that his 'girlfriend,' Naomi, had gone back to California to celebrate and Ollie couldn't get away from work to go with her. Not that Matt's family ever questioned it, and Matt never elaborated, they were used to his reticence.

The only topic Matt's family hounded him about was his relationship with Finn, and when were they going to finally get back together for good. His family believed that the engagement between Matt and Finn had been real, everyone had, including Bill. Matt and Finn had kept up the ruse for nearly a month after his father's passing and then called it off (amicably of course). Since then, he and Finn had kept up appearances and let his family believe they were in an on-and-off relationship. Only Matt's mother, Antonia, knew the truth.

"Matteo, come help me in the kitchen," Matt's mother called in Italian from the kitchen doorway.

"Sure, Ma."

"You look *bellissimo*," she said to him once they were alone. "As does Oliver. Things are good?"

"Si, Ma, *va tutto bene*."

"Ah, Matteo. I am so happy for you. He is so kind, and smart. And so handsome," she added slyly.

Matt beamed. "*Lo so, sono molto fortunato.* I love him so much," he added in a whisper.

"And I love you both. Make sure he sits next to me at dinner."

Ollie watched Matt carve the turkey, something he did every year, and then as he sat at the end of the table, while Ollie was in his usual seat next to Antonia. The chatter stopped when Matt made a toast. First, he teased his sisters, then he praised his mother, and then he turned his focus to Ollie.

"I'm also thankful for my right-hand man." He raised his glass. "He keeps me on the up and up, brings in the big bucks, and is only here, because I threatened to fire him if he didn't come," Matt laughed along with the table. "He always leaves these dinners feeling like he's been through the wringer. So be nice. I'd be lost without him," he added with a nod.

Ollie smiled and tore his eyes away to hide his pleased expression. To be acknowledged by Matt, even if just as a coworker, meant so much in that moment. He read the subtext to the gesture, and when he looked at Antonia's smiling face, he saw that she did too.

"What's it like working for my brother?" Lisa, Matt's younger sister, asked from Ollie's left at the table after Matt sat down and everyone began eating. "You haven't wanted to quit yet?" she teased. "He's so bossy."

Ollie chuckled. "No, it's been fantastic, I'm so lucky I happened to meet him when he was visiting Finn. Once I found out about his company, I kept leaving my resume all over her flat," Ollie lied.

Lisa laughed. "Do you live in Boston? Or are you more of Cambridge, Somerville, Allston kind of guy?"

"I live in Boston. I love it. How about you? You in the city?"

"No, I live here with Ma. My father never let us live anywhere else, and I guess some habits die hard. Plus, the food is amazing," she added and nudged Ollie's shoulder with her own.

Ollie took a bite of his food and nodded heartily in agreement.

After dinner, which was more like a late lunch and had enough food to serve an army, Ollie changed into the sneakers he brought and followed Matt's nephews and niece outside to play soccer. Ollie had talked Matt into letting him skip wearing a suit, instead wearing navy chinos and an emerald-green cashmere sweater that made the Mediterranean in his eyes shine more green than blue. Matt wanted to follow them and admire Ollie in action but forced himself to remain at the table where he had to listen to his oldest sister, Mary, praise the current president, and basically regurgitate the lies she was fed daily by her media outlet of choice. Matt bit his tongue, knowing that no argument, even with what he knew with his security clearance, would change her mind.

Matt turned his attention to Lisa as Mary said something else completely erroneous about the administration and gathered up plates around her. "How's work? How's the love life?"

"Work is work. The commute sucks, but there is a hot guy who gets on the train at the stop after mine and he's been making eyes at me. So, the love life could get interesting," Lisa replied with a grin and took a sip of her wine.

"Does he wear a suit?" Matt couldn't help the protective urge.

Lisa rolled her eyes. "You know, wearing a suit doesn't automatically mean someone's a good guy, in fact it could mean the opposite. Guys in suits, present company excluded," Lisa said as she swept her hand up and down in front of Matt, "are usually finance bros who don't care who they step on or bankrupt in their quest to make more money."

Matt nodded with a smirk. "So, he doesn't wear a suit. Please tell me he's not a bike messenger."

"You are an insufferable snob. You remember that Papa was a builder, right?"

"Yes, and he wanted better for all of us." Matt nodded even as he felt a twinge of discomfort remembering how homophobic his father had been, and how if he were still alive Ollie wouldn't be in his mother's house, in Matt's life. He took a breath and continued on. "That being said, Papa owned his own business, he was successful at it, and his level of craftsmanship is something rarely seen today. I'm sure your bike messenger doesn't come anywhere close to that."

Lisa laughed and shook her head. "I never said he was a bike messenger, you did! I don't know what he does, but he dresses nice, and he doesn't have a bike." She rolled her eyes.

"Who doesn't have a bike?" Theresa, the sister just above Matt in the sibling lineup, chimed in. Her pregnant belly grazed the table as she sat back down next to Lisa.

"Lis's new boyfriend," Matt teased. "When are you due again? Tomorrow?"

"Fuck you, Matt." Theresa threw her napkin at him. "I'm not due until early January. Right around your birthday. I pray he or she comes on any other day; we don't need another *Matt* in our midst." She stuck out her tongue.

"Hey now," Matt straightened indignantly. "I think another Matt is just what this family needs."

Lisa and Theresa looked at each other and laughed uproariously.

Matt frowned. "Oh, now we're back to bullying me? Why not loop Angela and Mary in and make it just like the good ole days." Matt looked through the doorway into the kitchen for his mother. "Ma, they're picking on me again," he called in Italian.

Lisa shoved him as Angela, the second oldest sister, reached across the table to smack Matt on the back of his head. "You're such a fucking tattletale, Mama's boy. Of course we have to bully you," Angela said with a grin. "You got away with *everything* while we suffered. Allow us this one pleasure." She held her fist up for Lisa and Theresa to bump.

Mary appeared in the doorway, blocking their mother's entrance. "*Bambino's* just crying wolf again, Ma," she said in Italian over her shoulder. "Don't fall for it."

She glared at Matt, a look that still froze the blood in his veins. She was just that much older and ruled the house with an iron fist all throughout Matt's childhood when their parents weren't home. Matt looked away and then stood, refusing to be put back into his birth order.

"*Bambino* does just fine without any of you," he said in a steady voice and waved his finger around.

His sisters cajoled and teased him as he strode out of the dining room. He took a deep breath and shrugged their ridicule off his shoulders. If anything, they kept him real, and he needed to embrace that, though he preferred how Ollie kept him in check with his subtle jabs, and a teasing nature that did more for his ego than his sisters reminding him of his roots ever could.

Matt exhaled and grinned to himself as he bypassed Mary with a narrowed gaze and then past his mother stacking dishes on the way to watch Ollie outside with his nephews and niece. He felt Mary's irritated eyes on his back and straightened his shoulders with a cocky shrug she was certain to have seen.

Matt stopped at the window of the back door and saw Ollie cheering on Mary's eleven-year-old son, Gino, who was kicking the ball around Angela's twelve-year-old, Max. There were two mismatched cardboard boxes set up in lieu of an actual net at one end of the yard, and a small boulder and a garden stake at the opposite end, and Gino was headed for the one Max's younger sister, Izzy, was guarding. Ollie called out a tip, something Matt couldn't quite hear, and Gino changed direction immediately and kicked the ball into the side of the goal left uncovered by Izzy. It bounced off the fence behind and Gino jumped with a fist pump in the air. Ollie gave him a high five and then said something to Izzy that made her smile.

"You should coach," Patrick called to Ollie. He was standing at the bottom of the porch stairs with his and Theresa's son, Joseph, on his hip. "Mike was saying they're always scraping for parents to step up and volunteer in the town league."

Matt watched Ollie sweep his hair from where it had flopped into his eyes as he looked at Patrick with a friendly grin. "I wish I had the time." His eyes flicked to where Matt was standing in the window of the door and flashed a toothy smile that was shy and borderline flirty before schooling his features. "My boss is a pretty demanding bast—I mean pain in the you know what," Ollie corrected his language as he glanced at the kids. "He's always checking up on me." He nodded with his chin to where Matt was standing.

Patrick turned and met Matt's eye as he opened the door. "Jesus. How long you been standing there?"

Matt shrugged. "Long enough to see Gino's goal. Just wondering if Beckham here was gonna be showing off like last year."

"You missed that," Ollie replied as he came to the stairs. "Is it dessert yet?"

Matt looked over his shoulder at the activity in the kitchen. "I'd say fifteen minutes or so. Chuck should be here soon."

Ollie nodded with an inscrutable expression and turned back to the lawn. "Okay, guys, we got about fifteen more minutes, let's see if we can score on Dominic."

Matt kept his eyes off the enticing curve of Ollie's ass in his snug chinos and looked at Patrick instead. "You want me to take Joe so you can play three on three?"

Joe went willingly to Matt, especially with the promise of dessert, and Matt went back inside the house with one last glance at Ollie who was demonstrating some footwork to his rapt audience. Finn was just arriving as Matt came back through the kitchen with Joe. He passed Joe off to Theresa and swept Finn into a tight hug.

"How's things, Chuck?" he asked with a quirked brow after kissing her lightly.

"Good. Busy," she answered in a way that shut down further questioning and then turned to greet another one of Matt's sisters.

Matt never got a chance to speak with Finn in depth, or barely at all after that brief exchange. Not even Ollie had a chance to get her alone to pry about her mysterious assignment. Matt was dying to find out more, especially since Finn had let slip over the phone that she was now seeing the FBI agent who had hired her. He couldn't just ask about Finn's new boyfriend in front of his family and she somehow managed to avoid being alone with either Ollie or him the entire visit.

Matt could tell there was something else bothering her and knew it was only a matter of time before he'd get it out of her. He managed to get her to agree to stay with him over her winter break (she could hardly say no with all his family listening in) and planned to get the full story while she was there.

11

You Can't
Handle the Truth

FINN STAYED WITH MATT AND OLLIE the day before Christmas Eve after dropping her German Shepherd, Jayne, at her father's in Wellesley. Matt heard the whir of the elevator just past nine at night, announcing her arrival, and went to the foyer to wait for her. It wasn't to ambush her, but he meant to send a message, and judging from her guarded response, she got the message loud and clear.

"Hey, Chuck. How's the haunted box?" Matt teased after hugging her hello and leading her into the living room where Ollie was waiting.

"It's not haunted," she scoffed. She took the glass of wine Ollie handed her with a kiss and then looked at Matt with a look that conveyed, 'not in front of Ollie.'

"Well, that's good news," Matt replied smoothly while wondering exactly what she was covering up. "How's your new beau and his government-issued shoes?"

Finn pulled a face. "You're such a dick. Yeah, he works for the FBI, but he's a good guy."

Matt pulled back as he noted the intensity of her tone. He wondered if she was hiding red flags or if she just wanted him to back off because she was tired. He sat on the couch opposite her and waited for Ollie to sit next to him while he studied her body language. He decided to continue with the teasing tone so she wouldn't retreat further.

"Whoa, Chuck. Didn't know you were serious about your fed." He grinned and took a sip of his martini. "I thought it was just a casual thing."

"You went from Guy to a government worker?" Ollie interrupted with a note of incredulity.

Matt turned his attention to Ollie and placed a calming hand on his thigh. It was strong and tense under his hand, and in that moment, Matt wondered just how much Finn's rejection of Guy had affected Ollie. Matt of course wished her relationship with Guy had blossomed into something more, because Guy was almost as incredible as Ollie and was someone he knew would treat Finn right. But he also knew Guy would never move to the States, and Finn would never move abroad again. Not just because Matt didn't want her to, but because Finn would never go far from her dad. Matt made a mental note to explain that to Ollie when they were alone.

"What's wrong with that?" Finn scowled defensively. "They do well, and, Luke, was a Major in the Army. He served nearly ten years before he retired," she said with a proud note in her voice. "He's really great."

"Army, Chuck?" Matt sighed and shook his head with disdain. "Talk about slumming it."

Finn rolled her eyes and picked up her wine glass with a pissed off attitude. "He was Delta, Matt."

Matt bristled. Delta was impressive, but he would rather come out to the world in a press conference wearing a pink tutu, than admit that to her. He scoffed and shook his head. "That means nothing to me. And Army-Navy, Chuck? It's a rivalry that goes back to the dawn of man." That bit was true. Truer than eggs with bacon, than stars with stripes, and certainly truer than wimps in green versus sailors in blue.

"What's Delta?" Ollie asked, looking between them and drawing Matt out of his military headspace.

"They're special forces, like the SEALs," Finn replied.

"Delta is *nothing* like the SEALs," Matt corrected firmly. "We had to support them more than once. They couldn't do shit without us."

"What is it with you military guys? Always feeling superior to the other branches and yet you all fight for the same side. It's ludicrous," Finn said, an angry tone in her voice.

Matt backpedaled, not wanting to risk a fight that would have her leaving. "Fine. I'll stop. I'm sure he's a great guy. Can't wait to meet him."

"That's never happening," Finn scoffed and stood.

Matt stood with her. "Don't be ridiculous, Chuck." He glanced at Ollie, hoping for a calming gaze and finding one of apprehension. "I'll be nice."

Finn ran her eyes over Matt, obviously checking the sincerity of his words. "Good night."

"This conversation isn't over, my dear," Matt called as she disappeared into the elevator. He looked back at Ollie who raised his eyebrows.

* * *

"Wakey, wakey," Matt said, touching Finn's shoulder. "We're running on the treadmills."

Finn groaned and tried to roll over.

"I'm gonna jump up and down on the bed if you don't get up," Matt threatened. "You have five minutes to get your ass upstairs. Don't make me come back in here," he called over his shoulder as he left the room.

Finn met Matt in his gym four minutes later. "Why does Ollie get to sleep in?" she grumbled.

"Because I kept him up late and it's Christmas." Matt grinned salaciously as he thought of just what he did to keep Ollie awake the night before.

"You *always* let him sleep in." Finn shook her head.

Matt shrugged. "I *always* keep him up late."

"Jesus. It would be nice if you slept in," Finn muttered under her breath.

"Just get on the treadmill and quit your bitching and moaning."

They ran in silence with one of Ollie's playlists playing through the speakers in the ceiling. Finn tried to keep up with Matt's pace on his machine before finally giving up and slowing hers down.

"So, tell me about your lover boy," Matt said, unable to remain silent any longer. "Am I gonna like him?"

Finn groaned. "Probably not. You never do. But you know what. I don't care." She made a face.

Matt laughed. "You're so full of shit. You know you care. And I don't hate everyone you date, I liked Guy."

Finn snorted and rolled her eyes.

"I promise, Chuck, I'll give him—Luke—a chance." He looked at her briefly. "Where is he from?"

"Wisconsin."

"Oh, Christ." He threw his hands in the air. "I just made you a promise that I now can't keep. He's from the *Midwest*?" He groaned and made a face.

There was nothing *actually* terrible about people from the Midwest, but Matt couldn't help but tease her.

"Fuck you. People from the Midwest are perfectly nice."

"I believe people from Wisconsin call themselves *cheese-heads* or *cheddar-heads* or some such nonsense.... No, Chuck. I can't. And he's Army?" Matt let out an exaggerated sigh. "What could you possibly see in him?"

Finn rolled her eyes. "He's a lot like you; that's what I see in him. Except he's not a snobby asshole," she added with a scowl.

Matt mulled that bit of information over, and then made a pensive sound. "A lot like me, huh? So, he's incredibly handsome and irresistible? Wildly successful? Has a gorgeous boyfriend with a British accent?" Matt raised his eyebrows mockingly. "Hm. Seems unlikely, and I think the boyfriend should be a red flag for you." He quirked his eyebrow.

"If I had something to throw at you right now, I would." Finn stuck her tongue out.

Matt smirked. "Where is he? Is he back from his assignment yet?"

"I told you, he couldn't say. And no, he's not back," she said sadly.

"Something feels off. The FBI sends agents overseas to some extent, but it's an appointment usually, not a random, last-minute assignment."

"I don't know what to tell you, Matt. I've seen his badge; he carries a gun. I've met his partner."

Matt looked out the window as he pondered Finn's answers. He slowed his pace on the machine. "You don't think he'd fake that do you? I mean, did you get a good look at his badge?" He paused and then corrected himself. "No, I suppose it would be a weird thing to fake in order to get you to translate something. If he was an imposter he'd have been just as successful pretending to be a history nerd. You would've eaten that right up."

Finn snorted. "The badges were real, and there's no way his partner Stan isn't a fed. You should see him. He gives off Josh Brolin vibes from *Men in Black 2*. Same suit and everything."

Matt tried to picture it and laughed. "Have you translated what they gave you? Did the contents of the box help?"

Finn shook her head and slowed her treadmill to a brisk walk. "It took me forever to get the damn thing open. I almost took a sledgehammer to it. It turns out it was a cypher lock and some of the symbols on the outside were actually buttons. I finally cracked the code the other night, but I was too exhausted to do much more than open it, so I didn't get a chance to look closely. I plan on going through it carefully when I get back. And as far as the cuneiform they've given me," she glanced briefly at Matt, "you're gonna think I'm crazy."

"I already think you're crazy for being interested in a cheddar-headed Army boy but try me."

"I told you Ned and I would have long, somewhat existential conversations about gods, and Mesopotamia, and Ancient Greece and Egypt and such. That Ned believed the stories weren't myths, he believed they were real. All of it, the gods, their offspring, Gilgamesh, the Annunaki, Hercules, Achilles, even Perseus, they were all real."

Matt frowned as he worried for Finn's sanity. "What are you talking about?"

Finn slowed her speed to the minimum and drank from her water bottle as Matt did the same. "Okay I'll try to keep this brief, knowing that you won't believe me anyway." She raised her eyebrows. "First, I need to back up and give you some context.

"Ned knew everything about the ancient world. He saw the gods in a completely different way from everyone else because instead of treating the myths and stories as lore, or anecdotes separated by civilizations and centuries, he saw that they were all the same stories. A recounting of history about the same gods, just in different languages.

"He wasn't completely alone in his theory. Herodotus, a Greek historian from the 400s BCE, believed that the Greek gods were the same as the Egyptian ones, just with different names. And, if you embrace that theory, then it's not a stretch to say they're the same as the ancient Mesopotamian or Babylonian gods."

Matt was following her, but also not, and Finn must've picked up on it from his expression.

"Think of it like this: the Greeks called their main god, Zeus, and the Romans called him Jupiter, and the Mesopotamians called him Enlil, but he was the same god to all of them, the god of the sky, the big cheese." She paused. "Like the word apple. That's the English word. It's *mela* in Italian, as you know, and *pomme* in French and so on, but they all mean the same thing. We've just given the gods different names because of language and culture and time." She shrugged.

"Okay, I'll buy that," Matt said and then held up his hands. "Not saying I believe they're *real*, but I get the name thing. So, what does that have to do with the translations?"

She took a deep breath. "The cuneiform is nothing anyone has seen before, and it's nothing I had seen before. That is, until I read through one of the journals Ned left me and found the same language. He translated some of it, mostly guesswork, I think. I don't know if any of it is correct; it's like reading Egyptian before the Rosetta Stone was found. But he said in his journal that it's the language of the gods." She stopped her machine and looked at Matt who was watching her with a frown. "How could there be a written language for or by something that doesn't exist?" She raised her eyebrows.

Matt held her gaze and then looked out the window at the buildings across the alley.

No fucking way gods are real. That's crazy talk.

"Chuck, that's just what Ned thought it was. Doesn't mean it is," he placated and looked back at her. "I think you're making leaps because you want it to be true, but it's far more likely that it's just an older civilization that we didn't know about or that we dismissed as not capable of written language, like the Neanderthals or something."

"I really doubt it. There're too many unexplained things, too many coincidences." Finn shrugged and brushed some stray hairs back into her ponytail. "We can agree to disagree. Only time will tell anyway."

Matt studied her face and knew that look. She was fully convinced and there was nothing he could say to change her mind. He sighed. "The bigger question is what the fuck does the US government want with these translations. I mean do *they* know what they are? It's just so sketch, and believe me, I know the US government. They're shady as fuck."

Finn smiled. "I don't really know. But what I do know, I can't tell you because Luke said this case is classified."

"I'm betting my security clearance goes just as high as your *boyfriend's*," Matt scoffed. "Spill it or I will be such a douche to him when we finally meet—"

Finn cut him off. "Fine. But you can't tell anyone, not even Ollie." She looked at the door. "Luke said the text he gave me is from stone tablets that they got from Hitler's war booty."

"What?!" Matt exclaimed with an incredulous laugh. He was certain he misheard her, but she wasn't laughing. "Okay, Indiana, calm down. That can't be true. Were the tablets in the *Ark of the Covenant?*"

Finn laughed and shook her head. "I know it sounds crazy, but Hitler was crazy. He was obsessed with all kinds of crazy shit.

"Don't shoot the messenger. I'm just telling you what he told me." She held up her hands defensively.

Matt turned his treadmill off. He was suddenly feeling real apprehension about what Finn was saying, about what she was getting herself into. "I'm going back to my gut feeling and say he's not a fed. I think you're mixed up with some fucking crazy person. I'm gonna need to meet him."

Finn pressed her lips together. "When he comes back, you can meet him. I think it would be more likely that he's a married fed rather than a crazy person, but I don't believe he's either. You'll see."

———

12

———

Tomb Raider

February 2019

"HEY, CHUCK. WE were just talking about you," Matt answered his phone and glanced through the glass door at Ollie studying his computer screen intently. He and Ollie were both working round the clock getting things tidied up for SharkFinn's year end. "What's up?"

"Okay, I know this is going to sound wild, but I need your help finding and getting something out of Mexico."

Matt widened his eyes and swiveled in his chair, turning his back to Ollie. "What? When?"

"I was thinking we could go in March, instead of the Caribbean. Would Ollie be mad?" she asked with concern in her voice. "Spring break is the only time I can get free from work until summer, and it can't wait that long."

"Well, I don't think he'll be thrilled. He really loves the islands, and beaches." Matt sighed wistfully as he pictured Ollie lolling naked on white bedsheets with the ocean breeze blowing over his golden body. "But I could take him another time or somewhere else," he added with a smile to himself.

"Good. Do you have any in-country contacts perchance? Like someone who could help get this thing I need and get it out without any… scrutiny?"

Matt frowned. "What? Is it a hundred kilos of black tar heroin or something?"

Finn laughed. "No. Nothing like that. But it is something I want to keep from the US government."

"Okay. This conversation's over. I'll see you in a week. I love you." Matt hung up and looked at Ollie through the door. He was gonna need to come up with a stellar (and discreet) destination to make it up to him.

* * *

"Hi, Trey." Matt heard Finn greet his driver from the side door of her Baltimore home. Matt had found Trey and his brand-new transportation company when Finn first moved to Baltimore and used him exclusively for all his travel needs in the DC area. Trey was former military and as obsessed with punctuality and discretion as Matt.

"Good to see you again, Dr. Hawthorn." Trey smiled as he got Matt's bag from the back and carried it inside. "Hello, Jayne," he added as Jayne wiggled her giant black body between him and Matt.

"Thanks, Trey. See you tomorrow at three." Matt shook his hand firmly.

"Thank you, Mr. Dion. I'll see you then." Trey smiled and got back in the car.

"Chuck. Get over here." Matt enveloped her in a hug and kissed the side of her head. "I need a run on your treadmill and then we can have dinner and a chat."

Matt sat across from Finn at her kitchen table, freshly showered in his US navy sweats and the Oxford hoodie Ollie gave him for Christmas the year before. Finn smiled as she looked him over. "You really are so handsome. You and Ollie; what a stunning couple."

Matt sighed and narrowed his eyes. "Seems like you're trying to butter me up. What's going on?" He shoveled some food into his mouth.

Finn laughed and took a bite. "I'm just so happy to see you. What? I can't pay you a compliment?"

Matt snickered disbelievingly. "So, what's going on with Mexico?" He took another bite and chewed carefully, seeing right through her casual tone. "I didn't mean to cut you off on the phone, but you can't talk about circumventing the US government over a cell phone with me. I have an encrypted phone for such matters, but you would need an encrypted line as well for it to mean anything. So, if you want to talk about sneaking contraband into the country, you need to do that that in person."

Finn nodded. "Right. Sorry. I don't want to sound like a crazy person, again anyway, but there's a pyramid in Mexico, in Tabasco, that has something I need, and I know I can't just waltz in there and take it, but it needs to be kept safe." She held his gaze. "It can't be left where it is."

Matt frowned. "What is it?"

"A tablet. Like the ones I'm translating for Luke, and like the one Ned left me in that box."

"Can't you just tell Agent Lover Boy where it is and let him get it?" Matt asked before taking another bite.

"No. I have no idea where Luke is, I haven't heard from him in months, and at this point, I don't know if he's even coming back. I got a message that said I need to do this."

Matt pulled his head back at that. "A message from whom? Chuck, what?"

Finn stood abruptly. "Are you gonna help me or not?" She took her plate to the sink and rinsed off the food with jerky movements. "Never mind. I have the money to do this without you."

"Whoa. That's not what I meant," Matt said placatingly as his mind raced. "I just need more information before I reach out to Arturo. He's gonna need to know what he's getting himself into."

She turned to look at him. "It's just a tablet at a pyramid called Comalcalco. I'm pretty sure I know the exact location inside the pyramid.

In and out, easy peasy, as you would say. But we need to go after hours to get it. And then I need to get it through customs without questions."

Matt looked away pensively. "It's just a grave robbery then? I mean no guns blazing or anything. Right? There won't be booby-traps or armed soldiers or some drug lord's pet hippos guarding this pyramid?"

"Right." Finn nodded emphatically. "No minefields, no machine guns, no pet hippos. In and out." She smiled. "The Mexicans don't even know this exists and will never miss it. And, if I'm right, *which I am*, this doesn't belong to Mexico. It belongs to the gods."

The gods?

"Oh, you're on about that again."

"Yes, Matt. So, will you help me or not?"

Matt closed his eyes, thinking if he said no, she would just do it anyway and could get hurt or worse. "Yes, I'll help you. I'll call R2 tonight."

She held his gaze with eyes full of relief. "Thank you. Is he trustworthy? He won't tell anyone?"

Matt grinned. "He was the best SEAL under my command, and I trust him with my life. It'll be good to see him again so soon. But we'll need to do some acting, that man misses nothing."

Finn smiled. "No problem. I can be whatever you need me to be, I only care that he keeps his mouth shut to his boss."

*   *   *

"We're not going to the Caribbean this year?" Ollie frowned unhappily when Matt got home from DC. He ran his eyes over Matt as he undressed in their walk-in closet. "And you and Chuck are going to Mexico without me? What?"

"I'm disappointed too, babe. Chuck needs my help with something, and we'll be staying with Arturo so you can't come. But I promise I'll take you somewhere remote, and sexy, just you and me. No staff or chefs or anything, but lots of vacation sex." Matt grinned and eyeballed Ollie just as carefully while he undressed across from him. "Pick an island."

Ollie couldn't help but smile at the alternative that Matt offered. He pursed his lips. "Okay. But I'm holding you to that promise. I should ask for it in writing, but you are so careful with your word, I know you won't break it." He looked at the bulge in Matt's underwear and then up at his face. "In fact, I seem to recall you promising me over the phone last night that you were going to rub your hard cock on mine, and then fuck me until I screamed." Ollie palmed himself over his briefs. "I've been limbering up my vocal chords all day."

Matt closed his eyes briefly and laughed. "I love you, Ollie. I love that you keep me honest and hold me to my word. It is so crucial that I follow through on my promises, especially to you," he said mock seriously and scanned his eyes slowly over Ollie's body. "However, I recall you saying something about peeling my underwear off and licking me until I moaned and begged. You're even more resolute about keeping your word." He raised his eyebrows expectantly as he crossed to the bed and grabbed a towel from his side table. He pulled back the covers, got in and then looked at Ollie expectantly.

Ollie chuckled low in his throat and straddled Matt, touching his tongue to his. "We'll both keep our word."

Matt ran his hands up Ollie's thighs as Ollie leaned forward and kissed him. It had been three days, and Matt's warm hands made every nerve ending in Ollie's skin awaken with a zing, particularly when Matt's thumbs teased into Ollie's briefs and grazed his balls. Ollie let out a small moan and rolled his hips seeking friction against Matt's hard length. He bracketed Matt's head with his forearms as he deepened the kiss.

Matt hummed in that pleased way that made Ollie's stomach flip and smoothed his hands from between Ollie's thighs to grip his ass. Matt pulled Ollie in tight as he flexed up into him and kissed along Ollie's jaw. He licked the shell of Ollie's ear and then nibbled the spot behind Ollie's ear that drove all rational thought from his head.

"God," Ollie whispered with a shudder of pleasure, "you keep doing that and you won't get your tongue bath."

Matt chuckled, his breath warm against Ollie's skin and slipped his hands under the waistband of Ollie's underwear to squeeze his ass cheeks tightly. Ollie met Matt's upward thrust with a downward one of his own and shifted his weight so he could kiss his way down Matt's neck and then chest.

One kiss for Matt's Adam's apple, two for his collarbones, two more for his nipples, where Ollie lingered to suck each one into stiff peaks, and then a tongue trail down Matt's hard body to his bellybutton. Ollie watched Matt's abdomen quiver, and his breaths come in short gust as he teased with his lips and his fingers. He looked up and found Matt watching him intently with pupils so big they almost completely obscured the bright blue of his irises. Ollie's cock flexed in his underwear, and he ground down against the mattress as he mouthed Matt's girth over the fabric of his boxer briefs.

"You're such a fucking tease, Oliver," Matt bit out in his gravelly voice. He threaded his fingers into Ollie's hair and gripped as he lifted his hips and moaned. "Take my boxers off and get your lips around my dick. I want it nice and wet."

"Oh, sure. You can edge me whenever you want, but god forbid I make you wait," Ollie scoffed and licked his bottom lip.

He had no intention of making Matt wait, because that meant he'd have to wait, and Ollie wasn't into that like Matt was. He shook Matt's hand out of his hair and eased Matt's underwear off. He kissed the jagged gunshot scar above Matt's right hipbone before planting kisses lower. Matt's cock flexed, almost with relief at being released, and lay hard and proud against his abdomen. The tip was glistening with pre-cum, and Ollie couldn't wait to taste it. Matt's cock was dark, and the even darker head was half-exposed from the foreskin. Ollie knew in a matter of minutes, it would turn purple and weep with excitement under Ollie's masterful tongue.

"Magnificent," Ollie whispered and then licked from the base to the tip with a flat tongue, tasting Matt's sweet flesh and then the salty tang at the top. "This fucking thing…." Ollie swirled his tongue around the head and then under the foreskin.

It was musky, but not too musky. Matt kept himself clean, almost obsessively so because he worked out so much, but there was always that delicious essence that was purely Matt and the scent and taste made Ollie's toes curl and his cock rigid and his heart flutter, all in ecstasy. Ollie opened wide and swallowed Matt down, wetting the shaft of his cock as he went. When the tip hit the back of Ollie's throat he paused, relaxed, and then took Matt deeper. His eyes teared, his breath caught, and his saliva glands went into overdrive, but the euphoria Ollie felt with Matt's cock buried deep in his throat was something he would never grow tired of.

Ollie heard Matt's moans, felt his hands on his head, Matt's fingers in his hair, and bobbed up and down as though his life depended on it. It was messy, and slurpy, and everything Ollie needed after three days apart. Matt fucked his throat as Ollie grunted and gasped around him. His cock was like steel in his underwear at the sounds Matt was making and while he was happy to take Matt's load down his throat, he far preferred taking it in his ass while he came all over Matt's chest, so he gently pressed against Matt's thighs.

Matt stopped pumping his hips as his chest heaved with passion. He ran his finger under Ollie's chin and forced his gaze. "On your back, and spread those legs," Matt commanded as he rolled his body up. "Let me see that beautiful bloom of yours."

Ollie slid off his briefs and lay back on the pillows with his knees to his chest, waiting with a grin for Matt to see what he had waiting as a surprise. Matt stroked himself as he waited for Ollie to get into position, and then busied himself with finding the lube, so it wasn't until he was back between Ollie's legs that he paused with his eyes locked on Ollie's ass. The smirk grew on his face at the same as his hand gripped the base of his cock.

"You little slut." Matt growled. "Fuuuuck," he dragged out on a breath as he reached down and spun the butt plug in Ollie's hole.

It was the toy Ollie had special ordered on a whim when Matt had been away on a business trip. It was navy blue, and shaped like a missile, with a gold trident stamped on the end. The trident matched the pendant on Ollie's necklace, which matched the trident tattoo on Matt's chest, and it had been one of the best purchases Ollie had ever made, because Matt loved it. He loved making Ollie wear it all day as a tease, he loved using it while swallowing Ollie's cock, and he especially loved to threaten Ollie that he would use it while fucking him (which Ollie told him in no uncertain terms that he was too big to do).

Ollie grinned at Matt's response and then threw his head back into the pillows with a moan as Matt began fucking him with it. He felt Matt's tongue around the toy and then on the sensitive flesh between the toy and his balls, and then his balls were in Matt's mouth, one at a time. Sucking and licking as he continued to slowly press the toy in and then pull it partially out, all while angling it so it brushed against his prostate. Ollie curled his toes and bent his knees as he gave over to the sensations and tuned everything else out.

Ollie felt Matt's hand on the back of his thigh as he pushed it into Ollie's chest and then Matt's lips on his calf. He lifted his head and met Matt's gaze.

"Have I told you lately just how much I love these legs of yours?" Matt asked as he kissed down Ollie's leg toward his ankle, all while continuing to push and spin the toy. "So fucking sexy." Kiss. "So muscular." Kiss. "So… hairy." Matt stopped to pull a hair from between his lips.

Ollie laughed. "My legs are not nearly as hairy as yours are. And I keep the parts that are normally in your mouth hairless, so quit your whinging."

Ollie flinched when Matt's open palm connected with the bottom of his ass cheek and then whined at the emptiness when Matt pulled the toy from inside him. Ollie watched Matt sit up and then spit into his hand.

"No lube?"

"Nah. You're wet enough from this," Matt held up the blue missile before tossing it on the towel next to Ollie, "and I'm not gonna last very long, so I'll be fucking my cum back into you."

Ollie huffed a laugh at Matt's salacious expression and then moaned as Matt gripped Ollie's ankle with one hand and guided his cock inside Ollie with his other. He held Matt's intent gaze as the burn of Matt cock stretching him took his breath.

"Breathe, princess," Matt murmured and kissed Ollie's ankle. "You take me so good. Look at you." Matt broke eye contact to watch himself sink into Ollie.

Ollie turned his head to look at their reflection in the giant mirror Matt had hung after they moved in. Matt looked glorious on his knees in the low light. Ollie watched the hollow in Matt's ass cheek deepen as the muscle flexed with his shallow thrusts. His cock flexed in response, and he licked his lip as he continued to watch, mesmerized.

"Like what you see?"

Ollie nodded without taking his eyes off the mirror. "You're fucking magnificent. Ahhhh." Ollie exhaled when Matt bottomed out and his groin was fully seated against him.

"You're the magnificent one." Matt groaned and began moving in long, slow thrusts. "Those beautiful rosy nipples of yours," Matt brushed his thumb across one and a zing went straight to Ollie's cock, "your absurdly soft skin." He smoothed his hand down Ollie's chest to his cock. "This spectacular dick." He gave it a quick stroke before gripping Ollie's thigh again.

He ran his hands down Ollie's thighs to his hips and held him close as he sped up his thrusts. Ollie looked at the muscles in Matt's biceps rounding in flex and the veins in his forearms standing out with exertion and felt the familiar tingle in his lower abdomen. He switched his gaze from their reflection to Matt above him. Matt was staring down at Ollie's torso, his eyes flicking from Ollie's cock to his nipples and then to Ollie's throat. Ollie waited for Matt to meet his eyes and then moaned at the intensity he found staring back at him.

Matt kept one hand on Ollie's hip and placed the other next to Ollie's head to capture Ollie's lips in a searing kiss. Ollie tucked his knees closer, resting his heels on Matt's lower back, and sucked on Matt's tongue. Matt's thrusts became erratic, and he sped up, clearly chasing his orgasm. Ollie slipped his hand between their bodies when Matt gave him room. Ollie focused on the moon pendant swinging from the necklace around Matt's neck above him and began stroking his cock in earnest. He smeared the pre-cum from the tip down the shaft and angled his ass lower so the curve in Matt's cock could rub that bundle of nerves even better.

"Oh, Matt… I'm gonna come," Ollie panted.

"Yeah, give it to me. Come on my dick and I'll be right behind you."

Ollie felt his eyes roll back as everything in his body went tense and then his pleasure burst free.

"Oh yeah, baby. Fuck that's so hot," Matt growled and squeezed Ollie's hip as he watched Ollie erupt all over himself. "I'm… I'm…." Matt's hips stuttered and he shouted something in Italian as Ollie felt a rush of warmth inside.

Ollie felt another pulse of cum pool over his thumb as his orgasm receded from its crescendo. Matt kissed him hard with heavy puffs of breath and rolled his hips until coming to a stop and resting on his elbows above Ollie.

"That was incredible," Matt said between kisses. "I love coming home to you."

"Felt so good," Ollie replied and watched Matt pull back then lean over Ollie's chest to drag his tongue through the splatter on Ollie's chest.

"Mm. Yum." Matt smacked his lips and rolled away.

Ollie grabbed the towel and wiped himself clean while Matt disappeared into the bathroom for a washcloth. He poked his head back into the bedroom. "I'm hungry. Got any leftovers?"

No cuddles then.

Ollie flopped back onto the pillow. The man was a walking stomach. "Yes. I made you a sandwich with leftover grilled chicken and brie. It's on the bottom shelf of the fridge."

"I'm the luckiest guy," Matt stated and pulled on a pair of grey joggers. His dick was still half hard and the material molded to it enticingly.

Matt kissed Ollie and left the room. Ollie thought about getting up to brush his teeth but in the end, decided it could wait.

13

Head Games

MATT TOOK A QUICK SHOWER after sparring with Finn in her basement gym the night before their trip to Mexico. SharkFinn's year-end wrapped up nicely at the end of February, with even better sales than projected, and Matt was in a stellar mood. He was putting on his US Navy t-shirt when he heard her doorbell ring and then Jayne barking. He heard men's voices in the foyer and pulled on his sweatpants with a frown.

"Who's at the do—" he cut off at the sight of two men standing in the foyer. Both were wearing nearly identical, off-the-rack suits and held themselves like former military. The older man, who looked to be in his forties and did in fact look a lot like Josh Brolin, was in charcoal grey, while the younger man, who looked to be in his late thirties, was in navy blue. They both turned their attention to him as he continued down the stairs. The younger man's impossibly handsome face was marred by a jealous frown, and Matt couldn't help his smirk.

"Jayne, place," he commanded with a snap.

Jayne immediately stopped fawning over blue-suit and went to sit in her spot next to the bottom step with her ears forward. Matt knew exactly who these two men were and couldn't wait to fuck with Luke.

If he wasn't such a frowny-faced, jealous knob (to use one of Ollie's favorite terms), Matt wouldn't have felt quite so compelled.

Matt stood close to Finn and put his arm across her shoulders, pleased when Agent Lover-Boy narrowed his eyes. He felt Finn flinch slightly under his hand and squeezed her reassuringly, also to keep her from stepping away.

Finn glanced up at him, her eyes tight. "Matt, these are Agents Stanton and MacEneas, from the FBI."

Matt looked at them and then back at Finn with a mocking expression on his face. "FBI?! What have you done now, Chuck?"

Matt grinned and released her shoulder to shake hands with Agent Stanton who had a firm grip and studied Matt with an impassive expression. Matt let go of his hand and took Luke's, shaking it with a vice grip that the agent matched. His bicep flexed just as hard as Matt's before they separated.

Matt quirked his eyebrow and fought a grin while receiving a cool glare in response. The animosity was coming off Luke in waves, and Matt had to admit, it was an attractive look on him. Clearly Luke had missed Finn and had expected that she would have missed him too. He probably wanted to make eyes at her and then promise that he'd return later without his partner. Matt almost felt bad about misleading Luke by being touchy-feely with Finn, but not enough to stop. He broke eye contact with Luke and came back to the conversation in progress between Finn and Agent Stanton.

"Yes, actually we're headed to Cabo." Finn said.

"We?" Luke snapped and then collected himself.

Luke's partner turned his head sharply at Luke's tone, and it was all the confirmation Matt needed that Luke's partner had no idea about Luke's relationship with Finn. It didn't seem like he'd look all too fondly upon there being a relationship, judging by the expression on his face.

"Yes," Finn replied with a slight quaver in her voice. "We go away every year."

Agent Stanton said something about getting in touch with them when she returned from the trip and then turned to leave. Luke gave

Finn one last parting glance before Matt closed the door behind them with a smug 'goodnight' thrown at their backs.

"What was that all about?" Matt asked when he turned around to face Finn.

"I could ask you the same thing," Finn spat angrily. "What was with you? You were being a dick."

"What?" Matt asked as innocently as he could manage. There was that anger again, and he was wholly unnerved by it.

Finn punched Matt's shoulder.

Hard.

"For fuck's sake. From the possessive arm around my shoulder to the knuckle-breaking handshake? I really expected better of you, especially after all this time," she scoffed irritatedly. "You know who that was."

"I know. I knew it from the minute I came down the stairs. Come on, you can't fault me for wanting to fuck with him a little to see just how authentic his interest is in you." He tucked a loose strand of her hair behind her ear. "And let me add, it's pretty damn authentic. I thought he was gonna punch me for a second there. Not that he would have been able to," Matt added with a cocky smile, hoping to diffuse Finn's anger.

Finn rolled her eyes but in a manner that conveyed displeasure like Matt had never seen from her. "Am I ever going to find someone who passes your muster? And for Christ's sake, at this point in my life, I wonder why I still care about your feelings on the matter. I really like him." She walked away. "And I haven't seen him in months."

"Hey, wait." Matt followed her into the kitchen. "I didn't say I don't approve… yet. He certainly is as handsome as you described," he mollified. "I just haven't had enough time to evaluate his character, and once I have the opportunity to do so, I'll let you know," Matt said with a laugh that he didn't quite feel. He wasn't sure how he felt about Finn actually settling down despite knowing it was inevitable.

"I am still single because you are such a pain in the ass about anyone I like." She shook her head.

"Chuck. Finn. You are one of a kind, and it pains me to think of you with someone who is not worthy," Matt stated, meaning every word.

"I get it, and I appreciate it," Finn responded earnestly. "And I love you, but you need to back off from my love life now. You have Ollie, and I want Luke."

"Hey, okay," Matt placated. "Why did you lie about where we're going? Tabasco is nowhere near Cabo, and besides, now that he's back, why not just have him go get the tablet?"

Finn looked at the floor and then back at Matt. "Because, as you said, I'm not sure what the government wants with them. And until I know more about what the tablets say, I'm not comfortable just handing it over."

Finn spun on her heel, effectively ending the conversation and Matt watched her leave with an unsettled feeling. After a pause, where he wondered what was going through Finn's head, he found his laptop and went into the living room. He was in the middle of responding to an email from his CFO, Fred, when motion in his peripheral caught his attention. He looked up to see Finn in the archway wearing a full-length Patagonia down coat, high-heel boots and slinging a large purse over her shoulder.

"Where are you off to?" he asked as he looked her up and down.

"I'm going to Luke's to fix what you did."

Matt frowned. "I didn't do anything. It's not like I stuck my tongue down your throat." Matt closed his laptop and tilted his head. "And, Chuck, don't forget, we leave first thing tomorrow. You're going all the way to Alexandria?"

"Yes, Matt. I told him I would wait for him, and then he comes back, after months away to find you here, practically pissing on me to mark your territory." She stared at him angrily. "He's seen the pictures on my mantle; he thinks we were a couple. I protected you before, but I'm gonna need to come clean with him." Her face softened ever so slightly. "You can trust him with your secret. You'll have to, because I can't just fix what you did over the phone. Plus, I really fucking missed him. He's a marvel in bed and I'd like to get laid, thank you very much."

Matt looked away with the usual sinking feeling around his sexuality being known and then frowned. He wasn't sure if he could truly trust

Luke, but based on the secrecy he and his partner had maintained up to this point, Matt felt somewhat confident that Luke could be discreet.

"Fine. Just be back by six thirty tomorrow morning at the very latest." He sighed. "And what time is the dog sitter coming for Jayne?"

"I'll be back by then for sure. And Sheila will be here in about forty-five minutes. Thank you, Matt. I love you." She kissed him and left.

Matt got up at five o'clock for a quick run through Finn's neighborhood where he admired the beautiful houses and the serenity of the cold late-winter morning. He showered, checked in with his pilots, and then made coffee and ate a big bowl of oatmeal. Finn came through the side door just after six.

"Well, well, well," he said as obnoxiously as he could. "It's been too long since I got to witness the Chuck walk of shame." He looked at her over his mug with raised eyebrows.

Finn paused. "Alright, calm down. You've never witnessed any such a thing. You don't let me date," she scoffed and dropped her bag into the barstool at the kitchen island.

"Well, I hope it was worth your while," Matt teased and quirked his eyebrow. "A man that beautiful has to have *some* glaring flaw."

"Oh, is that right?" Finn asked. "What's yours then?" she countered as she opened a cabinet and took down a coffee mug.

"Touché." Matt puffed out a sound he hoped was a laugh and looked back at his computer.

"To be honest, he's perfect," Finn answered, pausing wistfully. "He's smart, kind, and physically, *perfectly* formed." She looked sideways at Matt and gestured with both her hands.

Matt's eyes widened at the gap. *Agent Lover Boy was hung?*

"And he knows exactly what to do with it." She waggled her eyebrows.

"Well, I'm glad to hear he's not a pillow princess." Matt scoffed and put the image of Luke naked out of his head. "You have about fifteen minutes to wash all his bodily fluids off you and get dressed before Trey arrives," he said snapping his fingers.

14

Changes

OLLIE WOKE UP to a silent room, a silent house, and no coffee on his side table, same as the day before. He sighed unhappily as he rolled away from Matt's side of the bed and went to shower. He began doing his hair and stopped to press it back and flat to his scalp while looking at his reflection speculatively. He finished drying it, got dressed and poured a travel mug of coffee to take in the car.

"Call Pedro," Ollie said as he pulled out of his space and turned out of the alley.

The phone rang three times before connecting.

"You know it's only because you're so gorgeous that I would even answer at this ungodly hour," his hairdresser admonished in his slight accent. "When I gave you my number it was in hopes of a booty call, and you're about five hours too late for it to be that."

Ollie laughed. "I told you, Pedro, I'm not gay."

"Oh, child. My gaydar is never wrong. You just haven't realized it yet, and I'm waiting in the wings for you. I'm more than happy to guide you on your baby-gay journey."

Ollie smiled. Pedro was a terrible gossip, otherwise he would have just told him the truth, without mentioning Matt of course. "Anyway, I need a haircut. I want it all off. When are you free?"

Pedro gasped. "No! Oliver. I can't."

"Trust me. I'm texting you a picture of my cousin and I want his cut." At the stoplight Ollie quickly sent him the picture of Guy in his swimsuit from Lyon."

There was a pause. "Oh. My. God. Please tell me *he's* gay!" Pedro breathed. "I am keeping this picture."

Ollie chuckled as he considered Guy's reaction to being porn for Pedro. "Can you do it?"

"I have a cancellation this afternoon at four. I'll see you at the salon. You can give me your cousin's phone number in lieu of tip."

"He lives in Paris, and he's not gay either."

Pedro groaned dramatically. "Paris? He's French? You're killing me, Oliver. I'll see you at four, and bring more pictures."

Ollie laughed and hung up. "Call Naomi," he said pressing the button on his steering wheel.

"Ollie!" Naomi exclaimed when she met Ollie for dinner. "Holy shit! Your hair."

"Do you like it?" he asked nervously and ran his hand from the crown of his head forward.

Naomi hugged and kissed him before taking a seat across the table. "I do. You look so handsome. Like Charlie Hunnam when he cut off all his hair, minus the beard though."

"Thanks. That man is bloody beautiful." Ollie rubbed his jaw and wished he could grow a decent beard. He picked up the menu with a sigh. "I can't believe those bastards ditched us and went to Mexico." He dropped the menu and looked out the window. "It's absolute shite weather here. We should leave and let them find us gone."

"We should," Naomi agreed enthusiastically. "I can be packed in fifteen minutes." She waited for the server to put her drink down and for Ollie to order. "What are they doing there anyway? Finn was vague."

Ollie made a speculative sound. "They're on some secret treasure hunt, and Matt wouldn't give me any details either. That SEAL buddy of Matt's we met in September, C-3PO or whatever his stupid nickname was, is helping them, so I don't know whether to feel reassured that he's their back-up or *whatever*, or worried that they even fucking need it."

Naomi frowned and sipped her drink. "Yeah. That seems unsettling. I hope they're safe. Have you heard from Matt?"

"No. He called the night before they left and said Chuck's boyfriend, Luke, showed up with his partner in tow. So, he's back from wherever he was." Ollie waved his hand. "Finn doesn't want Luke to know where they're really going, for whatever reason, and Matt wasn't sure if they would track his phone, so he said he'd call me when he lands in five days." Ollie sighed. "We've never gone that long without speaking or texting."

Naomi covered his hand with hers. "That is a long time, but I'm here for you if you want to binge some trashy shows until the wee hours."

"What about Ray?" Ollie asked, dragging out the 'a' dramatically.

"We broke up. He wasn't over his ex." She shrugged and sat back in her seat.

"Well, *It's a Shame About Ray*. Can't say that I really cared for him."

"Yeah. I was fine with it too, and now that means I have more time for you." She smiled. "Are we playing tennis this week? Or do you just want to binge some trashy TV?"

"Yes, to both," Ollie replied as the server set down their food.

15

Love and Other Bruises

MATT WASN'T EXPECTED BACK for another two days, so he wasn't surprised to see the Maserati missing from its spot behind the townhouse. Matt took a long shower and dressed for work, putting on a crisp white Brooks Brothers shirt to set off the dark tan he picked up in Mexico and covering it with a charcoal grey Brioni suit.

Stacey and Kerry looked up with surprise as he came through the door to the office suite.

"Hello, Matt. You're back early. How was Mexico?" Stacey asked, composing herself in the blink of an eye.

Stacey was no nonsense and never gave away a thing. She'd been with Matt since the beginning but never pried into his private life or behaved in any other way than a consummate professional. If she hadn't, she'd have been long gone, and Matt paid her above and beyond any other admin in the company because of her discretion.

"Interesting… and fun. Thank you." He smiled and turned to face Kerry. "Is Oliver in?"

"No. He has a lunch meeting in the financial district and then a meeting next door with Brad at Goodwin Proctor, but he'll be back at three for an HR debrief."

"Okay, thanks." He turned back to Stacey. "Keep my day blocked. I've got a mountain of emails and work to catch up on, but feel free to schedule things for tomorrow if anything comes up. Don't tell Oliver or anyone else I'm here. I don't need them adding to my workload." He waited for Stacey to unlock his office.

Matt crossed to his desk and sat down to work. At three thirty he locked his office door and took a stack of paperwork into Ollie's office. Ollie appeared just before four and Matt put the papers on the cushion next to him. He watched Ollie turn to face him with a jolt as he closed the door behind him.

Ollie's face broke into a wide smile. "Matt!" He breathed happily and crossed the room.

Matt stood. He registered, vaguely, Ollie's open arms but he couldn't tear his eyes away from Ollie's hair. It was short.

Wicked short.

Ollie looked amazing; he was a sight for Matt's sore eyes, but there was nothing for Matt to run his fingers through and he clenched his hands briefly to keep the disappointment at bay.

"Ollie. What did you do?!" he couldn't help but ask with a frown.

Ollie smoothed his hand forward over his Caesar-style hair. "I cut it. You don't like it?" he asked, worry in every syllable. "I can't be a hipster forever. Even Beckham cut his flow. And you liked the look on Guy," he added with a hint of petulance.

Matt pulled Ollie into his arms and breathed deeply through his nose, pleased at the note of jealousy in Ollie's tone. He wasn't going to let a new haircut distract him from how happy he was to see Ollie, and as handsome as Guy was, he was nothing compared to Ollie.

"We can talk about the hair later. God, I missed you."

Matt pressed his lips to Ollie's and felt a buzz through his body. Ollie tasted of Earl Grey tea with an undertone of mint, and Matt couldn't help the moan from the familiar flavor. He ran his hands down Ollie's back, squeezed his ass and deepened the kiss. He pulled Ollie in tight and rolled his hips. Ollie met Matt's urgency with his own needy tongue as his hands roamed over Matt's body.

"I missed you too, Lieutenant." Ollie slipped his leg between Matt's thighs and moaned as Matt trailed kisses down Ollie's neck. "Christ, you look amazing. You're so tan, I feel like a ghost." He pulled his head back and looked at Matt. "I can't wait to see you naked."

"Lock the door. I know how you hate to be kept waiting," Matt murmured.

"Matthew, no," Ollie chastised and put distance between their bodies. "Kerry and Stacey are out there. And you aren't quiet, especially after five days without sex. Let's go home. I have nothing else on my calendar."

Matt groaned unhappily and palmed his throbbing erection. "Fine. But I wanted to fuck you while looking out over the water. Especially since we couldn't do it in the Caribbean this week."

Ollie hesitated, possibly seeing the appeal as he looked at the harbor behind him, and then shook his head. "Let me get my laptop and keys and I'll go first."

Matt kissed him one last time and went through the connecting door. He waited ten long minutes, pacing for half the time, before shutting down his computer and gathering his things. "See you in the morning," he said to Stacey and Kerry as he left.

"Christ, Lieutenant. Did you walk home?" Ollie asked teasingly as Matt appeared in the bedroom doorway.

"I offered to fuck you at the office." Matt shrugged throwing his coat and tie on the bench at the foot of their Alaskan king bed. He scanned his eyes over Ollie's mostly naked body as Ollie got off the bed. There was no mistaking Ollie's arousal in his tiny briefs; those fancy briefs from France that made Matt's mouth water. "Someone's eager to have me fuck his brains out. Christ, you brought out the big guns, didn't you?"

Ollie shrugged and stroked himself once over the white lace. "Says the man who was so eager to fuck my brains out that he was willing to risk our secretaries hearing us. I could at least restrain myself, though not once I got home, because, fuck, you are beautiful, and I missed looking at you."

Ollie stood in front of Matt and began undressing him hurriedly, kissing his lips, his neck and his nipples. He palmed Matt over his zipper and squeezed. "I'm so happy you came home early."

Matt tossed each layer of clothing onto the growing pile on the bench and stepped out of his pants as Ollie lowered to his knees. Ollie peeled down Matt's boxer briefs and hummed with pleasure when Matt's hard cock bounced lightly off his forehead.

"Yes, you magnificent thing. I'm happy to see you too."

Ollie nuzzled into the soft spot where Matt's thigh met his groin and breathed deeply through his nose. He rubbed his cheek on the soft skin of Matt's erection and then licked a swath up the shaft and over the tip. He pressed his tongue into the slit and lapped the bead of pre-cum that appeared. He looked up when he felt Matt's hand caress his shoulder and when his fingertips ghosted across his jaw to his chin.

Matt stared down at him with a soft expression as he pressed on Ollie's chin. Ollie automatically stuck out his tongue and opened wide. With a low groan Matt fed his cock into Ollie's mouth while keeping his eyes locked with Ollie's. He pressed his hips forward until he reached the back of Ollie's throat. Ollie relaxed against the pressure, closed his lips and ran his tongue all around Matt's cock to get it wet.

"Oh yeah, like that, baby," Matt whispered, his gravelly voice husky with lust as Ollie bobbed slowly up and down Matt's length, his cock sinking deeper into Ollie's throat with each down stroke. "God, I missed your tongue. Your throat." Matt squeezed Ollie's throat where he could feel his cock. He went to run his hands through Ollie's hair and could barely feel the strands between his fingers. He bit back a frustrated groan and decided now was not the time to complain.

"So, Ollie. What's with the hair?" Matt asked over dinner later, picking up a piece of tuna sashimi with his chopsticks.

"Do you hate it?" It was the third time Matt had brought it up and Ollie was really beginning to worry Matt couldn't stand to look at him.

"No, Ollie. I don't *hate* it. It's just wicked short. Did Pedro do it, or did you have to sneak behind his back?"

Ollie laughed with a modicum relief. "It took quite a bit of convincing, and several photos of Guy in his swimsuit, but he finally agreed."

Matt laughed. "Well, you're still beautiful, of course, but I liked running my fingers through it, gripping it." He paused with a lewd expression. "I even liked how much time you spent on it, making it perfect."

"It does feel weird this short. It's like I have a whole half hour in my day free now." Ollie ran his hand over his head. "It's as short as yours."

"Half hour?" Matt scoffed teasingly. "More like forty-five minutes. You can grow out the shaved sides if you don't want to look like a hipster, but grow it back," Matt stated firmly.

"Okay, Lieutenant," Ollie replied. He already missed the way Matt would grip his hair tightly when he fucked his throat, or kissed him like his life depended on it, so it was no hardship to agree. "How was Mexico, and seeing your creepy SEAL friend?" Ollie asked, changing the subject. He popped a piece of sashimi in his mouth and chewed slowly.

"Great. I'd never been to that part of Mexico before. It was pretty and the food was amazing. R2 did his best to keep his eyes to himself, considering that Chuck and I had to pretend we were a couple. Had to share a bed."

"Well, she's beautiful and she favors small swimsuits." Ollie laughed and tried not to think of Matt and Finn sharing a bed. He knew Matt would never do anything with her. "Did you find what she was looking for? Is that why you came home early?"

Matt narrowed his eyes in thought and chewed his maki. "We got it. It was a tablet with cuneiform on it. The weird thing was, the pyramid we retrieved it from was positively ancient, hadn't been entered in centuries, but the stone looked brand new." He looked at Ollie. "The whole thing was really bizarre, and we came home early because Arturo got a call from the Deputy Director of the NSA, telling him two of his agents were heading his way, and that Arturo was to take them to the same place he'd taken us. No doubt it was to get what we took. They're gonna be pissed when they find out it's not there." Matt mused cryptically as he looked at the curtained window over the sink. "Get this. The two NSA agents were Luke and his partner, Stan. Turns out they're not FBI."

Ollie sat up in his seat. "What? Why would he lie? And what is the NSA?"

"It's the National Security Agency. They spy on everyone. I'm not entirely sure what the hell they want with these ancient tablets but can't be anything good. She doesn't want to turn the tablet over to them because she's as worried about their motives as I am."

"Do you think she's in danger?" Ollie asked, his stomach unsettled with worry. "This Luke bloke wouldn't put her in danger, would he?"

"I have no idea, but I called my buddy at the Pentagon and I'm waiting to hear all about Chuck's new *bloke*."

"I hope it's all good for Chuck's sake. She seems to really like him."

"Me too, Ollie. If not for the fact I think Chuck would kill me if I said anything negative about him."

16

Motion

May 2019

IT WAS HORSE SEASON, and that meant more time with Bill. He and Ollie played tennis or squash at least three times a month, but when the horses were back from their winter in Aiken, it meant more time at the barn, more time retraining the horses to their riding style, and more time shooting the shit. Ollie was in Dover (at Bill's farm or at Sentry) at least three times a week and his body quickly felt the effects.

"I met Finley's new beau," Bill announced after a Wednesday match while they were dressing in the locker room of the clubhouse after showering.

Bill was favoring his right shoulder and had a slight limp on his left side but never complained. Ollie had aches from head to toe and couldn't imagine how Bill soldiered on without a word. That he brought up Luke instead of groaning as he bent to step into his underwear was astounding.

Ollie paused and then finished pulling his shorts on over his boxer briefs. "Is that right?" He zipped his fly and buttoned the button. "And?" He looked at Bill who was toweling his hair dry.

"Nice guy. Reminds me of Matt," he added and pulled his shirt on. "He's a lot older than I thought. He's gotta be at least ten years older than Finley."

Ollie hummed pensively and put on his shirt. Matt hadn't mentioned the age difference, so it must not have been glaring to him. "Does that bother you?"

Bill pulled a brush out of his bag and tended to his hair in the mirror. "Not really, no. All that matters is how he treats her, and he seems pretty head over heels for her." He put his brush away and watched Ollie begin to tame his hair, which had almost fully grown back. "And he's got a sixty-seven Shelby that he rebuilt himself, so he's A-okay in my book." Bill grinned.

Ollie ran a small dab of styling cream through his waves and rinsed his hands. He wasn't going to bother with the hair dryer since he was just headed home. "I'm not sure what that means, Bill." He chuckled and met Bill's eyes in the mirror. "Should I assume that's a car?"

Bill laughed. "Yes, Oliver. It's a type of Mustang designed by Carroll Shelby and first introduced in nineteen sixty-five. I'm partial to Chevy's myself, but the Shelby Mustang, particularly the first few models, is something to behold."

Ollie nodded thoughtfully. All he knew about old cars were things Bill had taught him, and while he had no desire to drive or own one, he appreciated Bill's old Jag and Finn's split window Stingray, both cars that Bill and Finn had rebuilt together.

"Well, Matt didn't hate him upon sight when they met, so I suppose that's promising." Ollie chuckled and tucked his shirt in.

"When did Matt meet him?"

"Back in March, when he and Finn were leaving for Mexico. I guess he showed up from wherever he'd been the night before they left."

"Finley and Matt went to Mexico?" Bill straightened from zipping his bag.

Ollie wondered briefly if he was meant to keep that a secret. "Yeah, they went without me and Naomi this year. To visit one of Matt's

SEAL buddies." Ollie figured that would be a safe detail. "Of course I couldn't go."

"Ahh." Bill nodded with a sigh.

"I can't complain. He took me to the Turks and Caicos instead." Ollie blushed lightly when he thought of that vacation. It had been brief but… thorough.

Bill barked out a laugh and patted Ollie's warm cheek. "Good vacation, huh?"

"Matt would die if he were here. Let's talk about something else. Like Sunday's match." Ollie picked up his bag and followed Bill out of the locker room. They nodded at the concierge as they left and parted ways in the parking lot with a hug.

17

Ignorance is Bliss

OLLIE'S PARENTS CAME to visit, along with his younger sister Cassie, who hadn't been to Boston since the previous summer and demanded that Ollie take her around to all her favorite spots in the city. Ollie wasn't surprised that Matt scheduled himself a trip to the West Coast and then Chicago for nearly the entire time. He knew that while Matt liked Cassie, he didn't trust her to keep out of his business and always limited how much time he spent around her.

Ollie wanted to feel indignant, but Matt wasn't wrong. He and Cassie had been quite close growing up; Cassie was always barreling into his room, talking his ear off, and nosing into his business. Though they'd grown up and apart, old habits die hard. She had nearly caught Ollie and Matt *in flagrante delicto* when she had come upstairs from Ollie's flat looking for him, despite believing the townhouse to be Matt's, which sent Matt into the stratosphere. After that incident, Ollie made sure to lock the floors of the elevator between his garden-level flat and the townhouse he shared with Matt any time she came to stay.

"Nice bloody car, Ollie," Cassie marveled when his GranTurismo unlocked with a chirp. "When did you get it?"

Ollie looked at the car and then at his sister. She had matured into quite an attractive woman, with her strawberry blonde hair, blue eyes, and wide smile that was a carbon copy of their mother's. She was wearing high-waisted short shorts, and a crop top that showed off her pale midriff in glimpses. She played tennis even more obsessively than Ollie ever had, and her body was lean and athletic.

"Last Christmas," he replied with a shrug. He of course didn't mention it had been a gift from Matt.

"And when did Matt get that?" She pointed at Matt's slate grey 911 turbo parked in front of their Range Rover. "I mean I'm assuming it's his."

Ollie nodded and got into the car. "I don't know, maybe last summer," he replied when Cassie got in and buckled her seatbelt.

"This is incredible. How much do you make?" Cassie looked at the immaculate interior and then turned in her seat to face him.

"Enough." Ollie pulled out of the space and drove out to Marlborough Street. "And Mum would say you're being crass." Ollie winked. "So, Harvard Square to get Millie a t-shirt, take some pics of you in Harvard Yard, and then a curry at that restaurant you liked last time? Anything else?"

Ollie merged onto Storrow Drive as he listened to Cassie rattle off what else she wanted to do around town. She was nosy, and never met a boundary she wouldn't absolutely obliterate, but she was his little sis, and he loved her. He just wished he could let her know about him and Matt, and while it killed him to keep the secret, he had to respect Matt's demand for privacy.

Ollie parked in the garage at the Charles and immediately missed the air conditioning of his car. He led Cassie through the hot sunshine to all the places she wanted to visit, starting with the Coop and ending with the Indian restaurant that Cassie had raved about the last time she visited.

They gossiped about friends from back home, Cassie caught him up on her new boyfriend, Roger, and her job, which was 'stressful' and how her boss was a 'complete wanker.' Ollie nodded and laughed, and the afternoon passed in the blink of an eye. They were headed back to Ollie's flat when Cassie casually asked about his love life.

"Nothing really to speak of." Ollie shrugged and focused on navigating through the ever-present Boston traffic. "Some dates here and there."

He felt Cassie's eyes and braved a look. Her face was full of skepticism.

"Ollie, you are the most monogamous person I know," she laughed. "You don't do 'dates here and there.' You're either seeing someone or you're not, and if you are, I don't get why you'd be cagey about it."

"I haven't really had the time to be committed." Ollie gave a little shrug and turned off the bridge over the Charles. "I'm not lying," Ollie lied.

Cassie snorted and then sighed. "Whatever. You don't have to say, but you're being weird. You've been weird since you moved to the States, so maybe you're becoming an American, and all I can say is, please don't." She laughed but with a serious face. "You might fall in love with one, but don't ever stop being British."

Ollie laughed. He'd adapted to the lingo of Boston, and loved living in America, but he could never give up his roots. Not just because he was so intrinsically British, but also because Matt loved it. Ollie knew this because Matt was always commenting in one way or another just how much he loved Ollie's accent, or his manners, or his way of being and Ollie would never give that up.

"Don't worry, Cass, I've no intention of becoming a Yank."

It wasn't until Ollie and his family came back from staying at Finn's beach house (Matt didn't want Cassie snooping around their house) that Matt came home. He'd been gone for seven days and while they'd texted and spoke on the phone, Ollie's skin felt itchy and too small for his body when Matt knocked on the door of Ollie's flat and came through to say hi.

The first thing Ollie noticed was how tired Matt looked, the second was how handsome he was despite the fatigue. Matt was wearing grey suit pants and a white Brooks Brothers button down with the top button undone and both items of clothing were tailored to his body with a precision that was borderline pornographic. Ollie knew with just a glance that Matt had come home, shed his coat and tie, and immediately made his way downstairs to see him. Matt had a hug and a smile for his parents, and a patient grin for Cassie's usual enthusiastic greeting, but it was the firm grip on Ollie's hand and the carefully guarded look Matt gave him that spoke volumes.

Ollie studied the way Matt's muscular shoulders rolled under the crisp fabric of his shirt as he joked with David, the way said shirt was tucked so carefully and neatly into his pants without bunching, and of course, the way Matt's suit pants curved around his ass like their only job in life was to cling 'just so,' and Ollie had the sudden desire to be an expensively-spun wool blend.

"You've got a bit of drool on your chin, big bro," Cassie said in a smug tone as she sidled up to him. "Are you allowed to crush on your boss in America?"

"Sod off. So do you." Ollie elbowed her gently and turned to busy himself with something or other while Matt made small talk with Ollie's parents. Ollie focused on schooling his expression and not on how he would sneak upstairs later to ride Matt's magnificent cock.

"Have you guys eaten?" Matt asked with a hopeful glance at Ollie.

"Yes, we went for an early dinner. I've got lasagna in the fridge, if you want to heat it up." Normally Ollie would do it for Matt, but Cassie would think that was too weird. He also left out the fact it was Matt's mother's recipe.

"I'll heat it up for you, dear," Ollie's mother stood from the couch. "You look positively knackered."

"Thank you, Maggie. I am pretty beat, and hungry."

"Just give him the rest, Mum." His mother might think it was too big, but Matt would eat it all.

"Not too big of a piece, please," Matt contradicted and then glanced at Ollie. "I have two contracts for you to review, if I can steal you away from your folks for a bit, and a full stomach will put me right to sleep."

Ollie stomach fluttered with anticipation, and he shifted his gaze to his phone to avoid looking at anyone, especially not Cassie. Matt wasn't worried about falling asleep, he didn't like to have sex on a full stomach, and he clearly didn't want to wait until everyone had gone to bed for Ollie to come up. Ollie guessed that was more from exhaustion than from desperation but either way he didn't want to wait either.

"Sure. I'll grab my laptop and meet you upstairs after you eat." Ollie stood from the couch and pocketed his phone.

Maggie brought a dish and fork from the kitchen and placed it on the table for Matt who sat down with a smile and a thank you.

"I'm gonna watch telly," Cassie announced to the room. "Will we see you tomorrow, Matt?"

"What time's your flight?" Matt asked and pulled out his phone.

"Eight pm."

Matt scrolled through his calendar and switched his phone off with a nod. "I can drop you all at the airport." He took a big bite and chewed with a pleased hum.

Ollie headed down the hall toward his bedroom, a quick (but thorough) shower at the forefront of his mind.

Less than an hour later, after Matt ate Ollie's ass for a good fifteen minutes, he was balls deep inside Ollie and groaning with pleasure. It had been a stressful trip with back-to-back meetings, barely any time for sleep and Matt had missed Ollie the entire time. He never slept well without Ollie breathing softly beside him or in his arms and this trip had been no exception. Seeing him looking so relaxed, and tan, with his family was like a balm to his restless, exhausted soul and he knew he couldn't wait until midnight to have him naked.

Now, Ollie was gloriously naked beneath him, the white of his ass that much more alluring in contrast to the rest of his tan body. Matt admired the marks that he had sucked into said pale skin in between feasting on Ollie's delicious bloom and felt a surge of possessiveness. There were four dark bruises and Matt wished he'd left a few more. He almost wanted to stop so he could decorate the inside of Ollie's thighs as well, but the sight of Ollie's hole swallowing his dick, the feeling of it clenching around him prevented him from doing anything but pump his hips.

"I'm not gonna last, princess," Matt said on an exhale that ended with a moan. "You feel so fucking good… I missed you."

Matt watched Ollie prop up on one elbow and snake his hand between his body and the mattress. Ollie turned his head to the side to sneak a peek at Matt and met his gaze. "I missed you too, Lieutenant. Now, fuck me like you mean it."

Matt growled and kneed Ollie's thighs wider for a better angle. Ollie wanted a railing, and Matt was more than happy to give it to him. He pressed one hand between Ollie's shoulder blades and gripped Ollie's hip with the other as he chased his orgasm with an intensity that had Ollie grunting.

"You feel incredible, and the view… I'm gonna come," Matt panted out and squeezed Ollie's ass in emphasis. "But I want you to wait and come in my mouth."

Ollie's arm slowed and then stopped with a moan. "Ungh, you shouldn't say things like that, if you don't want me to come."

Ollie looked over his shoulder with such a wrecked expression, Matt couldn't have stopped the surge of his orgasm if his life depended on it. Seeing Ollie undone because of him, knowing how much pleasure he was giving the man he loved, how much pleasure he took from Ollie in return was all Matt needed to tip over the edge and unload in Ollie's ass. There was a stream of Italian from his mouth, as though he was speaking in tongues, while his soul left his body and poured into Ollie's.

When the last aftershock of his blinding orgasm shuddered through him, he pulled out and smacked Ollie's ass to roll him over. Ollie's cock was so hard, and so red it looked painful, and Matt couldn't wait to soothe it. He paused to admire his cum dripping out of Ollie's ass before stuffing it back in with two fingers and a breathless smile.

Matt licked the length of Ollie's cock before sucking him to the back of his throat. Prior to Ollie, Matt had never had a dick in his mouth, he'd never wanted one there, it was *too gay*. But their first time together, back in Oxford, the heady scent of Ollie's pre-cum, the way it had leaked so effusively from the tip when Matt fucked him, had Matt desperate for a taste. He groaned around Ollie's shaft as another burst of pre-cum coated his tongue. The flavor was indescribable: a mixture of salty and sweet with a hint of something like an autumn day.

Apples? Mulled cider? The nectar of the gods?

Ollie's incoherent babbling brought Matt's focus back to getting Ollie off, not just savoring his taste, and he redoubled his efforts. Ollie lifted his head from the pillows to stare at Matt with eyes so full of lust Matt couldn't see the blue green of Ollie's irises.

"I'm gonna come. You ready?" Ollie asked, more rhetorically than anything because the next thing Matt felt was the hot spurts of Ollie's orgasm.

Matt swallowed and licked and stroked as Ollie clenched and shuddered and groaned through his massive orgasm. He closed his eyes and swirled his tongue slowly when Ollie threaded his fingers into Matt's hair to pull him off.

Matt collapsed into Ollie's groin and waited for Ollie to catch his breath as he caught his own. He kissed the soft spot where Ollie's leg met his groin, he sniffed the trimmed bush around Ollie's dick and sighed. Ollie's strong fingers loosened their grip and stroked through Matt's hair tenderly.

The love Matt had for Ollie suddenly radiated throughout his body like a shockwave that left his limbs tingling. Matt felt in that moment, in all his moments really, that he would walk through fire, slay dragons, or simply pick a field of flowers for Ollie if he asked it of him. Matt would do all that and more and wished he could verbalize it.

He eventually crawled up Ollie's body and kissed the side of Ollie's neck instead of trying to form the words for feelings that he bet Ollie knew anyway and ran his hands down Ollie's sides as he catalogued each bit that made up the sum perfection of Ollie's body.

Matt lapped the sheen of sweat on the column of Ollie's throat with his tongue before capturing his mouth in a deep kiss. "You taste like heaven," Matt whispered. "I wish you didn't have to go back downstairs."

Ollie brought his arms up and wrapped them around Matt's neck. "Me either. We could set an early alarm."

Matt heard the pleading in Ollie's tone but with Cassie in the building, Matt had no desire to risk it. Having Ollie up here now was already too risky. He rolled off Ollie and grabbed a small towel from the shelf of his side table and wiped his dick clean and then swabbed between Ollie's spread legs. He felt Ollie's eyes on him and eventually looked up when he was finished catching all the drips of his cum. Ollie's eyes were soft, like a calm Mediterranean sea, and Matt knew he didn't want to hear what Ollie was about to suggest. He tried to put that into his expression, tried to will Ollie to keep whatever it was that he wanted to say to himself, but Ollie either didn't see it, or ignored it entirely.

"We could just tell her," Ollie said softly, almost admonishingly. "Then we wouldn't have to sneak around."

Matt stomach clenched and then rolled. Cassie was practically an influencer on social media. Matt had looked her up not too long ago and nearly fell off his chair at the number of followers she had. She wouldn't mean to out them, Matt knew how close she and Ollie were, but having the information about her brother and the CEO of a nearly billion-dollar firm? How could she resist bragging?

"No," Matt stated firmly and let his wall come up and settle into place.

Matt used this method at work and with his family, though rarely with Ollie, but when he did, Ollie was always quick to respect the barrier. Tonight was no exception, though Matt didn't miss the twist to Ollie's mouth.

"One more day, Ollie. Then she'll go back to London, and her life and we won't be of any concern. We can't ever be of any concern to her," he added firmly. "Now, tell me about your trip to Nantucket to see Bill, and your polo match." Matt crawled back into bed and pulled Ollie into his side.

18

Army–Navy

IT WAS SEVEN O'CLOCK on Wednesday when Ollie finally put his work down for the day and closed the door of his home office in Truro. His parents had been gone for over a week, and he'd finally let his resentment about continuing to hide from Cassie fade. He stretched his shoulders and followed the short hallway to the kitchen where he pulled out the caprese salad he'd made earlier, a bottle of fig balsamic vinegar from Gustare's, and plates and napkins and joined Matt on the deck.

"Luke's coming to the beach this weekend," Matt said looking up from the grill as he flipped the chicken Ollie had marinated. "We're all going out on the boat Saturday."

"Oh. I finally get to meet this fake FBI agent," Ollie said as he put everything on the table and crossed to the mini fridge in the outdoor kitchen. "Bill liked him, but will I?" He took out two beers, popped the caps on the opener mounted under the counter and passed one to Matt.

Matt grinned and nodded his head. "Yes. I'm sure you'll find him irresistible. He's pretty hot."

"Should I be worried, Lieutenant?" Ollie pulled up with a mock frown and a real twinge of jealousy as he took the tongs from Matt. "Is your eye wandering already?"

"God, no," Matt replied, sitting in his chair at the head of the table with his beer. "He's your type not mine, I'm the one who should be worried." He quirked an eyebrow at Ollie and then flexed his spanking hand. "Anyway, you demand that I fuck you so much, I couldn't possibly have any more energy to spare."

Ollie laughed as he plated the chicken and put it on the table. "That's you, you horny perv."

"You love it." Matt winked.

"I do. I really fucking do," Ollie replied as he sat and spread his napkin in his lap.

* * *

Matt tied the boat up at the end of the yacht club dock and ran through the checklist of gauges and instruments. All he had on was swim trunks, his Rolex, and his silver necklace, and Ollie couldn't keep his eyes off him.

"You keep eye-fucking me, princess, I'm gonna untie the boat and take you out to sea so you can choke on my dick," Matt threatened with his back to Ollie. "I'm sure Chuck won't mind staying home with Agent Lover Boy."

"I'm doing no such thing," Ollie lied primly. "And for suggesting it, I'll have you choke on my—" He stopped when he saw Finn's SUV pull into the space next to Matt's car. "They're here," Ollie announced and stepped off the boat.

Ollie resisted the urge to lift his Ray Bans to get a better look at Luke and his stunning body as he approached the boat with a swagger that was just like Matt's. In fact, if not for the stick straight hair, that had a pair of sunglasses nestled in its strands, and the slight bow to his legs, Ollie would've thought it was Matt.

Luke was wearing a tight, grey t-shirt with the word 'Army' emblazoned across his chest, blue board shorts that came to his knees, and Reef flip flops. As he got closer, Ollie noted his blue-green eyes, his small straight nose, and his perfectly balanced mouth (just like Matt's) and the way his biceps bulged as he lugged a large cooler that Ollie knew to be full of food.

Matt was right: Luke was pretty fucking hot (despite the flip flops), and Ollie had to force his gaze away to stop from gawking. He turned to look at the boat as Matt appeared in the doorway of the cabin with a narrowed gaze.

Matt ran his eyes over Ollie's light blue swim trunks and short sleeve, white linen shirt that he was wearing unbuttoned. His muscular chest was waxed except for the dark blonde goody trail that began under his bellybutton and disappeared into his trunks, and his long muscular legs had Matt forcing his attention back to the approaching guests to keep from wanting to run his hands over their smoothness. He also wanted to bend Ollie over his knee and spank the ever-loving shit out of him for the way he was staring at Luke.

Matt studied Luke appraisingly as though he were Ollie, seeing him for the first time. Luke was maybe six two, just about an inch shorter than Matt and had a similar build, though Luke's muscles had a slight layer of padding. He was unquestionably handsome, and had a cocky swagger that made Matt want to punch him. When Luke met his eye and smirked, Matt shifted his gaze to Finn so he wouldn't act on the urge. Finn had a jug of water in one hand, a bag of magazines over her shoulder, and a floppy sunhat on her head. She was wearing a short, white crocheted cover-up over a navy-blue bikini and leather sandals and looked beautiful in a way that defied humanity.

Matt kissed her hello with a squeeze to her waist as Luke put down the cooler. He looked over her shoulder as Luke stuck out his hand to introduce himself to Ollie, and Matt had to fight a burst of irritation at Ollie's swoony smile.

"Agent." Matt pulled away from Finn and stepped between Luke and Ollie, breaking their handshake with one of his own.

"Dion," Luke replied with another annoying smirk.

Matt gripped Luke's hand and squeezed as hard as he could. He felt Luke's bones roll under his palm and saw Luke's nostrils flare before feeling his own bones doing the same under the pressure of Luke's returning squeeze. It wasn't until Matt noticed Finn rolling her eyes at Ollie that Matt released Luke's hand.

Matt shot Finn a quelling look and stepped back with a quirked brow that matched Luke's. He flexed his hand at his side and then swept his arm toward the boat behind him. "Welcome aboard." He took the water jug from Finn and stepped aside to let them pass.

Matt swatted Ollie's ass with his free hand when Luke and Finn were fully aboard the boat. "Wipe the drool," he commanded gruffly and shoved the water jug into Ollie's chest.

"I wasn't drooling," Ollie muttered unconvincingly while Matt untied the boat.

Matt strode to the helm with a harrumph and steered out into the bay where he opened the throttle and followed the buoys until they were well offshore. He dropped anchor, stripped off his shirt, and tossed it onto the table in front of Ollie. He was eager to submerge himself in the soothing saline of the Cape Cod Bay and maybe show off a little to bring Ollie's admiring gaze back to him.

He climbed up on the gunwale of the boat and looked over his shoulder at Luke. "Do you know how to swim?" Matt asked with a smug grin and then dove over the side with nary a splash.

Ollie crossed the boat and stood next to Luke and Finn while they waited for Matt to surface. Ollie knew to look as far away from the boat as possible and smiled at Luke's sharp intake of breath when he saw where Matt surfaced. Matt was treading water with what was probably a smug expression; he was too far from the boat to see clearly.

"I'm going in," Finn declared before jumping off the back platform. She made a beeline for Matt while Luke turned to Ollie as he pulled off his shirt.

"You swimming?"

"No. I guard the boat." Ollie ran his hand through his hair, which had grown in nicely.

Ollie swept his eyes over the expanse of Luke's bare skin. He was nearly as broad as Matt, but nowhere near as tan. The hair on his chest was light brown and tapered to a line that disappeared into his waistband just like Matt's. Luke had a tattoo of a skull with a pair of guns under it on his upper bicep, and a tribal tattoo on the back of his neck that Ollie noticed when Luke climbed on the gunwale of the boat. The sound of Matt's gravelly voice carried across the water, goading Luke to stop being such a pansy and just jump already.

After a big splash, Luke surfaced with a shout about the temperature, which of course spurred Matt to call him more names. Ollie watched them and listened to the banter for a bit before picking up his current read and settling down in the sun. He looked up a short while later to see Matt pulling himself onto the back platform of the boat in one easy motion. His muscles flexed pleasingly under the water rivulets that ran down his body.

Ollie licked his lips and put down his book. "Christ, you're positively magnificent. I love watching you in the water, coming out of the water. Just like Poseidon himself I imagine. The women at the aquatic center must swoon. How many drownings are you responsible for?"

Matt shook the water from his hair and picked up a towel from the stack on the table with a sexy grin. "And I love you sitting in the sun, with your blonde hair shimmering like gold." He wiped his face and kissed Ollie with lips that were cold as ice. "Mmm, you're so warm and tasty." He ran his tongue over Ollie's bottom lip.

"And you're freezing and salty," Ollie replied wrinkling his nose. He wiped the water that dripped from Matt's hair onto his face and kissed him again.

Matt ran his wet fingers across Ollie's cheek and down his neck as he deepened the kiss. Ollie was left breathless when Matt suddenly pulled away and looked over his shoulder at the sound of Luke's laugh close to the boat. Ollie saw Finn swimming rapidly ahead of him with Luke right behind her as Matt stepped away and finished drying himself off.

Finn and Luke went below to rinse off the salt water, and emerged ten minutes later, in their swimsuits and talking quietly. Ollie was totally engrossed in his book about closeted love in Communist Poland and ignored them as they slathered each other with sunscreen before going to the front of the boat. He felt Matt appear next to him and looked up, scanning his eyes over Matt's, cataloguing all the glorious ridges sexy tattoos, and then back at his face questioningly.

"You just missed the gun show and I'm not talking about his biceps," Matt said with his eyebrows up. Ollie looked up the side of the boat at Luke's back as he and Finn disappeared.

"Well, the only gun show I'm ever interested in watching or participating in is yours, Lieutenant," Ollie said with a sly grin.

Matt sat down on the other side of the table and put a foot up on Ollie's thigh. He held Ollie's gaze with a pleased smile. "I love you, Ollie."

Ollie rubbed Matt's foot and returned his heated gaze. "I love you too."

Matt moved his foot to between Ollie's thighs and stroked Ollie's balls with his toes. Ollie caught Matt's mischievous grin and squeezed his foot. "Don't be giving me a hard on, Lieutenant. We've got company."

"I wish we didn't. I love fucking you out here." Matt caressed Ollie's cock with the sole of his foot.

Ollie sighed. "I love it when you fuck me out here. Remember when we did it on the—" Ollie caught movement in his peripheral and flinched his hand away from Matt's foot at the same time Matt pulled it away from between Ollie's thighs. Ollie felt a flash of irritation that they couldn't be themselves on their own boat and forced a smile. "Forget something?"

"Nah, just needed a couple of cold ones." Luke gestured to the cooler.

Matt looked over his shoulder. "Join us."

Ollie recognized the tone for what it was, not a question but a command. He watched Luke pause and then lift the lid of the cooler. He took out a beer and sat down next to Ollie, opening it with the bottle opener on the table.

He took a long swig and raised his eyebrows expectantly. "Yes, Lieutenant?" Luke said with a note of mockery.

Matt studied him carefully and then shook his head. "You pulling rank, Major?"

Luke shrugged with a grin. "Just sounded like an order, and I don't take orders from a *Lieutenant*." He widened his legs to an obnoxious man-spread.

Ollie felt Luke's knee brush against his as Luke put his arm behind him on the back of the couch. It felt deliberate and oddly challenging. Ollie glanced between Luke and Matt and noted Matt's obvious displeasure with the move. Ollie stood and put distance between himself and Luke.

"Christ, I don't want to get caught in the middle of whatever this is, thanks," Ollie said with a shake of his head and took the opener off the table. He grabbed two beers out of the cooler and made his way to the front of the boat.

Ollie smiled to himself when Finn looked up and did a double take. "I didn't want you to die of thirst up here. They could be a while," he said with a smile as he opened and handed her a bottle. He sat in Luke's spot and looked around at the water and then the shore in the far distance.

"Thanks. Are they getting along at least?" she asked cautiously.

Ollie grinned. "I left them just getting started on their pissing contest." He opened his beer and put the bottle caps in his shirt pocket. "I feel confident that the cock-measuring portion will commence shortly. I wonder who'd win," Ollie added with a salacious grin.

Finn laughed and rolled her eyes. "Oh, god. The two of them, they're so similar." She sighed. "I just really want them to get along. I need them to. I *really* like him," she added softly.

Ollie patted Finn's thigh. "I think they will, lovey."

Just then they heard Matt's loud laugh, and looked at each other. "That was a laugh, right?" Finn asked with a panicked expression.

Finn and Ollie assembled a late lunch in the kitchen and brought it up to Matt and Luke as they lingered in the sun. Ollie could tell Matt was enjoying trading stories and jabs with Luke. They apparently discovered that they'd been in some of the same places at the same time and the shared experience seemingly loosened something in Matt. In fact, it was clear that Luke was surprisingly easy for Matt to talk to, and while it didn't appear that Matt was ready to give his final stamp of approval, Ollie could see that Matt was definitely thawing toward the man. It also helped that Luke was obviously head over heels for Finn and was treating her like a queen.

After lunch, Matt pulled up the anchor and began the journey back to shore. Ollie and Luke sat in the back while Finn went into the cabin to get her bag. Ollie watched Luke's gaze turn from soft and admiring to speculative and frowny as he tracked her. Ollie followed his line of sight and saw Finn had stopped to say something to Matt. She stood close, as she always did, and Matt's hand was on her hip. Their physical contact was so natural and frequent, it didn't bother Ollie like it was clearly bothering Luke. The only thing that bothered Ollie was that Matt didn't do it to him if anyone else was around, and especially wouldn't around someone like Luke.

"They're always like that," Ollie said quietly, drawing Luke's attention. "Don't ever let it bother you, because there's nothing sexual there. They have known each other for nearly twenty years, it's second nature to them. Besides, it won't do you any good."

Luke studied Ollie's face. "You said earlier that they were two sides of the same coin, and I get that. I don't want to come between them. I'm certainly secure enough in myself to not worry about another man, especially not a gay one." He flashed a grin at Ollie, softening the comment. "Doesn't mean I won't fuck with him, like he fucks with me. Every time he touches her, I'm gonna touch you." His grin broadened into a smile, and he nudged Ollie's knee with his own under the table.

Ollie chuckled at the thought, feeling a slight thrill. "Matt's secure too, but he's going to hate that. He's very jealous. I don't recommend it."

"If he's secure then he won't be jealous," Luke scoffed.

"That rule doesn't apply to me, agent. You see, that he doesn't touch me in front of other people, isn't because he doesn't want to; it's because he can't allow himself to. So, if you do something to me that he wishes he could but can't, then he'll see red. Please don't take offense if I flinch and step away from you. I won't mean any," he said softly.

Luke blew out a breath and nodded slowly. "Well, then we're just going to have to make him comfortable enough to touch you in front of me, so that I can touch you when he touches her, so he'll stop touching her." Luke let out a big laugh and Ollie threw his head back at the thought, drawing Matt's eye and frown. Finn came back towards them carrying a stack of magazines and sat next to Luke on the couch.

"What's so funny?" she asked looking between them.

"Nothing." Ollie laughed lightly.

Luke kissed Finn and stood. "Just gonna have a word with the captain," he said and went inside.

Ollie leaned forward and rifled through the stack of magazines until he found an *Architectural Digest*. He wanted to watch Luke and Matt have their conversation without being obvious about it. He felt Finn's eyes on him and turned his head.

"He's a nice guy," Ollie said simply. "I think Matt's going to approve."

"Oh, thank god!" Finn said with relief. "You really think so?"

"Yes. And I'll make sure he does." Ollie nodded. "They are quite similar as you said. I think they have a common background, not just with the military. I'm guessing Luke doesn't come from money either."

"No. Not at all. He had kind of a rough life," Finn said with a somber tone. "He's worked hard and is amazing at what he does. He's so honorable, and smart, and funny, and he's so damn sexy."

"He is indeed," Ollie agreed and raised his eyebrows in appreciation.

19

Truce

OLLIE UNPACKED THE boat fridge and gathered his things while Finn and Luke carried their bags and coolers to the car. He left Matt talking to a yacht club employee about cleaning the boat and put their things in the car. Ollie tossed him the key when he was done.

"Dinner at nineteen hundred?" Matt asked Luke and Finn.

"If you mean seven, then yes." Finn smiled. "We'll bring salad and wine." She gave Luke the keys and got in the passenger side of her car.

The car ride back to the house was quiet and Ollie felt his eyelids droop.

"Don't fall asleep on me, Oliver. I got big plans for you when we get home." Matt winked and turned the SUV into their driveway.

Ollie let himself into the house and heard Matt close the door behind them. Matt gave Ollie a knowing smile.

"You and your sun-kissed-self had better disrobe immediately so I can worship your body properly." Matt licked his lips as he stalked toward Ollie.

"Oh. Did someone get all hot and bothered on the boat? Did Agent Lover Boy rile you up?" Ollie asked with a tinge of jealousy.

"What are you talking about, Ollie?" Matt asked defensively. "You know my type. It's you and you alone. Or, maybe you're projecting? I saw you watching him. You like the way he sat next to you? Did he touch you?" Matt followed Ollie into the bedroom and took off his shirt. "Did you want him to touch you?" he asked in a low voice.

"Don't be ridiculous," Ollie said breathlessly as his pulse accelerated from Matt's tone and predatory movements. He pulled his shirt off, feeling suddenly constrained. "There's no one else on this planet who can make me feel the way you do, Matt, and I am desperate for you to touch me."

Matt hummed low in his throat and reached for him. "Jesus. I can't believe I made the whole boat ride without touching you and your glorious skin." He smoothed his hands slowly over Ollie's body and ran his fingertips over the back of his shorts. He exhaled audibly. "God, your ass." He kissed Ollie and swept his tongue through his mouth slowly as he guided him to the bed. "You want me to fuck you, Oliver?" he asked huskily as he slowly eased Ollie's shorts down.

"Yes, Matt. Hard and fast," Ollie breathed. "And then I think I want your mouth on me, but it's too soon to say."

Matt heaved Ollie onto the bed with a satisfied grunt and covered his body with his own. He nuzzled into Ollie's neck and began kissing his way down Ollie's body, biting Ollie's nipples into tight buds and then teasing them with his tongue. Ollie gasped and ground into Matt's chest, the friction of Matt's chest hair against his cock sent tingling shockwaves through his body. Matt ghosted his face over the light hair around Ollie's bellybutton and breathed in through his nose.

"I love the way you smell," he murmured and bent Ollie's knees into his chest.

"No, Matt. I'm sweaty," Ollie protested and tried to lower his legs.

Matt held him firmly in place with ease. "I love it. And all you did was sit on the boat." He grinned and dove in with his tongue. "I can still taste your bum balm."

"Nngh," Ollie moaned as Matt licked from his pucker to his balls and back again. "Christ, that feels incredible."

Matt made a sound of agreement and slid a finger slowly inside until he was buried to the knuckle. Ollie closed his eyes and surrendered to the sensation of Matt's talented tongue. It swirled, it lapped, it speared, driving Ollie insane with need. He felt another one of Matt's fingers join the first and moaned as Matt crooked them inside. Matt added a third, spinning and probing with them until Ollie was a begging, blathering mess.

Ollie lifted his head from the pillow with a drawn-out curse when Matt came up on his knees and sucked the head of Ollie's cock into his mouth. It was a fleeting sensation, as all too soon Matt was sitting upright and coating himself with a dollop of lube. Ollie held the back of his own thighs as Matt rubbed the head of his cock up and down Ollie's crack.

"Stop tormenting me," Ollie whined and rolled his hips.

Matt grinned evilly and then pressed slowly into Ollie with an intent gaze. Ollie studied Matt's face, the focus in Matt's eyes heating his belly as Matt held him down with his palm on the middle of his chest.

Matt looked down at Ollie's leaking cock as he began moving. "How's that feel? Worth the wait, Mr. Needy?"

"Yes," Ollie breathed and gripped Matt's forearm. "But I believe I said, 'hard and fast.'" Ollie quirked his brow.

Matt let out a low chuckle that turned into a moan as he gave Ollie what he asked for. The bed shook with the intensity of Matt's thrusts and Ollie had to brace himself against the headboard with one hand. Matt's cock began to burn inside him and rub against his prostate in the way that Ollie craved, and he felt the quaking that signaled the beginning of his orgasm.

"I'm so close," Ollie breathed.

Matt groaned in acquiescence and looked down at where they were joined without slowing his pace. "I wish you could see what I see, Ollie," he groaned in a husky voice before kissing Ollie's ankle on his shoulder. He pressed Ollie's other knee closer to his chest and hovered above him. "God, you're so beautiful. So perfect. You were made for me."

Ollie moaned and reached for his cock. It was impossibly hard and leaking precum like a faucet. Matt closed his eyes and bit his bottom lip, which meant he was on the verge. Ollie tightened his grip on himself.

"I'm gonna come. Don't you dare slow down," Ollie cried and called out Matt's name as he came in splatters over his fist and his abs.

Matt followed him over the edge, his hips jerking as he filled Ollie's ass so full he became slick. Matt gave a final thrust and then swirled his fingers through the mess on Ollie's stomach. He brought his hand to his lips and sucked Ollie's release from his fingers over and over until there was nearly nothing left.

Matt pulled out and watched the cum leak from Ollie's ass before pushing it back inside with his fingers. "I wish I brought the plug." He kissed Ollie's knee with a grin and then grabbed a towel from the shelf under his side table. "I'd make you wear it through dinner, keep you stuffed full of my cum." He cleaned them both before covering Ollie's body with his. "You are magic, Ollie," he whispered.

"And you fuck like a god," Ollie said between kisses. "I'm the luckiest guy."

Ollie rolled onto his side and Matt curled his body around him. Matt fell asleep listening to Ollie's even breathing and woke an hour later to a dusky sky beyond the window.

"I'll run to Mac's for lobsters. You get seawater for the pot and prep the veggies," Matt said, kissing Ollie as he left the bed.

"It really makes all the difference cooking them in water from the ocean. You're so clever, Lieutenant. Yet another reason I love you so."

Matt grinned. "I'm glad to hear it's not just because of my dick."

"Oh, that is the primary reason." Ollie grinned salaciously and then yelped as Matt pounced and tickled him mercilessly. "Stop! Stop! I can't breathe," Ollie cried, laughing as Matt's fingers ground into his sides. "I'd still love you if you had a pencil down there."

Matt stopped and backed away from the bed.

"But as a friend," Ollie added with a laugh as Matt pounced on him again.

Ollie and Finn danced to his playlist around the kitchen as they made dinner, stopping to sing along from time to time, which drew Matt and Luke's eye. Ollie smiled in response to Matt's wink, and him mouthing 'My, My, My,' along with the song when Luke wasn't looking. Matt pretended he didn't like Ollie's music, but Ollie knew Matt had a soft spot for Troye Sivan and knew the words to most of his songs.

Ollie scraped the chopped cucumbers into the large serving bowl filled with salad and stole glances at Matt and Luke on the couch. He couldn't help but notice their similarities, of which there were many, and how Matt's behavior was so different around Luke. It was just like when Matt's SEAL buddies were in town; he wasn't Matt-the-Machine, or CEO Matt, or even relaxed Matt, he was something else entirely. It had to be result of their shared experience in the military, and not just regular military, but special forces, and Ollie really hoped it wouldn't become a regular thing. It was a behavior that alternated between competition and camaraderie and was borderline annoying.

He carried the bowl through the living room and out onto the deck, followed by Finn.

"I can't tell if they're getting along, or if they're on the verge of tearing each other limb from limb." Ollie said to Finn as she put the steaming red lobsters on the table next to the salad.

Finn laughed. "I think they like each other. And it's a good thing too, because I don't just like him, I love him," she said softly and earnestly. "He's the one, I know it. And if Matt's not on board…." Finn shook her head with a wince. "I can't choose between them."

Ollie widened his eyes and looked into the house to see Matt and Luke clinking their beer bottles and laughing about something. "Well, it looks like we won't have to cross that bridge, god willing." Ollie nodded with his chin and looked back at Finn. "I'm so happy for you and I'll make sure Matt doesn't say shit about him," he added and squeezed Finn to his side as they opened the slider and announced that dinner was served.

They ate at the long wooden table on the deck with the ocean breeze keeping the bugs at bay. The string lights and votives twinkled around them while the sound of the ocean provided the perfect background to their conversation.

"What did you do in the summers growing up?" Matt asked Luke as he added his empty lobster shell to the others in the bowl between them. "What's the scene in *Wisconsin*?" he added with a friendly smirk.

"My mother's parents had a house on Geneva Lake, not the one in Switzerland," Luke shot a glance at Ollie with a grin, "and we would go for the whole summer until I hit middle school. My grandparents spoiled my brother and me. I had a few cousins who came too, and we would spend all day swimming or out in the rowboat catching fish and turtles."

"Sounds lovely," Ollie remarked and sat back in his chair with his glass of wine.

"It was. Nothing like this though." Luke gestured to the house and the beach.

"You think this is something, you should see where Chuck summered as a kid." Matt grinned and looked at Finn. "You should take him; use my helicopter."

Ollie didn't miss the brag, and neither did Luke, judging from his flinch.

"He's only here until tomorrow," Finn said sadly and put her hand on Luke's knee. "Next summer for sure." She smiled at him.

Luke returned the smile and nodded. "I can't wait."

"Speaking of only here until tomorrow…." Finn stood and pulled Luke to his feet. "We gotta run. Thank you for dinner."

They said their goodbyes and made their way to the beach.

Ollie watched Matt watch them disappear into the dark and stood when Matt stood.

"I'll clean the kitchen. You go wait for me upstairs," Matt said and waggled his eyebrows.

20

Midnight Rider

OLLIE WOKE IN THE NIGHT, disoriented and uncertain as to what roused him. He disentangled himself from Matt's body and went to the bathroom where saw a flash of light behind the curtain from the direction of Finn's house. He frowned and flushed the toilet and crossed to the open window for a better look. There was a faint odor of electricity or ozone on the breeze, but thankfully no smoke.

The nearly full moon illuminated the beach and Finn's house over the treetops. Ollie scanned the view and began to turn away when he saw movement between Finn's house and the water. There were two people, one of whom was Finn, and while he couldn't make out the man's features, he could tell it wasn't Luke. The man next to her was taller, leaner, and had long hair. They stood together for several moments, having a conversation judging from the body language and gestures Finn was making, before Finn turned to go back into the house.

The man watched her go and then turned his gaze toward Matt and Ollie's house. He looked up at the second-floor window as if he could see Ollie looking down at him. Ollie stepped back reflexively with a flutter of panic, but there was no way anyone outside could see in. Ollie peered around the windowsill in time to see another burst of lightning along the tree line and no sign of the mystery man.

Ollie shook his head with wonder. "What in the bloody hell?" He turned with a frown and went back to bed where he lay awake next to Matt for nearly an hour before spooning him and finally falling asleep.

Ollie dreamt he was in the yard, with the ocean behind him. Everything seemed normal except the sky, which was an eerie greenish yellow. He saw Matt sitting on their deck and waved, but Matt looked right through him. In the next moment Ollie found himself in front of Finn's house standing just to the left of the cabana bed in the sand. The gauzy curtains billowed sensuously in the evening breeze. There were shadowy figures intertwined with each other inside and Ollie couldn't help but step forward for a closer look. He saw an anchor tattoo on a muscled bicep and a blonde head like his own thrown back in ecstasy.

Just as he heard Matt call out his name in that way he did right as he orgasmed Ollie felt someone behind him. He turned to find a tall, blonde man of indeterminant age, with a face so beautiful it almost hurt to look at him, staring impassively back at him. His hair fell in waves to his shoulders and Ollie wondered briefly where the man's surfboard was. Ollie tried to raise his hand in greeting, but his limbs were too heavy.

"Who are you?" he asked, his voice loud in his ears.

The man smiled gently, an almost blinding flash of teeth and charm. "Just the messenger, here to tell you that you saw nothing, beautiful child of Ishtar." The stranger touched Ollie's forehead and Ollie was suddenly and completely awash with a sense of calm and joy.

Ollie woke several hours later and stretched his body languidly, the dream already fading like smoke on the breeze. He smelled coffee and Matt's body wash and rolled on his side to find Matt next to him in bed with his laptop on his thighs.

"As much as I love your notes, Lieutenant, I far prefer finding you in my bed like this, smelling and looking like heaven." He smiled and rubbed his eyes. "The coffee on the side table is an added bonus."

Matt grinned. "I should put ice it in because it's gone cold. Jesus, you slept way late; it's past ten. You have a polo match you need to get ready for. Good thing I packed all your stuff in the car and made sure the helicopter is waiting."

"I'm the luckiest man." Ollie drank his cold coffee and looked at Matt. "I feel like I was awake in the night, but I'm pretty sure it was just a dream."

"Hm. What did you dream about?"

"I can't remember. I think there was a man, or maybe it was a woman. And they said something about the movie *Ishtar*." Ollie took a deep breath. "Then they touched my head, and it was incredible, the calm I felt. I wish it were real."

Matt nodded appreciatively. "That sounds like a dream I would love. Work has me pretty stressed right now."

Ollie scanned his eyes down Matt's body. "I know a great stress reliever." He raised his eyebrows suggestively and pushed the covers off his body. He rolled onto his side facing away from Matt and ran his hand over his ass. "And I have just enough time to soothe you with it."

PART THREE

UNTIL THE END OF THE WORLD

21

Heartbreaker

October 2019

MATT'S PHONE BUZZED in his armband as he rounded the bridge over
the Charles River near Watertown to head back to Marlborough Street.
His breath clouded visibly in the cool, early-morning autumn air as he
checked the screen. He stopped running and tapped his earpiece.

"Hey, Chuck!" Matt answered breathlessly and continued walking
at a brisk pace, his long legs eating up the distance. "How's it going?"

He heard Finn take a deep breath. "I'm headed your way." There was
a pause. "I will be in Boston by two at the latest. Will you be home?"

Matt frowned at her tone. "Yeah, babe. I can be home. Everything okay?"

"Thanks. See you soon."

The call ended and Matt paused thoughtfully before resuming his
run. There was something in Finn's voice and Matt worried over it the
whole way home.

Matt left the Seaport, where he'd been too distracted to focus on work
anyway and waited for Finn back at the townhouse. He divided his

time between his home office and the kitchen where he checked the fridge a million times without taking anything out. His phone buzzed with a text from Finn saying she'd arrived, and he headed to the foyer to meet her. The elevator doors opened to reveal Finn, dressed in yoga pants and a zip hoodie. Her honey-blonde hair was in a messy bun, and she looked like she just rolled out of a bed she hadn't slept in in weeks.

She looks like shit.

Matt tried to smile soothingly but feared it was a grimace instead.

Finn's green eyes shone bright with unshed tears and her face crumpled when she saw him.

"Oh, Chuck." Matt pulled her into his arms as Jayne bounded out from behind her and wriggled around his legs. "What happened?" He kissed the side of her head as his stomach sank with apprehension. "Are you okay?"

Finn shook her head against his chest. "No. I'm not," she sobbed.

Matt tightened his arms around her, and rubbed her back lightly. "You're safe, sweetheart. I'm here. I got you; you know that. Tell me what happened. I'll fix it."

Finn took a deep shuddering breath. "Things have gone to shit."

Matt rubbed his hands down her back and then gripped her face lightly in his hands, wiping her cheeks with his thumbs. "What's going on?"

Finn blew out a breath. "Luke… I thought I knew him." She winced as tears spilled down her cheeks. "Things were great, and then he began… acting weird. He broke up with me in the middle of the night a few weeks ago and fired me from the job." She looked away. "Then, I, uh, needed to speak with him. He knew I was coming to see him, and…I caught him…with another woman. He didn't even flinch or try to come after me when he saw me." She shook her head angrily and met Matt's eyes.

Matt's gut tightened along with his fists. "That fucking bastard! Jesus Christ. Why did you go see him?" He frowned as he fought the urge to punch something. "If he had broken things off like an asshole, why would you go back to him?"

Finn slid her eyes away again, and fresh tears pooled. She swallowed roughly as her silence stretched. "I'm pregnant," she choked out and sagged in his arms.

Matt blew out a breath and pulled her against him as his mind raced. *Holy shit.*

He couldn't help the sound of disbelief. "Christ. Does he know?"

Finn shook her head against his chest.

"You gonna keep it?" he asked softly.

"I don't want to. I hate him," she cried. "I don't want to look at his baby every day," she sobbed and tightened her grip on the back of his shirt.

Matt nodded with understanding. "Okay, babe. I'll make an appointment. I'll go with you. I'll take care of everything."

Finn sagged against him with a soul wrenching exhale. Matt led her to the kitchen and sat her down. She looked gaunt and he mindlessly pulled a bowl of fruit out of the fridge with a silent thank you to Ollie for always having something fresh on hand. He gave her a fork and went to get her things from the car. He paused briefly at the sight of all the luggage before bringing them all inside. He left the large trunk in the back until Ollie got home.

"Why are you bringing all this stuff here? Aren't you still teaching?" Matt asked as he came into the kitchen. Finn was picking at the fruit she'd dished onto a plate. "And you've got that box from Ned with you... Why?"

She looked up with a guarded expression. "I've taken a leave of absence from work. I had to get out of Baltimore. I'm gonna sell my house."

Matt raised his eyebrows. "Awfully dramatic, Chuck. I mean he's a *dick*, don't get me wrong, I wanna fucking kill him, but why do you have to leave town?"

"I don't want you to get upset," she began which made Matt stiffen reflexively. "But... I was attacked in my office when we got back from Mexico in March, and then again at my house yesterday."

Matt stepped back. "What?!" he shouted as the blood roared in his ears. "Who? Are you okay?!" He gripped her shoulders and ran his eyes over her as his heart pounded.

"I'm fine," she placated with her hands up.

Matt dropped his hands and waited for her explanation.

"I was just a little roughed up. My neighbor came and scared them away." Her eyes flicked away. "But the trouble is that it had to do with the tablet that you and I got from Mexico, and I just wasn't safe in Baltimore anymore."

"Jesus Christ!" Matt's hands went to his head. "I knew that thing was trouble, and you should never have gotten involved with Luke or his partner. I can't believe he put you in danger," he said angrily and pounded the kitchen island emphatically with his finger. "If I ever see that man again, I will *fucking* kill him."

"We had no way of knowing that other people wanted it. It's just an ancient stone tablet." Finn shook her head as if to convince herself. "There was no reason to be fearful." She looked at Matt and looked as though she was measuring her words. "I translated what I could, with help from Ned's journal and from what I found in the chest. It's a story about infighting among the gods. The tablets make some sort of ring…." She trailed off and then nodded to herself. "I'll be safe now. I'm gonna stay with my dad until the house is sold and then I'll buy someplace new."

"No way." Matt shook his head at the thought of Finn at Bill's, where he couldn't protect her. "I want you here with me. Especially if there's some lunatic or lunatics out there after you or those fucking tablets." He frowned. "You'll stay here. You can have the whole third floor to yourself, or Ollie's condo. Though I'd feel better with you up here with us."

Finn held his gaze and then sighed. "Thank you, Matt. I don't know what I would do without you. Honestly." She stood and hugged him tightly. "I'm exhausted from the drive. I'm gonna go lay down, okay? Can you walk Jayne?"

"Of course." Matt kissed the top of her head and watched her disappear into the elevator with a worried frown.

He scraped the uneaten fruit into the trash and put the plate in the dishwasher. He shook his head as he thought about Luke, wondering how he missed the signs.

I'm gonna make that fucker wish he was never born, Matt thought as he went to the back door and found the spare leash he kept on a hook for Jayne. He didn't expect it would be as easy as doing away with Andy, but anything could be accomplished with the right determination and planning, and he already proved he had both in spades.

"I'm keeping it," Finn announced a few hours later from the doorway of Matt's home office.

He looked up from his computer in surprise and closed the browser before standing. "Okay, Chuck. What changed your mind?"

"I had a dream. About a house with a pool, and a little boy. I'm gonna name him Charlie."

"Oh. It's a boy? And you know this dream kid is your son?" Matt asked skeptically.

Finn nodded with certainty. "And he's gonna be beautiful, and perfect," she added with a small smile. "I need a house. Do you have a realtor?"

Matt nodded slowly and thought of the realtor who had rescued his life by finding him the townhouse they were standing in. "If you're sure...."

"I'm positive," Finn replied and spun on her heel.

22

Domestic Dictator

"WHAT IS CHUCK DOING HERE?" Ollie puzzled as they were undressing for bed, having arrived after a long dinner meeting. He ran his hand through his hair to smooth it after pulling his shirt off.

"She's moving back home," Matt replied with a broad smile that made Ollie suspicious. "And we're gonna buy a house and live together."

"I'm sorry, what?" Ollie straightened with a frown. He seriously hoped he'd misheard Matt. "You're joking. We're going to *live* with Chuck? I don't understand."

Matt looked at Ollie and shrugged that asshole shrug of his. "I'm not kidding. I'm looking for a place in the suburbs. We'll sell our part of the townhouse and keep your condo, for appearances, and for when we need to stay in town. Chuck needs me, Ollie. She's pregnant."

Matt was speaking at a pace Ollie suddenly felt incapable of following.

The suburbs?

Sell our beautiful townhouse?

Pregnancy?

"What?!" Ollie exclaimed, wondering at the excitement in Matt's eyes. "Our home? What? Why does she need you? What about Luke?"

Matt's eyes flashed with anger. "That fucking bastard put her in danger, dumped her, and cheated on her. He's not coming anywhere near her or her baby."

Ollie took a deep breath as he processed the information. "Christ. Poor Chuck. That's awful. He seemed like a really great guy."

"I thought so too," Matt said in a flinty tone Ollie rarely heard from him.

Ollie watched at Matt hung his pants on his side of the closet and measured his words. "And, that being said, I don't want to move." Ollie said carefully.

Matt stopped what he was doing and turned to look at Ollie. "She doesn't want to raise her baby in the city, and I agree. We've been here a few years, and it's been great, but I'm ready to move on. Don't you want a yard? Maybe a pool?" he added with a calculated smile. "You can have input, babe. I'll make sure you get everything you want at the new place."

Ollie twisted his mouth and counted to ten.

He can't seriously be doubling down?

Ollie took a breath. "But why do you, or rather we, have to uproot our lives to help her? Plenty of people raise children alone. We could help her of course, but we don't have to *live* with her." Ollie spread his hands and willed them not to shake. "Don't get me wrong. I want to help; I love Chuck," he said softly. "But I like living in the city. I like our privacy, our freedom. We'd be giving up a lot. Not to mention that this is a *huge* change, and you've made this decision without even consulting with me."

Ollie held Matt's cautious gaze and waited for him to speak.

"I have to do this for her, Ollie," he said after a beat. "Luke put her in danger. I don't want her living alone and vulnerable. Why should she be a single mom when she has me, us? I want to help her raise her child." He put his shirt in the hamper with a flourish that Ollie read as exasperation. "I said we'll keep your condo. We can come in and stay whenever."

Matt pushed past Ollie into the bathroom and began brushing his teeth at one of the sinks. Ollie watched him for a moment from the doorway. He ran his eyes over Matt's incredible body, took in every inch of his muscled physique just as Matt intended, before standing next to him at the other sink to brush his teeth.

Anger simmered in Ollie's belly as his body agreed with his brain for once. Matt was pulling out all the stops in hopes of getting Ollie to go along with his outlandish plan and every bit of Ollie was rebelling. The idea that Matt could make such a decision without discussion or even simply asking if it was something Ollie wanted, filled him with fury.

"I get that at work you operate unilaterally; your partner there is silent. But here," Ollie raised his eyebrows as he gestured around the space with his toothbrush, "your partner is not. I have a say."

Matt stared at him while the toothbrush buzzed in his mouth. "I had to be decisive. She was going to find a place on her own but she's not safe. Trust me in this."

Ollie straightened and turned off his toothbrush. "You're well aware that I don't normally question you. I've always trusted your judgement. It's just unbelievable that you haven't considered me at all in this. Not my wants or feelings. Like I'm some pet who follows you around without question." Ollie shook his head and clenched his fist around his toothbrush. "Like I'm bloody *Jayne*."

Matt spat and rinsed his toothbrush before placing it carefully on the counter next to the jar of cotton balls. "We're committed." He touched his moon pendant for emphasis and met Ollie's eye in the mirror. "And that's like being married, so of course I considered you."

Ollie narrowed his eyes. *Does he think our commitment ceremony gives him authority over my life?*

"But it's not a marriage," Ollie said peevishly. "And in any case, if it were, that still doesn't give you the right to make these life-changing decisions without consulting me."

Matt stared at him briefly with a calculating look. "You're right. I should have phrased it better. I should have asked for your input." He straightened and wiped his mouth on the towel. "But as you said, my judgement is sound. You shouldn't question it. I have always taken care of you, given you everything you ever wanted." He swept his arm around. "I love you. So, I'm moving, and I would like you to come with me. Is that better?"

Ollie's mouth dropped open of its own accord. He put his toothbrush down and rinsed his mouth. "You would leave me here and go live with Chuck if I said no?" he said slowly, his heart suddenly hot.

"No, Ollie. You would come to your senses long before that ever happened." Matt rested his hip on the granite counter and held Ollie's gaze. "And if you didn't, I would drag you to the new house by your hair."

Ollie exhaled, his displeasure audible as his brain rang the warning bell like a volunteer fire station reaching the county boundaries. "Well, I need to think about it." He left the bathroom, knowing Matt meant it more like dragging him out by the leash.

Matt appeared silently behind him. "Okay, Ollie. You have two months to think about it and then we're moving."

The rebellion bubbled over as he whirled on his heel. "You keep ordering me around without a thought for my feelings, or my wants and needs, and I'm going to move downstairs tonight." His eyes flashed.

"Why are you being so difficult about this?" Matt asked in a harsh voice. "I've said to you before, I owe *everything* to Chuck. She has done so much for me without a second thought, without any pushback. She gave me you." Matt held Ollie's gaze. "She didn't even ask this of me. I'm doing it because I love her, and I owe her, and it's the least I can do."

Ollie sighed angrily. "Is it too much for me to ask to be treated as a partner? Of course I know what she has given the both of us. It's not just the moving to the fucking suburbs and sharing space—which is weird enough—it's also the *baby*," Ollie said harshly and shook his head. "Bloody hell, Matt. That is the ultimate disruption. Our lives will be forever changed. I just think we should really consider that. I mean, have you done your *proper* OODA loop?" he scoffed, mocking Matt's military run-through technique, and picked up the glass on his side table.

"Yes, you are my partner and I do value your opinion. I love you, Ollie. More than anything." Matt followed him into bathroom. "Things will change, you're right. But only for the better, I promise. We'll get a house big enough that you won't ever hear the baby if you don't want.

You and Naomi can work together on the layout so you get everything you have here and then some. Make it however you want it. The bedroom can be soundproofed," he added meaningfully.

Ollie turned off the water and looked at him, studying his face carefully before sweeping his gaze down Matt's body. Matt knew just how to play him, and Ollie wavered between doubling down and giving in. Was he really against moving, or was it the way Matt announced the idea? He had the rose garden at the Cape, but wouldn't one at his permanent home be nice too? And maybe a tennis court of his own? And perhaps an attached garage so he didn't have to scrap off the ice and snow in the winter—not that he'd done that more than once or twice because Matt always did it for him if he wasn't traveling—and wasn't that (and all the other myriad things Matt did for him) enough to entertain the idea of moving?

"I need some time to think about it," he said finally and looked at the trident tattoo on Matt's chest. He dragged his eyes back up to Matt's face and found him watching him with a hooded gaze.

Matt ran his eyes over Ollie's body. "Let me know what I can do to convince you."

He came to stand behind Ollie and met his eyes in the mirror. He kissed Ollie's neck and the sensitive spot behind his ear. Ollie let his lids flutter closed, and he felt Matt's smile on his neck and then Matt's fingertips ghosting up his arms. Matt put the palm of his hand on Ollie's flat stomach and pressed his groin against Ollie's bottom. "I will do whatever it takes."

Ollie hummed low in his throat as goosebumps stood at attention on his skin. His brain wanted to stay mad, but his heart and body were helpless against Matt, as usual. He opened his eyes and licked his lips at the feeling of Matt's hardness growing against his ass. Matt was staring at their reflection intently and at what his other hand was doing on Ollie's skin.

Matt kissed the crescent shaped scar on Ollie's shoulder. Ollie shuddered lightly with the memory of how that scar got there especially as Matt ghosted his teeth over it. Matt continued to place open mouthed kisses up and down his neck and shoulder as he ran a finger under the waistband of Ollie's briefs.

Matt rolled his hips so his cock notched in the seam of Ollie's ass and his palm flexed on Ollie's stomach. "I love you, Oliver Turner. And I'm sorry I didn't ask you first."

Ollie's eyes flew to Matt's in the mirror and then he turned his head to look at him directly. He searched Matt's face for guile and found only sincerity. Matt never apologized for anything. Ollie could count on one hand how many times he'd heard that word out of Matt's mouth, and he certainly never used it with anyone else, not even Finn.

His resolve cracked and then shattered into a million pieces as Matt's lips descended on his own. Their tongues tangled and Ollie turned in Matt's arms to gain better access to Matt's mouth.

Matt pulled his head back after devouring Ollie's mouth for what felt like hours. "You interrupted me. I was just getting started with pleading my case," Matt said in a soft voice. "Turn around and look at yourself in the mirror. You're gonna watch me take you apart."

Ollie hesitated for the barest of moments before spinning on his heel. He decided he would fight for what he wanted … *after*.

"Not saying I've made up my mind yet, but you better make sure the house has bedrooms on opposite sides, and is soundproofed," Ollie said as Matt came out of the bathroom running his hands through his hair, "or you're going to make Chuck blush with your screams."

Matt grinned. "I can't help myself, Ollie. You feel too good." He climbed into bed and kissed him soundly. "I'm gonna buy a big ole house with horsehair plaster walls, so I don't ever have to keep it down."

Matt watched Ollie turn off his side light before turning off his own and rolled onto his back, waiting for Ollie to roll into his spot under his arm. He felt Ollie's lips on his nipple, and squeezed him to his side, his heart full of contentment.

He had miscalculated Ollie's response because he'd been lost in the euphoria of the plan. Luckily, he knew Ollie's weaknesses, and how to bring him around because he knew he couldn't live without Ollie.

Ollie was going to drag his feet for show, but Matt knew verbalizing the apology, as hard as it was to say the word, had the desired effect; he'd seen the shock in Ollie's eyes. Ollie would come to see that moving and helping Finn raise her baby was going to make both their lives better.

23

Barbie's Dream House

MATT'S DESK PHONE BUZZED, interrupting his work. "There's a Beth Bertrand on the phone for you," Stacey announced.

Matt pushed the speaker button with a smile. "Put her through."

He picked up the handset when the phone trilled. "Hi, Beth. Got something for me?"

"Hi, Matt," she replied cheerfully. "I have a couple of great houses for you to see. You have time today?"

"Yes. I told you time is of the essence. I've got a baby on the way," he added, smiling to himself.

Matt and Finn followed Beth through the second house on their tour and listened to her chatter about the features. Matt sensed Finn's distraction as they wandered through rooms that felt the same as the house Finn grew up in. It was big and beautiful, but Finn seemed unimpressed.

"What do you think, sweetheart?" Matt called her back to attention. "This kitchen is pretty amazing, and there's a huge yard; we could put in a pool. It's close to Ma and your dad."

Finn shrugged and nodded her head from side to side. "It's okay." She looked at Beth. "How many more houses do you have for us?"

"There are three more. Two in Newton and one in Brookline."

Finn nodded. "Okay. Let's keep looking."

Matt put his arm around her as they walked to his Porsche parked behind Beth's BMW. "You okay? You need some food or anything?"

Finn smiled lightly and pulled a bag of trail mix out of her purse. "I'm fine, lovey. Let's just follow Beth to the next place, and maybe stop to pick up something quick to eat after."

"Okay." He pulled away from the curb and followed Beth out of Wellesley Hills to Route 9.

Finn opened her eyes and stretched lightly with a yawn as Matt pulled up the emergency brake and turned off the engine.

"Oh, I can't believe I fell asleep." She looked around and sat up suddenly with a gasp. "Jesus Christ! Matt, this is the house!" she exclaimed and pointed excitedly out the window at the wrought iron fence and massive house beyond it on the hill. She put her hands on her head. "It's real! I can't believe it. Holy shit! Where are we?"

"We're in West Newton. The hill, I think Beth said it was called. What are you talking about?" Matt furrowed his brow and wondered at her exuberance. She'd been weird ever since she took on the project (with that fucking asshole whose name he never wanted to think of), and he worried again about Finn's sanity.

"This is our house. This is where we're gonna live," she declared, stabbing her finger on the car window emphatically. "The one from my dream."

Matt watched as she exited the car and pushed her way through the gate. She had described the dream she had the day she decided to keep the baby, but Matt hadn't really listened. He got out of the car and looked around, taking in the quiet neighborhood and the wooded landscaping.

There was a granite and bluestone path leading to the front door with a step every six feet matching the grade which was quite a sloping distance from the street. He hurried to catch up with Finn as he studied the yard around them. It was a mix of mature deciduous and evergreen trees, with rhododendrons and shrubs and flower beds which provided quite a bit of privacy from the street below. There was a walled garden off to the side next to the driveway, and a wide bluestone patio that extended on either side of the giant front door.

"This is pretty sweet, Chuck." He smiled and kissed the top of her head. It really was, and while Matt was eager to see the inside, he wondered if the walled garden to his left was filled with roses.

For Ollie.

Beth met them at the door and ran through the specs as they followed her through the house. "It's nearly two and a half acres which is completely unheard of on the hill. The property spans the block front to back, and the fence goes around the entire perimeter, with an inner fence around the large gunite pool, pool house, and hot tub.

"The pool house has a bathroom, small kitchen, and bedroom. There's an enclosed outdoor shower outside the pool house; all of these are accessed from the walk-out basement or through the side gate. The house was built at the turn of the last century, is twelve bedrooms, eleven full bathrooms, and two half." She rattled on. "It needs some work, but the systems are all new and there's a new roof with solar panels. There's also a four-car attached garage, a walled rose garden that's overgrown but easily tamed I've been told. There's just tremendous potential throughout," she finished with a smile that said she knew this was the house.

Matt looked at Finn with an inquisitive smile. He was already sold on the rose garden.

Fuck yeah!

But waited for Finn's response.

She nodded eagerly and Matt beamed.

"We'll take it, Beth. And we want to close as soon as possible," Matt stated as Finn put her arms around him and hugged him tightly. "I'll need your help finding a buyer for my townhouse," he added as he tightened his arms around her.

———

24

New Beginnings

"CONGRATULATIONS ON THE BABY, and the new house." Naomi raised her wine glass to Finn and then at Matt and Ollie. "Sorry about the asshole," she added to Finn before taking a sip.

Finn nodded with a tight smile and sipped her club soda. "I'm just gonna focus on moving forward. I've put my house on the market, my dad is over the moon about being a granddad, and I'll never let my guard down again with a guy."

Naomi made a sympathetic sound and squeezed Finn's hand. "You've always been great at reading people. I'm truly shocked. Are you sure he didn't just get caught up in something? Don't get me wrong; I am not trying to defend him, but from what you've said, it just sounds odd, like maybe he was possessed or something," she added with a laugh and took a sip of her wine.

Matt watched as Finn looked away with a slight frown. Something passed over her face that made him pause.

What the fuck was that look? What wasn't she telling him?

Matt glanced at Ollie to see if he noticed, but Ollie was draining his glass with his eyes closed.

"No, I think he was just a dick, and I didn't see it," Finn said firmly with a shrug. "Let's order dinner. Anyone else up for Mexican? I'm kinda craving it."

Matt held his tongue and wondered about confronting Finn later.

Matt knocked on Finn's bedroom door after Naomi left and opened the door at her invitation.

"Hey, you got a minute?" he asked as he stepped into the large bedroom and left the door ajar.

The blinds on the bay windows overlooking Marlborough Street were still open and Matt crossed the room to pull them closed. Finn was folding clothes from a laundry basket and putting them in the dresser between the closet and the bathroom. Matt looked around the room. It was one of the rooms in his house that he'd seen but never spent any time in. Naomi had done an impeccable job with the design and décor; it was cozy without being cluttered, and the colors were soothing. He stopped admiring her handiwork and turned his attention back to Finn.

"Everything okay, Chuck?"

Finn closed the drawer and turned to face him. "Of course. Well, as okay as can be under the circumstances," she clarified.

Matt sat on the foot of the bed. "What aren't you telling me?"

Finn straightened the small statue of a centaur that Matt had bought in Athens on a business trip and avoided his gaze. He had wondered what Ollie had done with it after he brought it home, but looking at it on the dresser, he saw how well it blended. How well it belonged in that beautifully understated room.

"There's nothing." Finn shrugged.

Matt scoffed and shook his head. He decided to change tactics. "You've been strangely quiet about that." He nodded with his chin at the open door next to where she was standing. "What's inside? You never did say."

Finn looked at the chest sitting where he and Ollie had left it in the middle of the closet floor. It was about the size of a steamer trunk, with a domed lid, and was covered in what Finn referred to as cuneiform.

To Matt, it looked like hieroglyphics, but he didn't understand the difference, if there even was one. The box was smooth like stone, but he and Finn had speculated, when they had unpacked it at her house in Baltimore, that it was more like petrified wood.

"Just a couple tablets; the one we got from Mexico and one that Ned had left inside."

"Can I see?" Matt asked.

"There's nothing to see. His tablet looks exactly the same as the one you saw in Mexico."

"What are you gonna do with them? Did that asshole ever tell you why the government wants them?"

Finn winced and shook her head.

"Shouldn't they be in a museum or something? They're old, yeah?" Something about the chest was unsettling and Matt wasn't sure he wanted it in his house.

"Yes, they're old, but no, they don't belong in a museum. I'm still trying to figure out what to do with all of it," Finn replied vaguely as she waved her hand and met Matt's eye. "I'm fine. Everything is fine. I'm just a little tired."

Matt stood and pulled her into a hug. She wasn't going to spill her secrets, and he knew better than to push. "Okay. Get some sleep. I'll keep you posted on the closing and the construction schedule." He kissed the side of her head and left the room with one backwards glance. The look on Finn's face could only be described as haunted and Matt pulled the door closed with a conflicted heart.

25

Concessions

"BLOODY HELL, MATT. This place is massive, and beautiful." Ollie marveled as they walked through the new house. He hadn't wanted to like it as much as he did, but it truly was a marvel, including the amazing rose garden he couldn't wait to get dirty in, and the expansive yard behind the garage that could easily become a tennis court. He glanced at the front of Matt's pants and then Matt's face with an amused sound. "Just like your cock, come to think of it."

Matt laughed and palmed Ollie's ass as they climbed the wide and elaborate front staircase to the second floor. They had to skirt around piles of tools and construction debris as Matt led the way to a large landing overlooking the first floor.

"Naomi's outdone herself again," Matt remarked appreciatively and spread the blueprint plans flat on the worktable in the center of the space. "Our primary suites are here, with guest rooms, and a home gym over the garage in our wing. While Chuck's rooms will be at the other end of the house, as you requested." Matt grinned. "And the nursery will be halfway between, as I requested."

Ollie looked at the plans and then at him with a sigh. "You're really looking forward to this aren't you? Helping Chuck with her baby."

Matt nodded with an earnest expression and led Ollie down the hall with a tight grip on his hand.

"You want children?" Ollie asked quietly, suddenly nervous as he paused in the hallway, tugging his hand out of Matt's. "I mean of your own."

Matt looked at the floor. "I certainly didn't before, when it was nearly a reality with Sam. And I've been so busy with work, and with you." He smiled at Ollie before grabbing his hand again and tugging him along the hallway and into the middle of the large suite that was to be their bedroom. "I never stopped to think about it. But now, with it on the horizon, really happening, I think I might. What about you. Do you want kids?"

Ollie shrugged. "Not really, no. But I'm only twenty-seven. I never really thought about it." He searched Matt's face. "I'm still reeling a bit from the disruption. Babies are noisy, and smelly, and needy." Ollie wrinkled his nose. "But I love you, and I want to help Chuck too. I truly hope this doesn't change our happiness, and our lifestyle. I fully expect you to show me affection here, cuddle with me in front of the telly, in front of Chuck, in front of the baby. I won't be a secret here. I *refuse* to be," Ollie added adamantly.

Matt took Ollie in his arms. "Of course. This will be our sanctuary, and Charlie won't be raised as a bigot," Matt said vehemently. "I know firsthand how much that sucks. It might take me a minute to…." Matt shrugged self-consciously. "But know that I love you." He kissed and hugged Ollie tightly. "I'll make sure that everything only gets better from here on out." He reached into his coat pocket and took out a small bottle of lube. "Now what'd you say we christen the place?" Matt squeezed Ollie's ass with a grin.

Unfortunately, the promises Matt made were conditional, as usual. When the house was nearly ready, and the townhouse had sold, Matt and Finn moved to Newton, leaving Ollie behind in his condo.

Because Matt didn't want the construction workers at the new house to know.

Who cares what the builders think?

Ollie couldn't help the resentment of having to continue to sneak around. He and Matt been together for more than four years, and he'd yet to hold Matt's hand in public or touch him like a lover would or should. Now he had to watch Matt touch Finn on a regular basis, and it suddenly bugged him immensely. He felt like a third wheel, and tortured himself with imagining all the canoodling Matt and Finn were doing when he wasn't there, even though he knew they weren't.

To make matters worse, when the townhouse sold, the new owners cut off his access to the roof. It had been his sanctuary even in the cold; full sunshine when he needed it most. His garden-level condo, with its extra lighting and expanded windows, was still dark compared to the upstairs. On top of that, Matt wouldn't spend the night because, *appearances.* He didn't want the new people to speculate. So, it was sex and a cuddle and then out the door, or Ollie sleeping in the new house and leaving at dawn before the workers showed up.

Matt invited Ollie's parents to visit and bought Ollie thoughtful gifts almost every day. He was doing things Ollie knew were meant to compensate, so, Ollie swallowed his complaints and reminded himself that the people they loved knew about them. That their relationship wasn't a complete secret. He reminded himself of these facts especially when Matt woke him with a tongue in his ass, or his mouth on his cock. Ollie also noted that construction was moving along at an impossible pace, and he surmised it was because Matt was paying them extra to finish ahead of schedule.

Ollie knew Matt was doing his best, and as such Ollie had little trouble putting on a smile and sharing Matt's enthusiasm about the custom bar, and the billiards room in the basement, and the barstools with the trident-shaped backs that matched Ollie's pendant and Matt's tattoo. He reminded himself it was a temporary disruption, and that everything would be right as rain once he officially moved in and reclaimed his spot under Matt's arm.

26

Bright Side

AS FINN'S BELLY GREW, so did her melancholy, and Matt did his best to distract her which for the most part worked. He kept her spirits high with daily runs, that grew shorter with the cold weather and Finn's fast approaching due date. Every time he found her gazing off into space with a sad look on her face, he wanted to hunt Luke down and kill him, *slowly*.

"How is it that you're even more beautiful than you were before?" Matt asked with a smile when he stepped into the kitchen and caught her staring out the window over the sink. He patted Jayne as she wriggled around his knees as though he hadn't just seen her five minutes before when he got home.

Finn pulled a face and looked down at her cumbersome body clad in stretchy everything. "You're so full of shit. I made you a martini, please drink it on my behalf," she said with a peevish scowl. "When is Ollie getting home? Does he want to eat with us?"

"He's got a dinner meeting with some clients he's vetting for me," Matt replied and held up his martini in cheers before taking a sip and smacking his lips. "Well done, Chuck. Almost as good as Ollie's."

"You should say that more around him," Finn said off-handedly as she turned to the stove to stir the quinoa.

"What?" Matt frowned and straightened defensively. "I tell him all the time."

"I've never heard you, not *really*. And I think he's bothered by me." Finn held up her hand at Matt's protest. "He loves me, I love him, but even though you may think you touch him in front of me, you don't really. And I imagine before I came along you touched him all the time in your own home." She furrowed her brow briefly and gestured around the room with her hand. "I don't want him to resent me, and I don't want you to feel as though you can't show him affection around me, in our home. I set you two up for fuck's sake. You used my flat in Oxford as a sex den. The guestroom stank like cum after you left, and those earplugs did fuck all." She laughed salaciously.

Matt looked away and felt his skin flush.

Finn came around the island and touched his arm. "Stop being embarrassed. There's no shame in being in love, and enthusiastically so." She smiled sadly. "I'm not going to faint if you kiss him in front of me or if you grab his ass or god forbid, dry hump him on the couch. But he will miss it if you don't." She raised her eyebrows meaningfully.

Matt held her gaze and then exhaled a small laugh. "You really should've gotten that PhD in psychology, Chuck. Thanks for the advice." He hugged her tightly and then startled at the kick against his stomach. "Jesus. He's a little brute," he said with a grin and pulled back with his hands on her stomach. He felt another kick. "Hey, bud. Can't wait to meet you," he said, bending down and laughing at the responding kick. "That must be the most amazing feeling," he said as he straightened.

"It is." She smiled, and then winced. "Until the little fucker puts his foot under my rib and presses like he's trying to break it." She rubbed her side.

Matt laughed softly. "Your belly is huge. What's your due date again?" Matt frowned as he contemplated just how large her belly was. She looked as big as any of his sisters in their last few weeks before delivery.

"May eighteenth. But according to the midwives and the measurements I'm due this month." She pulled a face. "Of course, that's impossible because I was on the Cape with you guys and just as celibate and miserable as I am now. The earliest it could have been was when Luke came in August, but I had my period after he left." She shrugged.

Matt looked at her belly again as he did the math. "That's a pretty substantial time difference, so maybe it wasn't really your period?" Matt relaxed against the counter. "Either way, I just hope this kid doesn't split you in two. You should have a C-section."

"I'd prefer not to, but of course I'll do whatever they advise. I don't want to be split in two either, Matt." She laughed.

27

Spring Forward

"HEY, CHUCK. HOW'S THINGS?" Matt asked when Finn answered her phone. "Just checking in."

"Fine. Jayne and I are doing our rounds of the 'hood. All the construction has ground to a halt because of the pandemic."

"Sounds idyllic. I feel bad but I love the peace and quiet," Matt said with a smile as he thought of the ease of his commute into the city. "Be careful. There are still some slippery parts on the sidewalks; there was a lot of black ice this morning."

"You're such a worrier, Matt. It's eleven and the sun has melted everything." Finn said with a smile in her voice.

"I'm not wrong to worry. I don't want the Richter Scales in Boston to go off unnecessarily if you fell. Think of all the panic there would be." Matt bit back a laugh.

"Fuck you," Finn laughed. "Remind me, *for the millionth time*, why I put up with you?"

"Nerds need love too, and I make you cool by association," Matt said with a shrug she couldn't see. He looked at the big storage bin next to his desk that was brimming with files. "Ollie and I are just grabbing things from the office. The place is a ghost town since the Governor shut everything down. We won't be long. Do you need me to bring you anything? You still craving Flamin' Hot Cheetos?" he teased.

"No," Finn scoffed unconvincingly. "I don't need anything. The shutdown is worrisome; I'm nervous about having the baby in the hospital. All those sick people. You saw *The Walking Dead*," she said quietly. "I think I'm gonna have him at home."

"What?!"

Is she fucking insane?

"Chuck, no. You're going to the hospital," Matt ordered as he stood from his chair and began pacing his office.

"Why? I'm not sick. I'm just having a baby. People have been doing it outside of the hospital since the dawn of man."

Matt frowned and shut down his computer. "We'll talk when I get home."

Finn made a noncommittal sound and ended the call.

Ollie made dinner and Finn joined them with a reticent air. Matt's irritation grew as she ignored his demands about the hospital with an increasingly closed off expression. He had been spending his minimal free time looking at birth statistics and infant mortality rates, and a growing panic was building inside him as her due date approached.

The Lamaze classes had been both thrilling and intimidating, and feeling the baby move inside her was miraculous in a way he never anticipated. Matt had been there for the christenings and birthdays of his niece and nephews, and he had watched them grow, but it was all with a sense of detachment. Things were markedly different with Finn's baby. Living with her, caring for her, and nesting with her made him feel as though it were his son she was expecting, and he couldn't help but act like a nervous father-to-be.

"Chuck, a million things could go wrong, and you should be somewhere you can be taken care of," Matt said decisively and took a bite of butternut squash risotto.

"Yeah, and there's a pandemic raging that's killing people. You want me to expose my newborn son to that?" she countered. "I'm not high risk, and the pregnancy has been smooth and easy. I know some people have to be in a hospital, and if I were high risk I would be there too. But I'm not. Don't worry. It's too soon anyway. Maybe the pandemic will be under control by the time he's born."

Matt made a sound of disapproval. "I won't change my mind and you will be going to the hospital."

Finn looked at Ollie and sighed.

"He's not wrong, Chuck. You should be where the doctors are." Ollie shrugged.

"Thanks, Ollie," she said sarcastically with a small frown and stood. "I'm going to watch TV. I'm tired."

"Good night, Chuck. I'll be checking on you later, as usual," Matt said as he watched her go up the back stairs.

"She's not wrong to be worried about the pandemic and the hospitals," Ollie said gently. "I agree with you, but I'd be pretty scared if I were her. Life and love are so fragile."

Matt held Ollie's gaze. "I know but there's no way around it and there's no other place for her to have a baby."

Ollie studied him silently for a moment. "You know, there's a real possibility that the hospital won't allow you in the room with her. I've heard they're only allowing patients, no companions. They're trying their best to minimize risk and exposure. Even in the maternity ward, they aren't allowing partners or fathers in."

Matt scowled. "Where did you hear that?" He stood and fought the urge to pace. He gathered up their dishes. "There's no way they can keep me from her side. They can try."

Ollie shook his head. "Okay, Superman."

28

Call the Midwife

MATT LOOKED AT HIS WATCH and scanned his eyes over Ollie's naked torso. "I'm gonna check on Chuck. I'll be right back to deal with all this, you sexy tease." He waved his hand over Ollie's body and left the room with a swift kiss. Ollie's chuckle followed him out the door.

Matt knocked lightly on Finn's door, in case she was asleep, and opened it slowly. He pulled up with shock at the sight of her bouncing lightly on one of the exercise balls from his gym.

"What are you doing?" he asked suspiciously, patting Jayne as she whined insistently at his knee.

"Watching TV," Finn answered in a tight voice.

Matt studied her carefully and then frowned as she began blowing out her breath with a look of pain on her face. He froze halfway into the room.

"Holy shit! Are you in labor?" He rushed into the room and took her hand. She gripped him tightly with a determined face and nodded, unable to speak. "What the fuck?! We are going to the hospital right now," he announced angrily. His belly tightened with fear as he imagined having to help her birth the baby by himself.

"No," she managed to choke out as the sound of the doorbell ringing interrupted them.

Matt looked at her questioningly. The contraction ended and she began bouncing again. "That's the midwife. Please go let her in."

"I'm not leaving you. Ollie will get it." He went to the door of her sitting room and bellowed for Ollie as Jayne ran down the front stairs barking.

Everything from then on happened in a blur. Matt and Ollie took direction from the midwife, Sherri, and if she had any question as to who Ollie was, she didn't let on. Matt had been accompanying Finn to her appointments and knew all the midwives in the practice. Of the four on the team, he was pleased Sherri was the one who came, as she had the most experience.

Ollie left the room shortly after Sherri arrived.

"I prefer a little mystery, Lieutenant. I certainly don't need to see Chuck's vagina, thank you very much." He wrinkled his nose. "I'm sure you'll wake me by jumping on the bed with excitement." He kissed Matt in the hallway and left as Matt, anxious to not miss a moment, dashed back into Finn's bedroom.

Matt took position behind Finn and rubbed her back while encouraging her with mindless words. In what felt like just a matter of moments, but was more like an hour, Matt found himself cutting the umbilical cord of her eight-pound baby boy. He wept at the beauty of the experience, and over the baby, who was perfect in every way. Charlie's eyes were wide open, looking at everyone, especially at Matt, or so it seemed.

Matt held him carefully and scanned Charlie's little body before letting Sherri tightly swaddle him in a light blanket. He was captivated with Charlie's tiny fingers and fingernails clenched in tiny little fists as though hiding something in his palms. He was so beautiful in a way he'd never seen or heard a newborn described. He had a perfect little nose, and pink bud of a mouth and his eyes were bright blue and rimmed with gold, like a blue moon solar eclipse. He stared back at Matt with equal wonder in his eyes. Matt laughed to himself as his eyes filled happy tears, suddenly overwhelmed with the love he had for this tiny human.

Matt passed him to Finn hesitantly, not wanting to let go. "He's so perfect, Chuck. I can't believe it." He smiled and kissed her gently.

He listened as Sherri ran through a brief list of things to look out for and then as she promised to return in the afternoon. Matt followed her to the door and hugged her impulsively before locking it behind her and taking the stairs two at a time. He couldn't believe how anxious he was to get back to Finn and little Charlie.

He climbed onto the bed and scooted next to her and took Charlie from her arms. "Born on the Equinox just after midnight. You're a perfect little baby boy, Charles Matthew Hawthorn," Matt said and kissed his tiny forehead gently. He looked at Finn and narrowed his eyes. "You're an awful sneak, laboring away without telling me." He shook his head with a wry smile. "Did you think I wouldn't notice?"

Finn smiled sleepily. "I told you I'd be fine. That we'd be fine." She nodded at the bundle in Matt's arms. "Now, you gonna give him back to me so I can feed him?"

Matt grinned and kissed Charlie's forehead again. "Only because he has to eat. Otherwise, I'd say no. He's so precious. I don't want to let go of him." He passed Charlie to her and watched as he latched on her breast. "What a beautiful thing," he remarked, barely aware that he was staring at Finn's naked chest. "I'm going to bed. Are you sure he's okay sleeping next to you?"

Finn nodded. "Safe as houses, Matt." She nodded at the side-sleeper bumpers Matt was squashing under his thigh.

"Okay. Call me if you need anything, I mean it. There's a water bottle on your side table, and I'll have Ollie bring you breakfast in a few hours. I love you so much, Chuck. You were amazing. So strong. I've never seen anything like it." He looked at her with soft eyes and kissed her gently when he stood.

Matt woke Ollie. His body was vibrating with excitement and need. "He's perfect, Ollie. The whole thing was so thrilling," he said quietly and kissed Ollie's ear. "And you look so sexy, all sleepy and tousled."

He sighed as he ran his fingers through the waves of Ollie's hair and pressed his erection against Ollie ass cheek suggestively. "Can I fuck you? You don't even have to change positions if you don't want. I'll do you just like this. I am so horny for you."

Ollie laughed sleepily and rolled onto his back. "Everything makes you horny. And of course you can fuck me. I've been kept waiting all night, for fuck's sake. You know how much I hate that." He reached up and grasped the back of Matt's neck.

Matt growled low in his throat and peeled off Ollie's underwear. He kissed a trail down Ollie's taut stomach and then lifted his legs until Ollie's knees were tucked into his chest. He wasted no time diving in.

———

29

———

Silver Linings

THE PANDEMIC DIDN'T GET ANY BETTER, in fact it got worse. The upside to all the bad news was Matt and Ollie could work from the beach house, and did so, well into the summer months. They spent their days on the boat, on the beach, and on the deck, in between zoom meetings, conference calls, and checking emails. They took turns spending the night at Finn's house next door to help with the night feedings, and despite Ollie's initial reluctance at being awakened in the middle of the night, he came to cherish the quiet time with Charlie who was such an easy, happy baby.

Ollie's parents came at the end of May and stayed until July after quarantining for ten days at Ollie's condo in the Back Bay. Naomi drove them out and spent the weekend at Finn's before heading back to the city to work with a slew of new clients who were clamoring for her services now that they were all stuck at home. Ollie was sorry to see her go, but was so happy to see his parents and hear word of how things were in the UK. His mother, Maggie, caught him up to speed on everyone's health and how his sister, Cassie, was miffed she couldn't join them because of work.

Ollie set his parents up in the first-floor guest suite they always stayed in when they visited and had cleared his desk in his home office for his dad, David, to use. The office was on the backside of the house and overlooked the rose garden that David had helped him plan and implement three summers ago.

"Thanks for letting me take over your office." David smiled, looking out the bank of windows at the roses in bloom. "What a view. You really made the garden flourish."

Ollie smiled, pleased with his father's praise. "I agree, and I'm happy to share. We're just so thrilled to have you."

David nodded slowly. "And how are you, Ollie? How are things? How's having a *baby*?"

Ollie looked at the open door and at the windows and then the door again. He strode across the room and closed it.

"Truly, it's all good," Ollie began with a smile, and then looked away. He didn't want to betray Matt's confidence, but he also had a hard time keeping things from his father. They had always had an open and trusting dialogue. "It was hard for a bit, I'm not gonna lie. I couldn't move with them until the new house was done…." Ollie sighed. "But wait until you see it. I got everything I wanted and then some, and things have been fantastic, even with the introduction of a baby into our lives. You'll see just how incredible Charlie is." Ollie rubbed the back of his neck and grinned. "I suppose everyone says that about their baby though."

"*Their* baby?" David said in a teasing tone.

Ollie scoffed. "You know what I meant."

"Of course," David replied and then sighed. "Well, I have to admit it was a bit shocking at first, when you told Mum and I that you were moving out of the city and in with Finn, but from the pictures you shared, the house looks to be palace sized." David chuckled. "And you've still got the flat in the city and this place…."

"Yes, and once things get back to normal with the world, Matt and I will be traveling all over again and it'll be nice to have Finn and Charlie, and Jayne, to return to."

Ollie's father made a speculative sound. "And when it returns to normal, what about your sister? Can she finally be told? She's going to want to come visit, and the lie is just going to that much more cumbersome."

Ollie twisted his mouth. It had been a while since Ollie last brought up Cassie being told, and Matt was still as adamant about keeping their relationship from her.

"He hasn't changed his mind. He's very private, and very used to being so. Cassie could accidentally let something slip to one of her friends, and a story like that could be sold for a lot of money. I'm sure she'll eventually figure it out, and it's better to happen organically, rather than to have a big reveal.

"With the exception of Cass, the people who truly matter know about us and that's enough for me. Plenty of celebrities live their whole lives in the closet with the ones they love. We're no different," Ollie said earnestly and then shifted the topic. "And wait until you see the kitchen he made me, he's really bending over backwards to make up for everything, truly. He always has."

David nodded and held Ollie's gaze. "He has made progress, you're right. We should focus on that, and he's a great guy. I have a lot of respect for him and am very pleased with how well he treats you. Especially considering the doubts I had at the beginning of your relationship." He sighed. "Just be sure you keep your voice, and don't always let him boss you around."

"I don't." Ollie replied defensively.

"Oliver." David pulled a face. "You do. And you always have with him."

Ollie slid his glance away with a frown. "Is that what you think?"

"Don't you?" David raised his eyebrows.

"I admit, I let him make decisions. But, Dad, he's got incredible judgement, and he was an officer in the Navy for many, many years. He's used to giving orders and having them followed." Ollie shrugged. "I am free to do what I want, *believe me*, and I exert my will in other ways. I am quite happy."

David put his hands up. "Okay, okay. I get it. I'm glad to hear you're happy. Now, scoot, so I can get some work done."

Ollie left the room with his brain buzzing. He thought he and his father were past the judgement and doubts that had plagued David at the beginning of Ollie's relationship with Matt. It was one thing for Ollie to take issue with Matt's controlling behavior, and something else entirely to hear his father's concern.

I'm not a pushover, am I?

30

Petty-coat Junction

"WHERE ARE YOU GOING?" Matt called from the couch when Ollie appeared at the foot of the stairs dressed in a Prada t-shirt and tailored shorts.

"Out. I can go out when I want," Ollie replied tersely and pulled open drawers in the kitchen.

Matt raised his eyebrows. "Okay. Of course you can. It's just that there's a pandemic and I'm not sure many places are open." He watched Ollie rummaging around. "If you're looking for your sunglasses, they're on the shelf under the key rack by the back door. Where they belong."

Ollie stopped what he was doing and looked at Matt with a peevish expression. "I can keep my sunglasses wherever I want to. You don't have to micro-manage me."

Matt opened his mouth and then closed it. He wasn't sure what Ollie was so pissy about, but he wasn't going to poke the bear.

Too hard anyway.

"If I let you keep your things wherever you left them, there wouldn't be an uncovered surface in this house, including the floor." Matt smirked.

"*Let* me, Lieutenant?" Ollie's entire body went rigid.

Oops.

This wasn't panda Ollie, it was the rarely seen grizzly Ollie, and Matt suddenly wished he'd never opened his mouth in the first place.

"I don't need your permission. This is my house too. I can keep my shit wherever I want, I can come and go whenever I want, and I can be whoever I want. This is my life, and if I want to be my authentic self, *no one*, not even you, can stop me." Ollie's chest heaved with anger.

Matt stood and took a slow step toward Ollie. His mind raced through the OODA loop of Observe, Orient, Decide, Act that he'd learned in the military as he approached Ollie. He wasn't sure what set Ollie off, but he knew somehow, he was at least partially responsible.

"It was a figure of speech, babe. I didn't mean you need my permission. You know I like things tidy, and if we keep everything in its place, then nothing is ever misplaced. If you want to keep your sunglasses, or any of your other shit, somewhere else, let me know," Matt said gently and swept his hand. "You just always seemed happy to let me decide."

"Right—I let you. That's more like it." Ollie's shoulders lost some of the tension.

"Is this because of the move? I thought you were okay with that. I thought you loved the new place." Matt rested his hands on the island countertop.

"It's not just that, Matt. Maybe I let you do too much. I don't like the idea of people thinking I have no say. I have agency," Ollie added emphatically.

Matt wondered who said something. There weren't many who could have, so if Matt had to guess it had to have been David. "Of course you have agency," he agreed. "You do everything, I would be lost without you, baby. I tell you that all the time."

Ollie ran his hand through his hair and nodded. "Damn right you would."

The fight seemed to go out of him and Matt could barely keep his relief to himself. "Have fun wherever it is that you're going. There are masks on the same shelf as your sunglasses."

"Thanks." Ollie gave Matt a quick kiss. "There are some open markets in P-Town. I think I'm gonna go look at art."

Matt's mind went back to Ollie's 'authentic self' comment. He knew Ollie had made a couple of gay friends in Boston, guys who didn't know Matt or about Matt, but Matt never asked Ollie about them. Matt had absolutely no interest in them or in the gay community in general; it was not a community he identified with. Matt always believed that Ollie was okay with that, and now he worried that Ollie was beginning to have doubts about staying in the closet with him.

"Are you planning to be *gay* while you're up there? Like out of the closet?" Matt asked cautiously.

Ollie frowned. "Well, I'm not going to hide it. I do that enough *everywhere* else."

The irritation was back, and Matt wanted no part of it. He held up his hands defensively and retreated to the couch where he'd left his laptop. "Have fun."

"I will."

Ollie returned in a better mood than he'd left in. He found Provincetown to be invigorating, even with everyone wearing masks and keeping their distance. Allowing himself to be visible, seen, amongst his community was something he didn't need all the time, but when he did it was a relief in many ways. He had perused the outdoor shelves at the bookstore on Commercial Street, chatted with a few people he met along the way, and purchased two paintings, one of a naked man done by a favorite local artist of his, and the other of a coastline that had three rock outcroppings that reminded him of the tines of a trident. He couldn't wait to show them to Matt and make him guess which one he was going to hang at the condo and which he was going to hang in the sunroom at the new house.

Matt was right where Ollie had left him, though now he had a plate full of crumbs on the coffee table and a half empty water bottle next to him. He looked over his shoulder and ran his eyes over Ollie and his packages.

"Have fun?" Matt asked.

"Yes. It was exactly what I needed."

"How much did your excursion cost me?"

"Enough."

Matt stood from the couch with a sigh and stretched his tall body. It was Ollie's turn to run his eyes over Matt. A delicious sliver of tanned skin appeared between the hem of Matt's US Navy t-shirt and the waistband of his low-slung gym shorts. Ollie loved Matt in a suit, but he loved beach bum Matt so much more. His shoulders flexed under the tight material as he lowered his arms and walked over to where Ollie stood in the kitchen.

"Was it crowded?" Matt leaned in for a kiss.

"Not like it usually is this time of year, but there was a fair amount of people around. The vibe was really positive."

"And prancy?" Matt teased.

Ollie rolled his eyes.

Matt snatched Ollie around the waist and dug his fingers into his tickle spots. "Did you just roll your eyes at me?"

"Stop! Stop! I can't breathe," Ollie gasped and writhed to get away.

Matt wrapped an arm around Ollie, pinning Ollie's back against his chest and dug his chin into where Ollie's neck met his shoulder. Ollie shrugged and tried to go limp to escape but Matt was too strong. Ollie was fit and muscular, but he was just no match for Matt.

"Please! No! Fine. There was so much prancing, they had to shut the streets down."

Matt stopped and loosened his grip enough for Ollie to step away after placing a kiss on his shoulder. Ollie caught his breath and subtly worked his way to the stairs.

"It was a competition to see who could do the best Lieutenant Dion impression," Ollie said and sprinted up the stairs. "A twink in a sequin thong won."

Ollie heard Matt's laugh and then the pounding of his feet on the stairs behind him as he fled toward their bedroom. Ollie felt a thrill and a burst of panic at being caught.

"Mum, Dad! Help!" Ollie cried.

"They're at Chuck's," Matt called from far too close. "No one can save you. That ass is mine, and I'm gonna paddle the shit out of it."

Ollie shut the door behind him and fumbled with the lock. It turned under his hand and he braced himself against the door to hold it shut, despite the futility. He weighed the option of running for the bathroom against staying put and decided neither option was viable.

Matt burst through the door shoulder first with an evil smirk on his face as Ollie reeled backwards. "You didn't really think you could get away, did you? Especially after saying that sassy shit." He clapped his hands together and then rubbed his palms together as if to warm them. "Was the thong-wearing-twink you, Oliver?" He quirked his eyebrow as he stalked Ollie into the room. "Let's see your moves."

"I'm not now, nor have I ever been a twink, Lieutenant."

"Not even at Eton? In your little suit and tie." He raised his eyebrows and then chuckled when Ollie felt the bed against the back of his thighs. "Surrender now and I'll go easy on you."

"Why do I have to surrender? You started it." Ollie skirted the edge of the bed. "There was no prancing. You know, you're just as gay as any gay man there. You shouldn't mock them."

Matt straightened with a frown. "I get that you like that community, but I have nothing in common with any of the alphabet mafia, or whatever they're called. I don't identify with them or that, and I never will." Matt tilted his head and adjusted himself in his shorts, drawing Ollie's eye. "Now, are you gonna take off your clothes or will I have to?"

Ollie wished for many things in that moment, but he also knew there was no forcing anyone into an identity, least of all *Matteo* Dion, and it wouldn't be right anyway. So, he reached for the button on his shorts with a small smile.

We'll cross that bridge later, Lieutenant.

31

Heaven's Only Wishful

THE DAYS FLEW and dragged in a way that defied actual time. Charlie challenged and exhausted and stunned them on a daily basis. Ollie's parents extended their visit twice before having to reluctantly leave the week after the Fourth of July. Maggie and David kissed Charlie a million times and promised to return as soon as they were able. Ollie drove them to the Hyannis Airport where SharkFinn's jet was waiting to return them to the UK.

"Give Cass my love and tell her I will see her soon." Ollie kissed his parents and hugged them tightly. "I can't begin to express how amazing it was to have you here. I'm so glad you were able to spend time with Bill on Nantucket, and at the club. So much has shut down, and yet enough has been accessible, I hope you find the same when you get home."

"It's been a dream, and we wish we didn't have to leave," Ollie's mother replied. "Let us know as soon as you know when you'll be back to visit, okay?"

"Of course, Mum," Ollie replied and hugged them again. He watched them board and waited for the plane to take off before heading back to the beach house.

"It's amazing how alert he is, Ollie. Look at him," Matt remarked as he stood over Charlie laying on his baby mat when Ollie finally returned and had hung up the car keys.

Charlie was staring up at the toys dangling over him as though he were willing them to come closer. It looked like the toys moved but Ollie noticed the slider to the deck was open.

"He is very clever," Ollie agreed and studied Matt's shining face. "Christ, to be honest, he's a marvel. And that he laughs and lights up when he sees me doesn't hurt."

"He loves you, Ollie. He watches you all the time," Matt replied with a grin.

"Oh, he watches you far more, Lieutenant. He has really bonded with you. It's sweet."

Matt beamed at Ollie and then turned his attention back to Charlie just as he rolled over onto his stomach, a technique he had quickly mastered at the end of June. Ollie had begun to worry that Charlie would roll himself around the living room every time he did it, when suddenly Charlie pushed his chest up off the floor and began rocking.

"Whoa! Ollie," Matt exclaimed, pulling Ollie's eyes away from Charlie. "Shit he's rocking like he wants to move. If he gets his knees up, we're in trouble." Matt pulled his phone out to take pictures. "We need to babyproof before he gets mobile."

Charlie started laughing and looked up at Matt with an almost proud expression. Ollie watched as Matt picked him up and tossed him in the air with a whoop.

"Is that normal at his age? I thought we had more time before he became mobile."

"I'm not sure, I don't think any of my sisters' kids did it this early, but I wasn't really paying attention. Great job, Charlie! We have to go tell Mommy." He looked at Ollie. "I'll be back."

"We're gonna be busy, aren't we?" Ollie called after him. "I'll look up what we need to keep him safe around here."

Matt and Ollie spent two full days babyproofing both beach houses. "We're not doing the entire house in Newton though, Lieutenant, that would take forever. We'll just limit the rooms this little terror can be in." Ollie grinned as he swung the gate he'd installed shut. "Definitely get some more of these gates."

"Agreed. We'll contain him in the kitchen and playroom and put gates on all the stairs." Matt looked out the slider at Finn sitting on the deck with Charlie and his toys. "She looks tired. I miss having your mom here, she was a big help to Chuck."

"She loved it. I think she really wants grandchildren. Cass better hurry up and get married." Ollie gathered up all the loose packing materials and missed the look on Matt's face.

Matt turned and put the screwdrivers back in his toolbox and took it to the utility room off the kitchen.

By August, Charlie was fully crawling and exploring, tasting, and teething on anything he could get in his mouth. He was curious about everything, pointing and making a sound that was distinctly questioning in nature. Objects, bugs, animals, people and occasionally something no one could see were all things he demanded to know about.

Charlie was an active baby, always in motion and Matt insisted on getting him in the water as soon as their pool opened and the temperature of the ocean in front of their house was tolerable. Matt swam for an hour every day after his run, and again in the evening. He or Finn would take Charlie in the pool every day at Matt's insistence, to train his natural reflexes. As a result, Charlie was a water baby through and through by the end of the summer, holding his breath, swimming with light assistance and able to grasp the edge of the pool and inch along to the stairs with Matt or Finn or Ollie hovering behind.

"Nonsense," Matt scoffed whenever anyone expressed concern, included Ollie's parents when they had been in town. "Babies can be taught to swim, and we have a pool, it would be irresponsible of me to not have him learn. First thing I showed him was how to get to the stairs, he's no dummy," Matt always added with a smile.

Matt and Charlie were in the pool during a lunch break in August, Matt had Charlie cradled to his chest and was dunking under the water and then jumping up. Charlie giggled ecstatically and mimicked Matt as he took a deep breath and dunked under with him again, repeating it several times before Matt waded to the steps with Charlie tucked on his hip.

"It's nap time," He announced to Finn who was reading a book in the shade. Matt took off Charlie's swim diaper and rinsed him in the enclosed outdoor shower before wrapping him in a towel and putting a diaper on him in the pool house when he was dry. He passed Charlie to Finn with kiss on the top of his head.

"Pa-pa." Charlie fussed briefly at being separated from Matt as he rubbed his eye with his fist and tucked his head under Finn's chin.

Finn looked at Matt over Charlie's head. "He's been saying that a lot around you. It's not just babble anymore, is it? You encouraging him?"

Matt held her gaze and hoped she wouldn't tell him not to. "Yes."

Finn nodded with a small smile and turned for the house.

He took a moment to think about the baby bug he'd been bitten by as he watched her disappear inside. Taking care of Charlie, getting up with him in the night, playing with him during the day, teaching him new things, and watching him master new techniques was pure heaven. Charlie was such an easy baby, always so happy, even teething, he was barely fussy, and so beautiful with his white-blonde hair and piercing blue eyes.

Matt's heart was overflowing with love for Charlie and he truly felt as though Charlie was his, which Charlie was, in every way except biologically. That Matt got to be Charlie's dad *and* be with Ollie, the love of his life, was perfection, and Matt had never been happier.

32

Pink Sky at Night

September 2020

"*SACRE BLEU*, I ACTUALLY CAUGHT YOU in *person*." Guy's voice teased down the line in French. "It's been like forever."

"I bloody spoke with you two weeks ago, you baby. Aren't your women keeping you entertained?" Ollie responded with a smile on his face.

"We're locked down here too, you idiot. Haven't been seeing any-one," Guy let out a heavy sigh. "How was your visit with your parents? Would've been nice to have flown on your boyfriend's jet."

"They were here for almost two months helping with Finn's new baby. You saying you would've been okay with changing diapers and getting drool on your clothes?"

"No to the diapers, but, *Olivier*, I am quite used to being drooled over," Guy replied in a smug tone.

Ollie chuckled. "You can visit anytime, you know that. I just worried it might be awkward now."

Guy made a small sound. "Bygones. Finn and I left things quite fine, and it's been almost two years. I've had plenty of time to get over her by getting under several different women, sometimes at the same time."

"Mon Dieu, Guy. Did you ring just to tell me of your debauched ways or was there a purpose to this call?"

"No, of course not. Just wanted to hear about the visit, what your parents thought about the new, unusual living arrangement of yours."

"It was grand, though a bit long, as you can imagine. They quarantined at my flat and then we went straight to the beach house, which I really need you to see when all this nonsense is done.

"We visited Chuck's dad on Nantucket for a week and spent a month at the Cape. We ate too much, then went back to our house in Newton and ate some more. Mum is mad for Charlie, and Dad worries too much about my happiness with the whole scenario. Kept pestering me about speaking up for myself, all whilst cooing over Charlie, like the hypocrite he is."

Guy laughed. "I've heard all about how adorable that baby is. My mum made me look at a thousand pictures of the kid. I think it was some kind of punishment for not knocking Finn up myself." Guy sighed dramatically. "Your dad is right to worry though. I mean, what the fuck? You're raising a kid that isn't yours or Matt's."

"We've been through this, Guy," Ollie interrupted irritatedly. "I know I complained a bit to you at first, but Charlie is a marvel. He's like perfect. And shut up," Ollie cut off Guy's scoff. "You have no experience with kids. This is different."

Guy laughed with a brittle edge. "Well, he may be cute and all, but not as cute as he'd have been if he were mine."

"No, of course not, Guy. But he'd be a pompous ass on top of it, poor thing. Your genes."

Guy chortled. "And you'd love him more for it. Be honest."

"I would. I'd have to because no one else on the planet would," Ollie retorted with a smile. "I'll see you over the holidays, god willing. Stay healthy, you gorgeous, pompous ass."

"I love you too, dear. Say hello to your stallion for me."

"I will. And you know he loves it when you call him that," Ollie laughed. "Too much maybe."

"Right. As long as he stays in your stable and remembers that mine is only open to fillies and mares."

"Goodnight, homophobe." Ollie shook his head.

"Not homophobic," Guy replied defensively. "Merely practicing self-preservation. His cock gives me nightmares."

"Matt's cock is a dream," Ollie responded in a sly voice, thinking of how he rode said cock that morning. "And I'll never share it, so don't worry about your stables or your pastures."

"Mon dieu," Guy replied with a cringe in his tone. "I need to go sterilize my ears now. My therapist will be sending you her bill. Bonsoir."

Matt heard Ollie on the phone in his office next to the sunroom and stuck his head in to say goodbye. Ollie nodded and blew a kiss with his phone to his ear. Matt wandered into the kitchen and found Charlie in his highchair with Finn reading a book at the table. He kissed the side of Finn's head and lifted Charlie out.

"I'm taking him to Ma's. I'll make sure he sleeps in the car."

"Is that today? I forgot."

Matt nodded and got Charlie's diaper bag from inside the playroom. He began checking it for supplies. "Yeah, just Ma and Lisa are there." He looked at Finn. "Can you pump? Or is there more boob juice in the freezer?" he asked with a grin.

Finn checked the freezer. "Take these. I'll pump while you're gone." She passed him two bags. "But he can have water in a sippy cup too, he's old enough to get by without boob juice."

"I know but he likes it, and it puts him to sleep. I haven't seen them in months, and Nona misses him; I'm planning on staying for a bit." He tickled Charlie. "And you have to try your Nona's lasagna, you are going to love it bud," Matt said in Italian. Charlie laughed and put his hands down to block Matt's tickles.

"Papa." Charlie exclaimed between breaths, laughing heartily.

"What?" Matt asked Charlie, with a mock serious expression. "You have to say uncle if you want me to stop."

"Uncle." Charlie repeated back.

Matt looked at Finn with a shocked expression. "He's picking up more words. Did you hear that? He's only seven-months old."

Finn nodded with a broad smile. "Who's a clever boy?"

"Mommy." Charlie reached for Finn.

"Get all his gear and bring toys. I'll feed him a little," she said and disappeared into the playroom with Charlie.

Matt's mother fussed over Charlie, cutting the lasagna into tiny pieces and speaking to him in Italian. Matt's sister Lisa came down and joined them in the kitchen. She began speaking English and Antonia interrupted.

"He calls you Papa, he needs to speak our language," she said to the two of them in Italian.

"I do, when I can," he replied in Italian. He couldn't add that he and Finn would only speak Italian to Charlie when Ollie wasn't around, so as not to exclude him.

"*Fallo*," she insisted.

Matt nodded with a sigh. "*Si*."

Charlie stuffed a fistful of lasagna in his mouth, his face already stained with tomato sauce. "*Bene*," he said.

Antonia looked sharply at Matt. "*Dio mio*," she exclaimed. "Did you hear that?"

"*Charlie e' brillante*." Matt grinned. "I told you." He looked at Charlie. "*Ti voglio bene*."

Charlie smiled and stuffed another fistful of pasta in his mouth.

"Who is Charlie's father?" Lisa asked. "He looks kind of like Ollie."

Matt laughed at the thought. "He's not Ollie's." He glanced at his mother.

"Well, whose is he, and why isn't he in the picture? You never said."

"Just a deadbeat. No one you need to worry about," Matt replied, hoping to shut her down.

"I think it's remarkable that you took her back and are raising another man's child. I didn't think you'd have it in you," Lisa said with a grin.

Matt held her gaze for a beat before pushing away from the table. "How 'bout you just focus on your own love life, Lis? Hm. How's the bike messenger?"

33

Red Sky Morning

OLLIE WAS IN his home office a week later, catching up on work when he heard the doorbell. He looked at his watch and wondered who it could be at seven o'clock at night. He jumped to answer it, knowing Matt was upstairs working out and Finn was putting Charlie to bed.

Jayne had stopped barking and was whining excitedly at the side window. Ollie peered into the dark as he flipped on the porch light and then wished at the last minute that he had ignored the bell. His hand paused on the doorknob as Jayne whined incessantly, and with an unsettled stomach, he opened the heavy door.

"Hello, Ollie," Luke said cautiously with a small smile. His deep voice was rough with nerves despite his casual posture. He was in jeans with a plaid flannel open over a plain t-shirt and looked like sex on a stick with his grown-out hair and leaner but still broad frame.

Ollie caught his breath and strengthened his resolve.

"Ahh. The infamous Agent MacEneas. I suppose it was only a matter of time before you darkened our door. Took you long enough. Really *too* long at this point, wouldn't you say?" he added bitingly.

213

"You're looking well," Luke replied in his deep voice. He extended his hand and broadened his tentative smile as he ignored Ollie's words. "Is Finn here? I'd like the opportunity to explain myself."

Ollie took a deep breath and, after a moment's hesitation, stepped back from the door, sweeping his arm as an invitation.

Ollie heard footsteps behind him as Luke stepped in. Luke's expression immediately changed to one of pure unadulterated love and aching need that nearly took Ollie's breath away. He turned to see Finn standing in the hallway to the kitchen, like a rabbit trapped in headlights. She nearly retreated, and Ollie couldn't blame her. He was overcome with the memory of Matt showing up on his doorstep in Oxford all those years ago after breaking his heart; how it had been both devastating *and* thrilling to see him again.

"Finn. Wait," Luke called to her, breaking the spell and her retreat.

Finn hesitated, and with a shy glance at Ollie, she crossed the large foyer and stepped out onto the porch with Luke, The door closed softly behind them. Ollie stood lost in thought for a moment before returning to his office. Matt was going to be livid. Ollie closed his eyes with worry. He was thankful that Matt didn't have a gun, but he did have large fists, and unrestrained anger when it came to Luke.

Ollie stood in his office, unable to focus with his stomach in knots. He worried for Luke and wondered if he should go upstairs to head Matt off. He sped into the foyer to do so and found Luke and Finn standing back inside, talking softly while Jayne whined quietly at Luke's knee. Ollie stopped and made to turn to go through to the kitchen and up the back stairs when he heard Matt's angry voice above him.

Oh *shit*.

"What the *fuck* are you doing here?" Matt growled as he descended the staircase. His face was a storm cloud of epic proportions, and his body was rigid with fury.

"Matt!" Finn and Ollie cried in unison.

"I came to talk to Finn." Luke paused, adjusting his stance defensively. "This is between her and me." He gestured with his hand.

Matt scoffed derisively. "You need to get the fuck off my property." He stopped at the bottom of the stairs next to Ollie and flexed his hands before crossing his arms. "Now."

"Matt. Stop, please," Finn implored and put her hand on his crossed arms. Finn caught Ollie's eye and pleaded silently for him to help her. "Matt," she said again quietly. "I know you're upset, but I need to hear what he has to say. No," she continued over Matt's protests. "We're going downstairs." She released Matt's arm and turned away.

"Come on, Luke. One drink and then you'll go. Okay?"

"Okay. Yeah, of course," Luke agreed and looked at Matt. "Listen, Matt. I get it. I'd hate me too but let me have a chance to explain. I owe it to Finn, and I deserve the opportunity to redeem myself."

Matt scoffed. "The only thing you deserve is a beating, or worse. Don't fucking speak to me." He turned and stalked angrily away. Ollie watched Finn lead Luke through the hidden basement door in the wainscotting under the stairs and then turned in search of Matt.

Ollie paused in the doorway to the kitchen. Matt was standing in front of the sink facing the windows and suddenly covered his face with his hands. Ollie tentatively crossed the room and put his arms around Matt's waist.

Matt flinched and pulled Ollie's arms away. His grip was painful around Ollie's wrists. "No, Ollie." His voice flinty with anger. "Don't."

Ollie stepped back and leaned against the island as he stared at Matt's tense back. Matt took a deep breath and let it out and he gripped the edge of the counter as he looked out the window into the night.

"That fucking bastard. That *motherfucking* bastard." Matt shook his head. "Why did she let him in?"

Ollie swallowed, his throat clicking with nerves. "I let him in."

Matt turned around and widened his eyes. "What?! Why the fuck did you do that?" he shouted. "You know what he did. You know what happens next."

Ollie quivered slightly with fear and took a deep breath. "I let him in for same reason I let you in all those years ago. You should have seen his face when he saw her. It was the same as yours," Ollie said softly.

"You didn't let me in; I forced my way in," Matt scoffed.

"Luke would have too. I saw it in his face. He came all this way. Do you think he would just leave with a shrug and 'sorry to have bothered you,' if I turned him away?" Ollie furrowed his brow. "Would you have?"

Matt's jaw ticked. He flared his nostrils and went up the back stairs without responding.

Ollie tossed and turned most of the night, waking when he heard Charlie on the monitor and Matt leaving the bed. Matt had barely spoken more than four words to him and had brushed off his advances, leaving Ollie feeling out of sorts and doubting himself. As always in times like these, his inner dialogue picked up.

You couldn't have turned Luke away, his heart placated. *It was just like when Matt came back for you.*

Luke is going to fuck everything up, his brain warned. *Matt knows that and you should too. You should've shut door. You should've called for Matt. He would've made Luke leave.*

No way, his heart countered. *There might've been blood and harsh words, and no way was Luke going to leave without seeing Finn.*

That's all well and good, but what about me? his body, wheedled. *Why am I being punished for something you two did?*

Ollie squeezed his cock in solidarity and rolled onto his side with a sigh. He strained to hear what Matt and Finn were discussing in angry whispers over the baby monitor before finally falling back to sleep.

34

Sailor's Warning

MATT WOKE BEFORE DAWN and went for a long run up Heartbreak Hill. He followed the carriage road of Commonwealth Avenue, went around the Chestnut Hill reservoir and then back home, past the large high school and up the hill. The sight of Luke's navy blue, 1967 Shelby Mustang still parked in front of the house made his blood boil.

He let himself in through the side door and went through his morning routine on autopilot. Ollie was still asleep and didn't stir when Matt put a mug of coffee on his side table. Matt paused to scan his eyes over Ollie's naked form then turned to the bathroom, stripping off his sweaty clothes on his way.

"Morning, Lieutenant. Can I wash your back for you?" Ollie asked as he opened the shower door five minutes later, startling Matt out of his angry musings.

Matt's dick twitched in response to Ollie's erection, which was standing at attention and seemingly hunting for him like a divining rod.

He handed Ollie the soap. "Sure."

Matt watched Ollie turn on the second shower head and the side sprayers. Ollie lathered his hands and waggled his eyebrows when he caught Matt's heated gaze. Ollie nudged Matt to turn and face the wall.

"Your body is so beautiful," Ollie praised softly as he traced his fingers lightly over the ridges of Matt's muscles, from his biceps, down his back, and over the curve of his ass. "If I were a poet, I would write volumes to fill every library in the world." He kissed Matt behind his ear. "If I were a painter, I would fill the walls of every building with your portraits." He kissed Matt's shoulder. "And if I were a musician, I would sing myself hoarse." He ran his tongue up Matt's spine.

Matt chuckled as his dick grew hard. "You trying to woo me out of my bad mood, Oliver?"

Ollie hummed and ran a soapy hand over Matt's erection. "It's working, isn't it?"

Matt closed his eyes and put his hands on the tile as Ollie slowly and thoroughly lathered his back and sides. He let out a small moan as Ollie smoothed his fingers into his crease and over his taint. Ollie pressed with his fingers and took a step closer, his erection pressing against Matt's ass cheek as he stroked Matt hard cock with his other hand.

"I love feeling you like this," Ollie said, his voice husky with need. "I love when you let me." Ollie's finger slipped into Matt's hole slowly and found Matt's prostate with ease.

Matt bucked into Ollie's hand, his body alternating between thrusting back onto Ollie's finger and then back up into his fist. He never wanted to bottom for Ollie (again) but he enjoyed letting Ollie have his fantasy.

For a little while anyway.

Matt let Ollie add a second finger, kissing him over his shoulder as Ollie ground his dick against Matt's ass cheek, before he turned in Ollie's arms. He gripped Ollie's head in his hands and kissed him as the hot water coursed down their bodies. He dug his fingers into Ollie's hair and pulled his head back for access to Ollie's neck. He nibbled and kissed his way to Ollie's collarbone.

"You know just what I want, and you're gonna give it to me, aren't you?" Matt breathed into Ollie's ear. He bit his lobe and smiled when Ollie cried out with a moan.

"Yes…. God, yes."

Matt wrapped his hand around Ollie's erection and fisted them both together, capturing Ollie's moan in his mouth. He rubbed his thumb across the tips of their cocks on the final upstroke and then pressed the slickness he'd gathered between Ollie's lips.

Ollie's tongue circled Matt's thumb as his eyelids fluttered. "Suck," Matt ordered. Ollie cheeks hollowed. Matt hummed and rolled his hips. "So good for me." He removed his thumb and caressed Ollie's cheek. "So perfect." Matt's heart fluttered and burned hot with passion when Ollie's cock jumped in his hand and his eyes flashed with heat.

"Would you like me on my knees or with my hands on my head facing the wall?" Ollie panted.

Matt growled low in his throat and reached for the clear bottle on the shower shelf. "Hands on your head. I did like the way you looked the last time, but I'm not gonna hurt you," Matt replied as Ollie turned and did as he was told. "Such a turn on. Your body, your compliance. You want this, my love?" Matt pressed his hard length between Ollie's cheeks and ghosted his nose along the side of Ollie's neck before nipping him gently with his teeth.

Ollie nodded with a shudder and goosebumps sprang up on his skin. Matt slid his fingers between Ollie's legs and then lifted Ollie's leg to prop his foot on the built-in bench. Ollie moaned, but with restraint, and Matt didn't know if that was real or an affect Ollie was putting on to heighten the tension. His fingers were laced tightly on the top of his head, and his forehead rested against the cold tile.

Matt coated his fingers and began working Ollie open, deciding at the last minute to use only two.

Maybe I'll hurt him just a little. I am still mad at that fucker, Luke.

Matt could see the eagerness in Ollie. His widened stance, his short gasps of breath, his impossibly hard cock between his legs. He ran a fingertip down Ollie's spine and then crowded into his space, feeling the heat of Ollie's skin.

Matt paused with his dick just pressing against Ollie's tight hole and kissed Ollie's neck as he gripped Ollie's hip with his free hand. "This hole is mine. I get to use it however I want," he gritted out and pressed his hips forward. He expected (and heard) Ollie's gasp when he didn't pause after sinking the tip of his dick inside.

Instead, he gripped Ollie's hips tightly and thought of how perfectly his hands fit there, how perfectly his thumbs fit into those beautiful indents at the base of his back and thrust all the way in. Matt's eyes locked on Ollie's bent arms and admired his beautifully defined muscles, the way his silver necklace shone brightly against his golden skin. Matt began moving in long determined strokes and ran his hand over Ollie's thigh and squeezed.

The white scar on Ollie's shoulder caught Matt's eye and he moaned in ecstasy. Fueled by the sight, he increased his pace. He squeezed Ollie's hips tighter and hoped to leave fingerprint bruises in his flesh. Ollie was silent but pressed back eagerly and angled his upper body toward the wall. Matt reached up and grabbed Ollie's right wrist tightly, squeezing until his fingertips turned white.

"I changed my mind," Matt whispered. "Okay?"

"Okay," Ollie answered eagerly as Matt took one of Ollie's arms down and twisted it behind his back.

Matt leaned forward with a moan and pressed Ollie's arm up. He bit Ollie hard, right over the scar, and cried out loudly as the orgasm washed over him nearly without warning.

Matt hugged him tightly. "God. I love you so much, Ollie," he panted as he pulled out, spun Ollie around, and dropped to his knees.

Ollie put his hand back with the other on his head as he came in Matt's mouth within seconds of his tongue touching him.

"I'm gonna have a word with Agent Smug. Be ready to leave in twenty minutes."

Matt put on his suit coat and left, headed for the basement guest room. Ollie's shoulder and wrist throbbed mildly, along with his asshole, as he sprawled contentedly across the bed in his underwear. He was happy for the small victory with Matt and hoped he had eased some of Matt's anger. He dozed lightly and then left the bed to get dressed with only moments to spare.

Ollie found Matt waiting in his Porsche, the nose of which was pointed impatiently down the driveway. Matt skimmed his eyes over Ollie's lavender Brooks Brothers shirt and black Tom Ford suit pants. Ollie folded his tall body into the passenger seat and put on his seatbelt.

"What?" Ollie asked as Matt studied at him with an inscrutable expression.

Matt shook his head lightly. "You are breathtaking. I'm the luckiest man." He leaned across the car and kissed Ollie softly. He pulled back and looked at the muffin in Ollie's hand. "But you are not eating that in here."

Ollie grinned rebelliously and took a bite. "You can punish me later."

Matt raised his eyebrows and made a low sound like a growl. "You can count on that."

He pushed the button for the window, took the muffin from Ollie's hand and chucked it into the bushes.

Ollie sighed. "I'm hungry."

"I'll buy you a new fucking muffin in town," Matt said putting the car in first and rolling down the driveway as the window went up.

"Nothing will be open," Ollie pouted.

"There's food in my office fridge. Or I can feed you my cock." Matt quirked his eyebrow with a grin.

Ollie hummed thoughtfully at the image of getting on his knees in Matt's office and turned up his playlist.

The offices were empty as usual, because of the lockdown. Matt had thought being away from the house would be less distracting, but he couldn't get his mind off Luke, and Finn, and Charlie. He knew that if Finn didn't get Luke out of the house right after he and Ollie left, then the cat would be out of the bag the minute Charlie woke from his morning nap, and there would be no getting rid of Luke. He pressed his fingers to his eyelids, telling himself his eyes were watering from the applied pressure.

After three hours during which Matt got barely anything done, he hustled Ollie into the car and headed home.

"Fuck!" Matt shouted as they came up the hill later and saw Luke's car still parked in front of their house. Ollie stayed silent as his stomach dropped. "Join me in the gym."

"To run?"

"To keep me from killing him."

Matt pulled the car into the garage and got out with a slam of his door. Ollie made for the stairs to the house as Matt went to pick up the packages that had been left on the side porch. Ollie went into the kitchen and began filling two water bottles. He looked up as Finn and Luke came down the stairs looking freshly showered with their hair still wet. Luke had his backpack on his shoulder and Ollie prayed that meant he was leaving. Matt came through the door with an irritated air and dropped the packages on the kitchen island before striding through the archway to the front hall.

"I'll see you upstairs, Ollie," he said over his shoulder, ignoring Finn and Luke.

"Do you want something to eat?" Ollie said and suppressed a shiver at Matt's tone.

"No, Ollie. Get upstairs," Matt called.

Ollie looked at Finn, who was pale with worry, and shook his head. "He's in a *really* bad mood. I can't imagine what's gotten him so upset," he said bitingly and looked at Luke before walking out.

Ollie was afraid to go upstairs, but he was afraid not to. Matt's anger was unfamiliar, and it was only a small consolation that it had nothing to do with him. It did, however, have everything to do with Matt's heart, and Matt was fiercely, *violently*, protective of that particular organ. Ollie dragged his feet and took his time going up the stairs.

Ollie changed into workout clothes and carried his trainers and the bottles into the gym next to their suite. He found Matt in a pair of shorts, pounding away on the hanging bag. Ollie stopped to admire how Matt's muscles flexed with each punch before turning down the volume on 'Head Like a Hole.'

"I really think you ought to go for a run."

Matt looked over his shoulder at Ollie. "Is he fucking gone yet?"

Ollie nodded. "Yes. I heard his car drive away."

Matt pressed his lips into a thin line. "I'm surprised I didn't hear it, even with the music. That thing is obnoxiously loud." Matt took the water Ollie offered.

He took a long drink. "Ollie, stop looking at me like that. I'm not going to hurt you."

Ollie exhaled and held his gaze. Matt took another long drink, sweeping his eyes slowly over Ollie's body and back to his face. "But you keep looking at me like *that*, and I will have you on your knees."

Ollie smiled gently with relief. "You keep banging away on your effigy of Luke, whilst I hit the treadmill, Lieutenant. I will get on my knees for you later."

Matt came back to the suite with Charlie in his arms and put him down in front of the low bookcase full of books and toys. Ollie put his towel on the bed, looked at Matt and then pulled up at the expression on his face.

"Well, what did she say?" Ollie stepped into his underwear and a pair of joggers and crossed to the doorway between the rooms as Charlie pulled himself up on the shelves and began pulling out books and toys. He gurgled happily when he found a shape sorter and dragged it down. Matt sat on the floor next to him and opened the hatch and dumped the shapes out.

"She said he was undercover, and had to behave that way, and that it took so long for him to find her because she had been wiped from the NSA system, and online." Matt twisted his mouth. "She accused me of doing that," he scoffed. "As if I could get into *that* database."

"No way." Ollie frowned and sat on the other side of Charlie who turned to pat Ollie's leg before returning to the sorter. "What kind of undercover bullshit could that have been? He just *had* to cheat on her?"

"That's exactly what I said. You know, I gave him the benefit of the doubt in the beginning because of Chuck and how crazy she was for him, but I should've known better. There's something wicked shady about him," Matt spat, his Boston slang slipping in with his anger. "I don't want his influence on Charlie, and he certainly isn't capable of raising him the way we have been."

"Raising him? Did Chuck say she was leaving?" Ollie asked, his stomach dropping at the thought.

Matt shook his head. "She said she's not going to leave, but there was a big unspoken 'yet.'"

Ollie winced at the look on Matt's face.

"I'm not giving either of them up without a fight, Ollie." Matt kissed the top of Charlie's head. "And you're going to help me."

Charlie reached up and patted Matt's face. "Papa," he said with a drooly smile.

Ollie felt tears behind his eyes as he held Matt's gaze.

35

Decisions, Decisions

OLLIE WATCHED FROM the kitchen window as Matt and Charlie splashed in the pool that Matt kept open despite the falling leaves. He'd cranked up the heat as the days began to cool so that he could continue to swim with Charlie. It had been nearly two weeks since Luke reappeared in their lives and Matt's mood hadn't improved.

"They still out there?" Finn asked, startling him. "I came down to get him for his afternoon nap."

Ollie turned and looked at her in the doorway with a curt nod. "What's going on, Chuck? You and Luke getting back together?"

Finn took a deep breath. "I haven't made any decisions. I'm in touch with Luke, but I don't know when I'll see him again."

Ollie made a noise that he tried to keep from sounding like a harrumph. "You just going to string them both along then? How fun for us all."

Finn widened her eyes. "What? How dare you!"

"How dare you!" Ollie countered angrily. "You see him out there. This is destroying him. He loves Charlie more than his own life, sometimes I think even more than me. He can't focus on work, he barely sleeps.

You need to pick a side, or at least fill Matt in on your grand plan. He's too scared to ask you, but I'm not."

Finn watched Ollie with a stunned expression as her eyes filled. "You think this is easy for me? That it's not destroying me too? I am absolutely torn between them. I have Luke calling me every fucking day, begging me to come see him, to let him come *here*. And then there's Matt spending every minute with Charlie, as if I'm going to steal him away. Luke is his father, and Matt has been his father. I love them both. How the fuck am I supposed to choose, Ollie?"

Tears spilled down her cheeks. "If I cut Luke out, I'm sure he'll fight and win some type of custody, and then it's flying Charlie to DC every other week?" She questioned with a frown. "And if I take Charlie to DC to be with Luke, what happens to me and Matt? Don't you see, Ollie. I will keep limbo for as long as possible and know that I do it entirely for Matt's sake, which is incredibly unfair to Luke. He shouldn't be second fiddle, but he is."

Matt came through the archway from the front hall with towel around his waist and Charlie wrapped in a towel in his arms. He pulled up with a frown at Finn's tearstained face.

"What's going on?" he asked and looked at Ollie. Charlie kicked his legs with excitement and leaned forward toward Finn.

"Nothing," they replied in unison.

Finn took Charlie and disappeared up the back stairs at a brisk pace.

Matt watched her leave and turned a cool gaze to Ollie. "Okay, *Georgie Porgie*. Why the fuck was she crying?"

"I only asked what her plan was." Ollie shrugged defensively as her words echoed in his head.

Matt scoffed. "That can't be all you said to her."

"Matthew, I'm only concerned because you are so distraught. I love you, she needs to know what this is doing to you, to us." He walked around the island and pressed his cheek to Matt's bare shoulder and hugged him tightly. The last thing he wanted was for Matt to be mad at him.

Lighten the mood.

"And who is *Georgie Porgie*? Is he from *Gilligan's Island*?" Ollie asked as though he didn't really know.

Matt chuckled. "It's an old English nursery rhyme, how do you not know it? You're literally from England."

"Oh, Christ. You and your dusty references. Maybe you should've been at Oxford studying with Ned." Ollie shook his head and left the kitchen with a sassy swagger he knew Matt couldn't resist.

Matt looked up at a knock on his open office door after dinner. Finn walked in and closed the door quietly behind her.

"Hey, Chuck." Matt stood and came around his desk. "What's up?"

She chewed her lip briefly. "Can I use your plane this weekend?"

Matt narrowed his eyes. "Where you headed?"

Finn's eyes flickered away briefly. "DC."

"No," he answered simply.

Finn's eyes flashed. "Fine I'll rent a plane. I don't need yours." She turned to leave.

Matt grabbed her bicep. "No. I don't want you to go."

She frowned at his hand on her arm. "I know you don't. But you don't get a say."

Matt winced, dropping his hand. "Don't I? I've raised him as my son. I don't want him to go."

"I know, Matt. But he's not your son. He's Luke's. And Luke wants to see him," Finn said quietly.

"Fuck Luke!" Matt shouted. "I don't give a shit about what that fucking asshole wants. He's just gonna break your heart again. I don't want him anywhere near Charlie."

"You think he's just going to go away?" She shook her head angrily. "He wants to see his son, and he wants to see me. Matt, I love him."

Matt turned his gaze to the windows for several breaths as he tried to calm the turmoil boiling through him. Finally, he looked back at Finn. "You should remember what he did to you because I sure as shit do. You don't need him, Chuck. You have me. You have Ollie."

"No, you have Ollie. And I know I have you, but I don't *have* you. And I have needs. Luke loves me. I love him, and I'm going this weekend."

He rolled his tongue through his mouth unhappily. "Fine. You can use the plane, but I want you home Sunday night."

"Thank you."

Finn closed the door behind her. Matt stared at it for a long time before going back around his desk.

———

36

Plan B

"PACK A BAG. We're going to the Cape this weekend," Matt announced after breakfast on Thursday.

"Great." Ollie smiled and looked at the stairs. "Chuck and Charlie coming?"

Matt stood and put the dishes in the dishwasher, his body language suddenly stuff. "No. They're going to DC." He dried his hands and left the kitchen.

Ollie stared at the empty doorway pensively before leaving the kitchen on a mission. Ollie found Finn in the side yard pushing Charlie in the bucket swing of the elaborate playground set Matt had picked out.

"I hear you're going to DC."

Finn looked at him warily and nodded.

Ollie tickled Charlie's legs as he swung to him and smiled as Charlie giggled madly.

"Get back here. I'm going to get you," Ollie teased when Charlie swung back to Finn. Charlie kicked his legs and squealed, laughing as he swung back toward Ollie. Ollie tickled him again with a laugh. He looked at Finn who was watching him with a small smile. "I'm sorry about the other day. I love Matt so much. I worry for him. I should've thought about what it was doing to you." Ollie tickled Charlie again.

Finn looked at him with soft eyes. "Thank you, Ollie. I understand. I would be angry too if I were you. I love you."

"I love you too. And I love this little guy." He turned his gaze back to Charlie. "Yes, I do. So much I might eat him up the next time he comes my way," he said in a singsong voice while wiggling his fingers and chomping his teeth at Charlie, who shrieked and giggled again, his happy laugh filling the air around them.

* * *

Ollie unloaded the cooler and a bag of magazines and other things that weren't stocked on the boat from the back of the car while Matt rowed the little dinghy out to the mooring. It was a gorgeous fall day, and many of the anchored boats that were usually in the harbor were already gone for the season.

Ollie sighed and watched Matt's muscles flex pleasingly under his shirt as he rowed, and thought of how tense Matt had been, knowing his light mood was covering a deep worry. Matt secured the dinghy to the mooring and boarded the boat. Ollie watched as he unlocked the sliding glass door and disappeared inside. The engine roared to life a moment later and Matt came back out with his four-foot flagpole with a medium-sized American flag stacked over a similar-sized Navy SEAL flag. He screwed the pole into the holder on the back and untied the boat.

Ollie was so happy they had gone to the beach, tension aside. Matt's melancholy mood about Finn and Charlie being in DC seemed kept in check by the ocean air. Ollie too was worried about her trip. The thought of living without Charlie was unbearable, never mind the impact it would have on Matt and what Charlie's absence would mean for them. Ollie looked at the horizon and thought again about the surrogate website he visited when Matt was out for his run the other day. He knew Matt would want a child to fill the hole left by Charlie's absence. Ollie closed his eyes at the thought of hiring a stranger, while also pushing away the persistent thought of not being enough for Matt.

Ollie woke slowly, aware first of Matt's body spooned around his, and then of the rocking of the boat. The salty ocean air filled his nose, and he was unsure if it was coming from Matt or from upstairs and outside. It was a heady, delicious scent that was difficult to isolate. He looked out the window next to the bed which was so close to the water line it was disconcerting. He closed his eyes, reveling in the moment with Matt behind him and listened to the waves lapping the boat. He sat up in a panic at the sudden sound of an airhorn. The rumble of the nearby engine, which he could now discern, must have been what woke him.

Matt sat up as well, also instantly alert. He rolled out of bed and pulled on his shorts.

"Stay here, Ollie. No matter what." He opened the cabinet of the side table and pulled out a handgun, and with a quick glance at Ollie disappeared out the door and up the stairs.

Ollie dressed hurriedly and waited at the bottom of the stairs with his heart pounding. He heard Matt's deep voice calling across the water but couldn't make out the words. It sounded like he was assuring someone of something, and then he heard laughter. After a moment Matt appeared at the top of the stairs, shirtless and gorgeous, with the gun in his hand pointed at the ground.

"Why do you have a gun?" Ollie asked, still shocked at the sight of it.

I hope he doesn't bring that home to shoot Luke the next time he appears, Ollie worried half-seriously.

"I always have one on the boat. It's to keep you safe." He smiled at Ollie. "Anyway. It was nothing to worry about. They thought we were stranded or abandoned."

"Who?" Ollie frowned.

"The Coast Guard," Matt replied with a grin.

"Christ. Were we about to be boarded? I was naked!" Ollie panicked. "I told you, Lieutenant that we shouldn't have come out so far. Was it the US Coast Guard or Portugal's?"

Matt threw his head back with laughter. "Ollie, sometimes you're so blonde. We are in sight of land. *American* land. Portugal is more than three thousand nautical miles from here."

"I know that, Skipper. I was teasing." Ollie rolled his eyes.

"Skipper?" Matt puzzled and came down the stairs. He put the gun in the side table and closed the cabinet door.

"Oh, yeah. I watched your silly little *Gilligan* show. Pretty funny actually. You watched that but don't like *Mr. Bean?*" Ollie twisted his mouth. "The professor could make a radio from a coconut but couldn't get them off the island that was three hours from shore?" He raised his eyebrows.

"I never said I watched the show," Matt said as he came toward him. "I told the sailors I had a hot, naked blonde down here, and I was mostly right." Matt scowled at Ollie's clothes. "Who said you could get dressed?"

Matt scooped the lobster and oyster shells into the garbage and loaded the dishwasher. They'd stopped at Mac's market on the way back from the boat and had a quiet dinner in the kitchen of the beach house. Ollie felt Matt's eyes on him and glanced up in time to see a twist to Matt's mouth.

"What's up, Ollie. You're in and out again; you have been all night."

"You have been too, Lieutenant. I'm sure it's for the same reason."

Matt looked away with a flinch and left the room. Ollie watched him leave with a heavy sigh.

He poured two glasses of whisky and found Matt in the upstairs living room, in front of the large window looking out over the ocean blanketed in darkness. He handed Matt his glass and sat next to him on the couch.

"She loves you too much. She won't leave," Ollie said quietly, hoping he was right but not truly believing his words.

Matt furrowed his brow briefly. "She loves him more, though she should know better. He's exactly what I worked so hard to protect her from all these years." He looked down at his glass. "She's blind to everything with him. I suppose I was too. How could someone be so convincing, and not be a complete psychopath? How did I miss it?"

Ollie winced. "Darling, I don't think you missed anything. I don't think, and you don't truly think, he's a psychopath. Because he's not. He's human. We all make mistakes." Ollie paused. "I've thought about it. Maybe Luke had a moment of weakness. You of all people should be more sympathetic, Lieutenant."

Matt closed his eyes and swallowed roughly. "There wasn't a baby hanging in the balance with us when I fucked up; it's not the same." He opened his eyes, finished his whisky in one swallow and stood. "I won't ever give Charlie up. And you're going to help me keep him if it comes to that." He strode away into the bedroom.

37

Worst Case Scenario

"MORNING," MATT SAID to Finn as he came into the kitchen of their shared home later that week.

Finn jumped with a yelp and turned from doing dishes to meet Matt's concerned frown.

"You okay, Chuck? You've been on edge since you got back from DC."

"I'm fine." She looked away. "Just lost in thought about that article I've been working on. I need to turn it into the editor. The deadline is looming."

"God, you haven't finished that thing? The three people who are going to read your article on gods in ancient Mesopotamia being real must be pacing the halls of their psych ward in sleepless anticipation."

"Shut up." Finn shook her head with a laugh that softened her tense body and dried her hands. "It's not that far-fetched, *believe* me," she murmured and then straightened. "I'm gonna borrow your office downtown to get some work done. I need silence. Is that alright?"

"Of course. Let me get you Ollie's swipe card and my key."

Ollie ended his afternoon conference call and followed the sound of Charlie crying. He found Matt pacing agitatedly in the basement with a red-faced Charlie in his arms.

"Cor, he's been crying for a while now. Did he hurt himself?" Ollie asked with a concerned frown.

"Not that I can see. Ollie, you gotta watch him, I have to go to the office. Chuck's not answering her phone, and I think something might've happened." He looked at Charlie sobbing on his hip.

Ollie took Charlie from him with a nod. "Shite. I've got him. I'll calm him down and warm some milk. Go find Chuck."

Matt kissed Ollie swiftly and took the stairs two at a time with Jayne on his heels.

Ollie kept calm as he jostled Charlie's stiff body gently. "Let's go, big man. You're okay; let's go cuddle with Puddy and a book." Ollie carried him into the kitchen and searched for the blue washcloth-sized blanket with a stuffed head that Charlie carried everywhere.

Matt sped down the highway to the Seaport, fully focused on getting there and finding Finn, and hoped she just had her phone on silent in her purse. He pulled into a spot out front which pre-pandemic would've been impossible and leapt out of his Porsche. He swiped into the building and then raced off the elevator and into his office suite where he found his door wide open. The lights were still on and there was a mess of papers on his desk and scattered on the floor. He saw her purse on the credenza behind his desk as he focused on her phone which was left next to his computer. He picked it up and frowned at his missed calls and a missed text from Luke.

With growing panic that he tried to quell, he checked the bathroom and Ollie's office and turned up empty. He powered down his computer, picked up her purse and locked the doors. He called her name down the hall and then made his way out of the building. He had his phone in his hand ready to call the police, when it rang.

"She's here," Ollie announced breathlessly.

"Is she alright?" Matt's heart bounced with relief as he started his car and sped away from the curb. After a beat of silence, the phone switched to the car audio. "What happened?"

There was a pause. "The whole thing was rather odd, to be honest. Charlie stopped crying like a few minutes after you left. Just looked at me like he didn't even know he had been crying, and then ten minutes later, Chuck barreled in. She was…weird and had definitely been crying. She wouldn't talk to me. She just took Charlie and went upstairs. All she said she was that she was fine and to leave her be."

"I'll be home in less than ten minutes. Fill a bottle with ice water for me. I'll see you soon." Matt ended the call and focused on getting home and getting some answers.

Ollie handed the ice water to Matt with a kiss and watched as he went up the back stairs with Finn's phone. He let Jayne outside and waited for her bark to come back in before going upstairs. He put his phone in the bedroom and went to check on Matt and Finn. Ollie stepped silently into Finn's sitting room and saw Matt through the door, sitting on the bed next to Finn as he spoke softly with her. Charlie's little body was a lump on the bed next to her.

"Of course. You look tired, and he's out like a light." He heard Matt say as he crossed the room. "I'll check on you later."

Ollie watched Matt close the bedroom door quietly, backing out of the room with his eyes on Finn and Charlie.

He exhaled sharply when he turned. "Ollie!" he cried softly. "You scared the shit out of me. What are you doing?"

"I just wanted to check on her. How is she?"

"She's fine, outwardly, but she's keeping something from me." Matt led Ollie into their wing and closed the door to the sitting room behind them. "It obviously has to do with Luke. Whatever happened, made her leave my office with nothing but her car key."

"That's so weird. What could've it have been? Do you think he broke up with her again?"

Matt shrugged with a frown. "Anything's possible with that fucker. She denied that it had anything to do with him, but I don't trust her." He clenched his fists. "And I *absolutely* don't trust him."

Ollie brought his hands up to Matt's face and kissed him gently. He needed to diffuse the situation before Matt worked himself up. "I don't trust him either, but I'm just so glad everyone's okay. I was really worried today."

Matt's shoulders lowered and he placed his hands on Ollie's hips. "Me too, baby." He closed the distance between them and kissed Ollie again. He deepened the kiss before pulling back. "I'm just gonna lock up. Go get your magic stress reliever ready for me," Matt said and patted Ollie's ass as he turned to leave the room.

Ollie grinned with relief and headed to the bathroom.

Matt went for his run the following morning, made a mug of coffee for Ollie, who was still asleep (of course), and took a quick shower. He went down to the kitchen for oatmeal and coffee dressed in his favorite lounge pants and a white t-shirt, when he heard someone on the back stairs. He closed the cabinet expecting Finn and did a double take when he saw it was Luke barefoot in a t-shirt and jeans with Charlie on his hip.

"Luke," he stated as his brain raced. It took all his effort not to jump across the counter and punch him.

"Hey, Matt," Luke said with a smirk. "How you doing?"

"Papa," Charlie said happily and leaned out of Luke's arms toward Matt.

Matt felt a deep sense of pleasure at the dismay on Luke's face before continuing to wonder why Luke was standing in his kitchen at seven in the morning on a Sunday.

"What does this brute eat for breakfast?" Luke asked in a casual tone. He lifted Charlie in front of him and tossed him in the air with his biceps flexing as Charlie giggled ecstatically.

Matt watched him with a frown and ignored Luke's effortless appeal. It was clear what Finn saw in Luke, but Matt only saw a cloud of red gathering around his peripheral vision. He took down a small pot hanging over the stove and measured in the water and oat bran to keep himself from acting on his rage.

He nodded to the highchair against the wall. "Pull that up to the island."

Luke did as he was told, putting Charlie in the seat, and then sat in the barstool next to him.

"Give him some of these to occupy him while I make his hot cereal." Matt slammed a box of organic o-shaped cereal down on the island in front of Luke.

Luke startled and then shook some out on the tray in front of Charlie, who immediately began shoveling them into his mouth with his tiny fists as his eyes flitted between his food and Luke and Matt. Matt continued to move around the kitchen as he mulled over what Luke's appearance could mean.

Matt got down a mug and poured coffee from Ollie's over-priced and elaborate coffee maker and put it in front of Luke. He then poured himself one and took a sip before setting the mug down on the island between them.

"Thanks. This is good," Luke complimented after taking a sip.

Matt braced his hands far apart on his side of the island, flexed his muscles and shrugged his shoulders up to his ears as he studied Luke. Luke held his gaze with a quirked brow as Matt relaxed his shoulders after a moment with an exhale and turned away to the stove.

This fucking guy, Matt thought as he clenched his teeth. *I want to punch that smirk off his face.*

A lot.

Matt took a deep breath and turned back to look at him again. "When did you get here?"

"Late last night," Luke answered. "Didn't Finn tell you I was coming for the weekend?"

"It's Sunday." Matt scoffed.

Luke stared back at Matt with an unwavering gaze. "My weekends aren't often traditional ones."

"Where's your car?"

"I flew."

Matt made a thoughtful sound before turning the stove off and adding mashed banana and yogurt to Charlie's hot cereal. He walked around the island and nudged Luke out of his stool with his hip and sat down. Luke moved to the next barstool and watched him feed Charlie.

That Luke was here out of the blue, could only mean that something did happen to Finn at his office and whatever it was had to do with the smug asshole sitting next to him. It was no coincidence. Matt wondered if she had been attacked by the same people who attacked her in Baltimore and if it was Luke who had led them right to her door.

"He's gonna eat all that?" Luke asked with disbelief, interrupting Matt's thoughts.

Matt narrowed his eyes but then smiled at Charlie. "He has a huge appetite. He's a ball of energy all day long. It's really no wonder." He glanced at Luke who had a strange expression on his face, and went back to feeding Charlie. "Did Finn say anything to you about what happened yesterday?" Matt asked casually after a pause and watched Luke from his side-eye.

"No. Did something happen?" Luke asked with concern.

Matt looked at Luke's mouth and bit back a retort before turning back to Charlie. "That thing on your face lies pretty effortlessly," Matt said quietly. "I'm not surprised though, to be honest. The work you do, the government you work for. Don't forget, I worked for them too, and I can spot a steaming pile of bullshit from a mile away. I can shoot it too." He shook his head and looked again at Luke. "Whatever the fuck you told Chuck, to win your way back into her life and her bed, just know that I'm onto you," he warned angrily.

He watched Luke's throat bob as he swallowed and then as he leaned back in his barstool. Matt held his gaze a moment longer, wanting to unnerve Luke, before looking back at Charlie who was making hungry noises. "Get the fuck outta here. I got this," he commanded without looking at Luke.

Luke hesitated as though he wanted to say something but then thought better of it and stood.

Good, Matt thought as he watched him disappear up the stairs.

Ollie appeared in the playroom doorway an hour later. He was wearing one of Matt's Navy t-shirts and tight grey sweatpants that outlined his perfectly sized package. There was a very strong chance Ollie was going commando and Matt kept his smile to himself at the thought.

"I missed you in bed," Ollie said with a sly grin. "How's Chuck? Have you seen her?"

Matt scanned his eyes over Ollie and took a breath. "I haven't seen her. But Agent fucking Smug is back."

Ollie raised his eyebrows as his mouth dropped open. "What? When did he arrive?"

"He said last night, but the cameras show him arriving around four this morning. And the camera on the gate showed him talking to some guy out in the street." Matt frowned. "There was a bit of interference and a blinding flash which damaged the sensor. I have to replace it."

"That's bizarre. Was it a neighbor or someone he arrived with?" Ollie puzzled.

Matt thought about the knife he saw Luke draw from behind his back before re-sheathing it and knew he could never mention that detail to Ollie. There's no way Ollie wouldn't freak out and Matt needed more information before bringing Ollie into the mess that was Agent Smug.

"I don't know who it was, but it seemed like someone he knew."

"Do we need to worry?"

Matt stood and took Ollie in his arms. "You don't have to worry about anything, princess. But I still don't trust him. He makes one wrong move, and I'll fucking kill him."

Ollie gasped and pulled back. "Don't be ridiculous. You won't kill him. He's in the NSA."

Matt made a noncommittal sound. He still hadn't decided whether or not he was going to *deal* with Luke.

"I finished the front section of *The Globe* if you want it." Matt picked up the paper from the coffee table and handed it to Ollie before leaving the room.

$$38$$

Rock 'Em Sock 'Em Robots

MATT WAS IN HIS OFFICE when he heard the floorboards creaking as someone walked through the front of the house. He stood and followed the sound into the main living room where he found Luke looking at one of his Warhol paintings.

"It's real," he said from the doorway as he studied Luke carefully.

"I didn't think it wouldn't be," Luke responded somewhat peevishly. "You don't strike me as the kind of man who would have copies. I mean other than Ollie."

Matt narrowed his eyes and wondered at his meaning. "Do you mean because he looks like Chuck?" He shrugged when Luke shot him a look. "I guess I have a type. Maybe she does too." He scanned his eyes over Luke's body pointedly and decided then and there that he would *deal* with Luke. "You bring any workout gear with you?"

"Yeah. I have sweats but I didn't grab my sneakers."

"What size are you?"

"Twelve and a half," Luke answered.

Matt felt his eyebrow flicker involuntarily and managed to avoid dropping his eyes to Luke's crotch. "Get changed and meet me in the gym." He turned and left the doorway without waiting for an answer.

Ollie came back from lunch at Bill's, where they discussed their tennis match, which Bill had won, Charlie, and how much they missed their horses. He heard voices coming from the open door of the gym and stopped with his mouth open when he saw Matt and Luke circling each other on the mat and dripping with sweat and blood. Their shirts were stuck to their muscled bodies and their faces were clouded with anger.

"By the way, you been fucking ordering me around all day. I thought I told you I don't take orders from a *Lieutenant*. Especially ones that let themselves get shot," Ollie heard Luke say in a hard tone.

Ollie gasped lightly. *Oh no he didn't.*

He saw Matt scowl darkly and feared for Luke. "Yeah, but you did everything I said and came up here anyway. So clearly you do," Matt said with a smirk and swung at Luke's right cheek.

Luke dodged Matt's swing and came up with a punch to Matt's side. "I came because I couldn't wait to beat the shit out of you. I can't wait to punch that smirk off your face."

"Dear god," Ollie called, wanting to deescalate what he was witnessing. Luke looked over at him and Matt blindsided him, catching Luke on the jaw, and causing him to stumble back.

"Allow me to remove the smug expression off yours," Matt said and bounced a step back.

Luke regained his footing and charged at Matt, who ducked under Luke's swing. Luke avoided a punch to the gut and turned back to land a blow on Matt's mouth, splitting his lip and snapping his head back. Matt shook his head and blinked furiously.

"Boys, not the faces!" Ollie shouted. "Stop it! What on earth are you doing?"

Both men stopped to catch their breath and wipe their brows. They studied each other with grim expressions. Matt finally nodded and extended his hand to Luke with a tight jaw.

Luke grasped his hand. "Not bad for someone trained by an organization that calls their entry-level grunts seamen."

Matt grinned and blood dripped from his lip onto the mat. "And the Army calls their's privates. What's your point?"

Matt handed Luke a towel and followed him to the door. Luke gestured at his feet.

"Why did you ask me for my shoe size if we were going to spar barefoot?"

"Our run tomorrow," Matt answered, taking the tape off his hands and dropping it into the trashcan next to the door.

Luke groaned and took his tape off as well. "Okay, but don't be all, 'we run at dawn.' I prefer midday."

"No problem, pussy," Matt scoffed and walked past Ollie, who turned to follow.

"What in the bloody hell was that all about?" Ollie asked in an angry tone once they reached the room. Matt stripped his sweaty clothes off under Ollie's watchful gaze and stepped into the shower. "Your beautiful face. Did he break anything?"

Matt closed his eyes and washed carefully, avoiding the soreness in his side from Luke's kicks and punches. His face was already swollen, and he knew he was going to have a sizable black eye. "Maybe just a rib."

"What?!" Ollie shouted, his voice echoing off the marble. "I wasn't being serious. You fought each other so viciously that you think you have a broken rib? Bloody hell." He threw up his hands.

Matt watched Ollie leave the bathroom in a huff and then touched his side gingerly, taking a deep breath to test it. It wasn't broken, but it was going to hurt like a motherfucker for a day or two.

"Get me some ice please," Matt called loudly and then grunted in pain from the effort.

He washed himself carefully and then stepped out to dry off. He hung the towel neatly before putting on sweatpants and a t-shirt with a zip hoodie. Ollie appeared in the dressing room with a bag of ice in a kitchen towel and shook his head with disgust as he turned to leave. Matt followed him while holding the towel to his eye. "Nothing's broken."

"Well, thank god for small favors. Because you look awful." He ran his eyes over Matt with a disdainful expression. "I can't believe you."

There was a knock at the sitting room door. "Come in," Matt called.

Finn stalked in with an angry expression darkening her beautiful face and closed the door behind her. "What the fuck is the matter with you?"

"Chuck—"

"No! Don't 'Chuck' me. You are a barbarian. You both are. I don't know what the hell I was thinking getting involved with either one of you. This stops now. Or I take Charlie and I fucking walk." She glanced at Ollie. "Maybe Ollie and I both walk and live happily ever after in a violence-free zone. People might think we're *Flowers in the Attic*, but Christ, it's preferable to this nonsense."

She spun on her heel and slammed the door.

Matt stared at the door for several moments before looking sheepishly at Ollie. "You wouldn't. Would you?"

"What on earth is *Flowers in the Attic*? Is that also from the sixties?" Ollie sighed heavily and then shook his head. "Never mind. I bloody well should; she's not wrong. But how could I? I love you so much it hurts. I should seek professional help for my addiction."

Matt smiled as relief flooded his belly and then winced from the pain. Ollie scoffed and shook his head again.

"I love you, Ollie." Matt paused and then straightened his shoulders with resolve. "He deserved it. I won't apologize for that."

Ollie put his arms around Matt and hugged him loosely. "I swear to god, you better still be able to fuck me. I doubt my cock is going to get much from your mouth the next few days."

Matt laughed and slid his hands down Ollie's back and then whined when Ollie pulled away.

"Oh, I wouldn't laugh if I were you. Yours won't get anything from mine either."

Ollie scanned his eyes over Matt's body in that sassy way of his that, unfortunately for Matt, meant business.

They gathered for dinner around the long table between the kitchen and the family room after Charlie went to bed. Matt and Luke sat scowling at each other with their twin swollen eyes while Finn and Ollie studied them with their twin looks of disgust.

Finn shook her head at them both while she opened a bottle of white wine. Matt looked sheepishly at Ollie, who was watching him with his eyebrows raised, and then stood to escape Ollie's judging gaze. Matt grabbed a bottle of bourbon from the butler's pantry near the back stairs and poured two generous glasses before returning to the table. He passed one to Luke.

"You should be ashamed of yourselves," Finn scoffed when everyone was seated and settled. "You look awful. Both of you. You better not go out in public."

"I'm going into work tomorrow. But I'll be home for our run at three," Matt said and held Luke's gaze. "You'll have plenty of time to go see Bill while I'm gone."

Finn turned her head with an incredulous expression. "What are you talking about?"

"I called your dad." He glanced at Finn and then back at Luke. "I can't wait to hear how you explain yourself to him, and I want you to do it with my handiwork all over your face."

Ollie saw a pleased expression cross Matt's features and wondered if Matt had actually called Bill, as Bill hadn't said anything to him during their tennis match.

Luke narrowed his good eye and made a sound. "Maybe you should join me, so he can see my shiner on yours as well."

Ollie turned his eyes to Luke to gauge his intent before shifting them back to Matt. Ollie felt a flash of fear for Luke at the look he saw on Matt's face. Ollie rubbed the bruises on his wrist and felt Luke's eyes on him. He put his hands in his lap before turning to meet Luke's speculative gaze.

"You had no right to call him," Finn said angrily, interrupting the silent appraisal. "It is my decision to make, and I was going to do it when I was ready."

"Finn, it's fine." Luke said quietly and covered her hand with his. "I need to. He's not wrong."

Everyone turned their attention to their plates and ate in silence.

Matt and Finn cleared the table when they were done and left Ollie and Luke to finish their drinks. Ollie was lost in thought about the fight he witnessed in the gym. Matt may have been beating on Luke, but Ollie wondered if he'd have rather been fucking him violently instead. He might not be Matt's type, but he was walking sex appeal.

"What was that all about?" Luke asked.

Ollie snapped out of his reverie and found Luke staring at him with a shrewd expression on his face. It took him a minute to realize that Luke was referring to the bruises on Ollie's wrist and perhaps even the flash of fear he'd clearly misinterpreted. He felt himself blush.

Shit, he's perceptive.

"Nothing." He picked up his wine glass and finished the last swallow. "You know, you're lucky all he gave you was a shiner. I'm quite certain he wanted to do far worse to you," he said after a moment with a small smile.

Luke furrowed his brow and looked at Ollie with his lips parted. Ollie couldn't tell if it was that Luke was speechless, or about to say something.

"I'm glad you're back to make things right with Finn," Ollie said, changing the subject and standing in case Luke wanted to dig deeper. "I hope it can be made right. I told you before, they're a package deal. You need to make things right with Matt too."

"I know, Ollie," Luke said solemnly. "I'm trying."

Ollie found Matt later, brushing his teeth in just his Tom Ford trunks. One side of his beautiful face was swollen and red, and the left side of his torso was already a nasty shade of purple. Ollie frowned in sympathy and took down a bottle of pain reliever.

"I've had three of those already," Matt said spitting and rinsing his brush. "But bring them to the bedroom. I'll need more in a few hours."

Ollie brushed his teeth methodically and watched Matt. "You do find him attractive, don't you?" He turned his toothbrush off. "Don't get me wrong, I wouldn't kick him out of bed for eating crackers, but you would much rather have been fucking him angry-Matt style than just beating on him. It was all over your face at dinner." Ollie wiped his mouth.

Matt frowned. "No, I would much rather have been killing him and burying him six feet under."

Ollie believed they were both right but sighed. "It doesn't matter either way because he'd never let you. I was just pointing it out because I didn't care for it. I'm the only one you fuck, angry or otherwise." He held Matt's gaze in the mirror.

Matt gave him a slow smile, careful with his lip. "You're mine, I know."

Ollie shook his head at Matt. "You're mine, and don't you forget it," he declared and left the bathroom. He put the bottle of pills next to Matt's glass of bourbon and hoped Matt didn't plan on mixing the two.

He climbed into bed as Matt took off his underwear and turned off the overhead light.

Ollie made a pensive sound for effect and straightened the sheets. "If you plan on fucking me, please turn out your side light. You look like the *Elephant Man.*"

"Oh, him you know, but not *Georgie Porgie?*" Matt shook his head laughing. "Get over here, cowboy. I wanna give you a ride. It'll be nice having you do all the work for a change." He turned off his sconce. "And I saw that eye roll."

Ollie chuckled as he straddled Matt.

I know nearly all your dusty references, Lieutenant, Ollie thought as he leaned down to kiss Matt, *but it's so much more fun to tease you.*

39

Dear God

"YOU BACK FOR your run with Luke then?" Ollie asked when Matt poked his head into Ollie's home office.

"Yeah. Just wanted to check in about the Portland deal before I left," Matt replied as he straightened his hoodie.

"It's all good. They want both of the new products and are eager to pay for the added services."

"Fantastic." Matt swept his eyes over Ollie. "And of course they did. Who could say no to you?"

Ollie's grin turned filthy. "When you come back, don't shower." He flicked his eyebrows.

Matt pulled up. "Seriously?"

Ollie hummed. "Have fun on your run," he replied and turned his attention back to his computer screen.

Two hours later Ollie heard a step on the front stairs and then the front door shut, followed by Jayne whining. Judging from the whine, it was clear Finn had left the house, probably to get the mail, and he wondered where Matt and Luke were.

Probably having another pissing contest.

Less than ten minutes later Ollie heard the side door in the kitchen slam shut and then the sound of raised voices. He paused his typing to listen. It sounded like Matt and Luke were having words.

Fuck's sake, Ollie thought with a frown, *they still at it?*

He heard them thudding up the back stairs and then nothing. Ollie was hesitant to investigate, not wanting to come between them if they were having another fight. He strained to hear sounds of struggling or walls shaking, and decided they must have gone their separate ways. Ollie hoped Matt would come in search of him.

Ollie finished making his edits on a contract and was about to go looking for Matt and his deliciously sweaty body when he heard a thud on the floor above him. Ollie shot out of his chair and ran for the stairs, knowing the sound came from Charlie's room which was directly above his office. He took the stairs two at a time with his heart racing and realized on his way up that he never heard Finn come back inside. He found Charlie crawling to his bedroom door sobbing. His face was beet red, just like the last time he'd had a crying fit like this.

Ollie picked him up carefully and cradled him gingerly, checking for injuries and looking him over for blood. "Big man," he soothed. "You can't get out of your crib; you could hurt yourself."

Charlie didn't respond to Ollie's gentle probing for injuries, just continued to wail and point at the door. He kept saying 'mommy' between sobs.

"Shhh, darling. You're okay. Mummy's okay. Let's go look for her."

Ollie hugged Charlie and rubbed his back as he left the room in search of Finn. Her suite of rooms was empty and smelled faintly of ozone. Charlie continued to wail as Ollie walked to the other end of the house and called for Matt in their rooms before checking the gym. He felt the floor vibrate as the garage door opened beneath him and heard Matt's Porsche roar to life.

"What in the bloody hell?"

Ollie went to the window and saw the Porsche race down the driveway. He headed down the stairs to the kitchen with a frown, his mind racing as he continued to try to soothe Charlie.

"Jesus, is Charlie okay?" Matt asked when he bumped into Ollie coming around the corner. He took Charlie from Ollie's arms. "Get a bag from the freezer," he ordered Ollie.

Ollie hesitated momentarily before springing into action. His brain was a blender of questions.

"Who took your car?" Ollie asked in an incredulous voice as he opened the freezer door. "Where's Chuck?"

Matt slid his glance away like a guilty felon and turned to the sink. "Luke needed it. He… took Chuck somewhere."

Ollie frowned. "Why didn't they just take her car?"

"Ollie, I don't have time for your questions right now. Please thaw the milk and put it in a bottle," Matt ordered.

Ollie took Matt's spot at the sink and did as he was told, rebellion welling inside. Once the bottle was ready, he handed it to Matt and held his tongue about feeding Charlie in his state.

Charlie drank the bottle while hiccupping, and then cried again before throwing up all over Matt.

Hmm, *didn't see that coming.*

"You better shower. My tongue bath offer was for sweat, not regurgitated breastmilk," Ollie said as he took Charlie from Matt.

Matt shot him a look and went upstairs. He reappeared ten minutes later to take Charlie, who was beginning to tire but still crying. He sang in a low voice as he carried him to the couch in the playroom when suddenly, Charlie stopped crying and pushed himself away from Matt's chest to look at him.

Matt smiled. "Hey, bud. You okay?"

Charlie held his gaze. "Mommy. Daddy."

Matt nodded with a smile and shifted Charlie to his knees. "Yeah, Charlie. Papa has you. You okay now? You scared me and *Père*," Matt said, using the French word for father they had decided on for Ollie.

Charlie craned his neck to look at Ollie with a smile as he sat down next to Matt. "Come here, big man."

Charlie leaned into Ollie's arms and hugged him, as Matt watched with soft eyes.

"I love you both so much. I'm so glad he stopped screaming," Matt added in a whisper.

"Me too. I wonder what it is that upsets him so. He stopped crying this way last time, like a switch." Ollie kissed the side of Charlie's head. "What troubles you, Charlie?"

"Mommy and…." he said something unintelligible against Ollie's neck.

Ollie pulled Charlie back to look at his face. "Mommy and what honey?" He looked at Matt out of the corner of his eye and turned his head at Matt's wide-eyed expression. "What is it?" Ollie frowned. "You look like you've seen a ghost."

Matt shook his head and blinked. "What? Nothing. Just glad he stopped crying." He looked at Charlie with a grin that was more like a grimace with how fake it was. "You must be hungry, bud. You threw up all over me, and you've been wailing for nearly an hour now. Want some food?"

He swept Charlie out of Ollie's arms and left the room.

Ollie watched his back with a puzzled frown. *What are you hiding, Lieutenant?*

40

Subterfuge

OLLIE WOKE TO HOT COFFEE on his side table and a note about a run on Matt's pillow. He rolled over languidly and sat up to drink and heard the shower running through the open bathroom door. He put down his coffee and slipped into the bathroom to join Matt. He opened the shower door with a smile and then startled as Matt jumped into a defensive stance with a grunt.

"Jesus, Ollie. You scared me." Matt gasped and wiped the water gently from his bruised face.

"Sorry. Why're you so jittery?" Ollie stepped in and took the soap to wash Matt's back.

"I was just lost in thought, babe, and you're up early." Matt made a sound of pleasure as Ollie smoothed his soapy hands over his skin. "God your hands feel so good on my body."

Ollie smiled. "Your body feels so good under my hands."

Matt toweled off and dressed in suit pants and a button down, with a vintage XMI tie. He ran a small dab of Ollie's hair serum through his hair with his fingers and tousled the short waves just the way Ollie liked it. He checked his reflection in the full-length mirror on the wall and left the room, palming Ollie's bare ass cheek on his way out.

Ollie took his time dressing and doing his hair. Once the swoop of his bangs was perfect, he made his way to the suite door and stopped when he heard voices on the other side.

"She's much better; she's going to be fine," Luke was saying. "I'll be interested in what Isi has to report. Can you get Ollie out of here? He can't know."

"Of course. We're going to the office. We'll be out of your hair for most of the day. Oh, there's Chuck. Bye."

Ollie jumped away from the door and made it to the bedroom. He was utterly and totally confused by what he overheard as he hurried away from the door.

Who is Isi? What happened to Finn?

When the door to the hallway opened, he turned and made like he was just coming into the sitting room and watched Matt pull up short at the sight of him.

"Oh, hey, babe," Matt said smoothly. "Let's leave in ten, okay? I just gotta grab my charger."

Ollie narrowed his eyes as Matt passed him. "Okay."

Ollie stepped into the eerily quiet hallway and stopped at the top of the stairs, straining to hear anything as he looked toward Finn's suite.

We wanted it sound proofed, he thought with a sigh before heading to the kitchen to make a quick batch of cheesy eggs with spinach.

He pushed a plate toward Matt when he came down the stairs. Matt looked at his watch, then grabbed the plate and began shoveling the eggs into his mouth.

"Is there toast?" he asked, just as the toaster dinged.

"Do you want jam on yours?" Ollie asked as he spread the butter.

"Sure."

Matt ate four pieces while Ollie finished his one, leaving all the plates and utensils and food on the counter.

Ollie left the kitchen and wondered how to broach the subject of what he'd overheard, without giving away that he'd been eavesdropping. "I'll see you in the car."

Matt stayed behind to clear everything away, just as Ollie knew he would. Ollie smirked to himself when Matt eventually came out and folded himself into the Porsche.

Matt gave him the side eye and started the car. "You got a piece of toast hidden in your sweater, Oliver? What is that look for?"

"No." Ollie continued to swipe through his phone and ignored Matt.

Ollie felt Matt's suspicious gaze run over him before Matt backed out of the garage. He turned the car around in the side spot and drove down the hill.

"We have to stop for gas," Matt said as he turned onto Washington Street.

Ollie glanced at the gauge and saw that it was nearly on fumes. "Where'd they go? You filled the tank two days ago and we've not been anywhere."

Matt glanced at him without turning his head. "I don't know. I didn't ask."

Ollie frowned incredulously and put his phone in his lap with a huff. "Something weird is going on, Lieutenant," he said irritatedly. "You two were beating each other to a pulp two days ago, you said you wanted to kill him, and now you're letting him joyride in your car that you don't even let *me* drive, and you don't ask him where he's going? Just 'here are my keys and drain my tank.' I'm not an idiot." Ollie thinned his lips in anger.

Matt pulled into the gas station and handed his credit card to the attendant. "Fill it with premium please." He put the window back up and looked at Ollie. His eyes searched Ollie's face as he seemingly picked his words. "To be honest, Ollie, I don't really know or have any answers for you. It's classified and turns out his security clearance is lightyears above mine. He asked to borrow my car, which is faster than Chuck's, and said he couldn't tell me anything, that I had to trust him. So, I did.

He outranks me, and old habits die hard. Also, knowing that what he does for the NSA keeps us all safe, I happily gave him my keys."

Ollie felt his mouth slowly open in shock as he listened. He looked out the windshield and then back at Matt. He nodded slowly in understanding. He knew he wasn't going to get any real answers, and he was fairly certain he wouldn't want to know the truth in this instance anyway.

"Okay. Okay. I get it, but you should've just told me that instead of being an evasive weirdo. I'm your partner; you can trust me. I hate it when you keep secrets from me, Lieutenant. We've been through this."

"I know I can trust you, baby. I love you, and I'm sorry for not telling you. Luke asked me to keep it under wraps," he said quietly and put his window down to take his credit card from the attendant.

"I want you here for Christmas this year, Ollie. So, I've arranged for the plane to take you to London early, to celebrate with your family, and then bring you home in time for actual Christmas." Matt looked at Ollie as they sped down the Mass Pike.

Ollie closed his eyes. "Okay, sounds nice. You're sure it's for me, and not to just be rid of me?"

Matt glanced sharply at him. "What are you talking about? I know you want to see your folks; you go every year. But this year I want you home for Charlie's first Christmas."

"Okay, I just wondered if it had to do with Agent Smug, and his secret operation." Ollie smiled to cover his skepticism.

"No, Ollie. Just me selfishly wanting you for Christmas this year."

$$41$$

Winter Solstice

IT WAS COLD and raining in London when Ollie landed and met his driver. The raindrops on the window of the Range Rover looked like a crowd of faces desperate to get in where it was warm and dry, huddling together and then streaming away in disappointment when they couldn't, as the SUV sped down the A4.

The driver pulled into his parents' driveway and Ollie looked up with a smile at the large, cream-colored, semi-detached house that he grew up in. He followed the driver, who carried Ollie's bags to the front porch, and then pressed a generous tip in his hand.

"Thank you. See you on the twenty-third."

The door opened and his father ushered him in with a beaming smile. "It's frightful out there. Get inside." He hugged Ollie once the door was closed.

"Hello, Dad. You're looking well." Ollie smiled. "Where's Mum?"

"She's just run to pick up Cassie at her flat; she'll be back soon. If you want to get settled. I can help you with your bags."

"This one stays down here, it's filled with presents from me and Matt." He pointed at the large, hard-sided suitcase. "And I can carry this one up. I'll just go change for dinner. Think I'm going over to Ivan's after."

"Ah, Captain America," George announced obnoxiously as Ollie walked into his best friend Ivan's flat several hours later. "You wear anything from the homeland anymore?" he added with a grin.

He'd known George and Ivan since Eton, and Sahil, who was sitting on the couch next to Ivan since undergrad at Oxford. They had been a close foursome ever since Michaelmas term their first year, despite pursuing vastly different studies. Sahil was a cardiac surgeon, Ivan studied finance, and George majored in marketing.

"Yeah, yeah. I got my Ritchie trainers on and the Harrods underwear your father gave me." Ollie laughed and hugged George. Ivan and Sahil stood for hugs and back slaps. "You guys ever gonna stop dressing like you've just come from algebra class?"

"Fuck off, Mr. Moneybags. We're not flush with cash and can't just buy a whole new wardrobe," Ivan scoffed and waved his pale hand. "Besides, we're just hanging in; no need to get all poshed up." He ran his eyes over Ollie's bespoke shirt, submariner Rolex, and Prada jeans.

"I dress with respect, and you guys do just fine, especially you, Viscount Leopold." Ollie shook his head and waved his hand around Ivan's spacious flat.

"Living in London isn't cheap, Ol," Sahil chimed in, his smile flashing white in his tan face. "Ivan got this place from his granny; we live very frugally."

"One of several places of residence he had to choose from," Ollie teased. "But Boston isn't cheap either. Speaking of Boston, when are you guys coming to visit me?" He looked around the living room. "You've all been to the states since I moved and came once like four years ago for half a second before ditching me for the Rotten Apple."

Sahil looked at Ivan. "We were planning to come last summer, but the fucking pandemic happened. Now who knows when it'll be safe to travel."

"Let us use your company jet, and we'll come whenever." George grinned, his dimples softening his square-jawed face.

Ollie shrugged. "Maybe. I'll have to ask my boss. Perhaps next time I'm here for business. I'll plan ahead and let you guys know so you can get time off and fly back with me."

"That would be amazing, Ollie!" Ivan said. "What the fuck is it like flying private? Is that the only way you go now?"

"It's bloody incredible. There's a bedroom, two bathrooms, couches, a kitchen, Wi-Fi, a flight attendant usually. Fits nineteen." Ollie grinned and opened another beer.

"Cor! What the fuck, Ol?" Sahil shook his head and widened his dark brown eyes. "You are definitely flying us over on that sweet bus. Do whatever it takes to get your boss to say yes. Don't suppose he's gay?" Sahil mimed a blow job with his hand and tongue in cheek.

Ollie laughed. "Oh, I wish. You met him, Ivan."

"Right. You couldn't take your eyes off him. No wonder he left the pub abruptly with his bird, Finn." Ivan laughed. "Clearly, you've stopped doing that or he would've fired you by now. Sexual harassment and all."

"I have a boyfriend. Haven't got time to stare at my boss anymore," Ollie lied and sipped his beer to cover his smile. He really wished he could just tell them, but Matt would lose his mind.

"Speaking of boyfriends. When I was in New York last year for work, I could've sworn I saw Andy-the-Asshole." George opened two beers and passed one to Sahil. "He disappeared two years ago, right? But they never found a body. Shady wanker probably faked his death because he fucked the wrong guy."

Ollie's body went cold as he straightened in his chair. "What do you mean you saw him? Where? Did you speak to him?"

George shook his head. "No, I was at a club after a dinner with some coworkers on our last night there and I saw him, or someone who looked like him. Guy had bleach-blonde hair though. We locked eyes, and then someone walked between us, and he was gone. That's why I thought it might be him. If he's changed his identity, and recognized me, then he definitely wouldn't have wanted me to get a better look."

"Do you think he faked his own death?" Sahil mused. "Why would he? Was the wanker in trouble with the law?"

Ollie's mind raced as the guys speculated. *Could he still be alive?*

Ollie thought about Andy's laptop and wondered again why Matt had it. The box it had been in was no longer in Matt's office; it had disappeared not long after Ollie had discovered it.

What had Matt been doing with it? And where was it now?

It's at the bottom of the ocean, his brain said quietly. *Why else would it have been in a box labelled 'boat?'*

"Ollie?" Ivan called.

Ollie snapped out of his thoughts. "Yeah? Sorry, was just thinking about the poor guy they arrested, if Andy is still alive."

"Oh, Christ. I didn't even think about him. Andy's a fucking tosser if he's alive and letting that guy rot in jail," George scoffed.

"All I know is that he was determined to stay in the US, but he couldn't get a visa. Maybe he's turned criminal or got himself an American identity," Ollie replied. The scar on his shoulder tingled suddenly as he thought about whether he should tell Matt or not. "Either way, let's talk about something else. I don't want to waste another brain cell on that asshole."

42

Nightmare Before Christmas

IT WAS THE DAY AFTER the winter solstice, and Ollie was having a nightmare. It came in confusing flashes until Ollie found himself surrounded by graffiti covered walls and nearly ankle deep in broken glass. The space was cavernous and there were three men fighting under a spotlight. Ollie moved forward for a closer look and discovered the light was coming from one of the men, through cracks in his skin. He wasn't sure why, but the sight was terrifying in a way that froze him in place. Suddenly, the fighting finished with a burst of light so intense it was like an atomic bomb and all that remained were two men, and Ollie realized they were both Luke. Ollie cringed as he waited for a blast of heat that never came.

The next thing Ollie knew he was on a balcony and Andy had Charlie in his arms. "Your boyfriend broke into my house and stole my computer," Andy's hair was a garish blonde and his eyes sparkled like gold. "He tried to have me killed."

Ollie opened his mouth, but no words would come out. He tried to make a grab for Charlie, but his limbs were like lead.

"Tell that cunt, eye for an eye, you fucking bitch," Andy said with an evil smirk and tossed Charlie over the side.

Ollie woke up with a scream, the bedsheets all tangled around him. He peeled them off his arms and legs and sat up with a heaving chest, thoroughly disturbed and rattled. There was a knock at his door.

"Are you alright, Ollie?" his father said as he opened the door. "I heard screaming."

"It was just a nightmare, but I'm fine, Dad. So sorry to have woken you." Ollie swiped a hand over his face and stood. He pulled a robe over his sleep shorts. "I'm just gonna get some water. Go back to bed."

"Do you want talk about it?"

"No, Dad. It wouldn't make sense, it barely made sense to me."

David touched Ollie's shoulder and gave it a gentle squeeze. "Goodnight, son."

Ollie used the bathroom and drank a glass of water as he calmed his racing heart. He looked at his watch and did a brief calculation before texting Matt.

> Hi babe. I miss u.
> Is everyone ok? I just
> had a terrible dream.

The text bubble appeared and then disappeared. His phone rang a second later. Ollie closed his eyes with a smile.

"Good evening, Lieutenant," he said as his body flooded with relief.

"Hey, princess. You okay? Everyone here is fine, great in fact. Never better," Matt replied in a happy tone.

"Oh, I'm so glad to hear it." Ollie blew out a breath. "I miss you so much, and really wish you were here, wrapped around me."

"What was the dream? I don't think I've ever seen you have a nightmare."

"I know." Ollie paused. "How could I with you next to me?" Ollie swallowed, uncertain how much to tell Matt over the phone. "It was crazy. First, I was in some sort of warehouse where there were people fighting. I thought it was you and Luke again, but then there was a blinding explosion, and the two men who remained were both Luke, but not. I don't know how to describe it. Then ... Andy was there."

There was a long pause.

"And?"

"We were on a balcony, and he was holding Charlie. And his eyes were weird, like glowing suns. And he... he threw Charlie," Ollie whispered. "I tried to jump. I tried to save him, and I *couldn't*."

There was another pause and then Matt blew out a breath. "It was just a dream, baby. Charlie's here. He's perfectly fine. Andy can't hurt Charlie; he can't hurt us. He's dead."

Ollie clutched the phone tight against his face as his emotions warred with what George had told him.

"What is it?" Matt asked as the silence stretched.

"They never found the body. How do you know he's dead?" Ollie whispered.

"Well, I don't know for sure, but they arrested someone, and they wouldn't have done so if they didn't have enough evidence to indicate some sort of foul play...."

"I wish you were here so I could hug you and tell you in person that everything is going to be alright," Matt soothed. "It's been a long week without you. Can you come home early?"

Ollie sighed at the same time that his stomach flipped with anticipation. "It's only two more days, and we haven't done presents yet. But... I could ask my parents if we could celebrate tomorrow morning so I can hop on the plane and be home in time for dinner, and then bed..." he trailed off suggestively. "Do you promise that Charlie is okay?" he urged, needing to hear Matt's reassurance again.

"Charlie is perfect, and sound asleep. It was just a bad dream. All of it. I'll call the pilot in the morning," Matt stated. "I miss you and can't wait to have my hands on your beautiful body. You know I will keep you safe, right?"

Ollie closed his eyes and welcomed the thrill that pulsed through his body and erased the worried tension. "I know, and I can't wait until your beautiful hands are all over my body. I'll see you tomorrow, Lieutenant."

"I love you so much, Ollie."

"I love you too, Matt. So, *so* much."

EPILOGUE

OLLIE DESCENDED THE stairs after the customs check and strode toward the parking lot with purpose. Matt was leaning against the side of Ollie's Maserati, wearing a wool car coat and a smile on his handsome face. He gave Ollie a handshake and a tight one-armed hug before putting his bags in the trunk.

"You look amazing, Ollie. What's different?" Matt asked gazing at him briefly before starting the car.

Ollie shrugged and ran his eyes over Matt's body. "Nothing. You look amazing too. I just think it's been forever since we've been apart this long. I know I missed looking at you. I can't believe we would go more than a month between seeing each other when I was in school." He shook his head. "How did we manage?"

"Lots of video phone sex." Matt grinned and drove out onto the main road.

The ride home was both quiet and chatty. Ollie filled Matt in on seeing everyone, leaving out what George said about seeing Andy, while Matt told him about Charlie's latest achievements.

When Matt exited the highway, the silence set in. Ollie was desperate to be home and, in their bed, and began to feel out of sorts again; the memories of that nightmare still niggling in his brain. Matt must have sensed Ollie's eyes on him and reached over to squeeze Ollie's thigh before turning up the hill into their neighborhood.

The garage door slid closed behind them, and Ollie leapt out of the car just as quickly as Matt did to properly greet each other with a deep kiss. Matt's hands slid to Ollie's ass and squeezed until Ollie moaned.

"Bloody hell, it's good to be home."

"It's so good to have you home, Ollie. I can't wait to strip you bare and celebrate you tonight. I promise, this New Year's celebration is going to be a doozy." Matt smiled with a secret behind his eyes. He led Ollie into the house and went back for his bags.

Finn was in the playroom off the kitchen with Charlie and stood up to greet him when he came through. Charlie pushed himself to his feet and toddled behind Finn, excitedly calling 'Père!' Ollie hugged Finn quickly before scooping Charlie up and kissing him exuberantly.

"He's walking unaided now?" Ollie exclaimed. "I've only been gone a week, and when I left, he was still holding onto furniture."

"Progress waits for no man," Matt said with a grin when he reappeared with Ollie's bags and tickled Charlie's belly.

Ollie held Charlie tight as he listened to Finn catch him up on what he missed; how Luke had been there for a few days, and his partner, Stan, had come for a bit as well, but that they had to head back to DC.

"Luke will be back, and Dad will be here for Christmas, of course. You can join us at my uncle's for Christmas Eve while Matt's at his mom's for the feast."

"Sure, whatever." Ollie watched Matt carry his bags up the back stairs. He wished that he could partake in the feast of the seven fishes with Matt and his family but that was a pipe dream he never saw coming true.

Ollie passed Charlie back to Finn with a kiss and promise to watch him in the morning after breakfast. He made for the stairs and shut the door to his and Matt's bedroom suite with a determined flick in his wrist.

Matt was waiting for him, with an expectant look on his face. Ollie stripped off his clothes and left them in his wake on the way to the bed.

"I washed up in the bathroom on the plane, but proper sex will have to wait until I've had a chance to clean out my pipes," Ollie said and wrapped his arms around Matt, who had stripped off his clothes as quickly as Ollie had.

Ollie sighed as their bare chests came into contact, Matt's chest hair a welcome tickle on his torso. Matt smoothed his hands up Ollie's back with a hum and bent to trail kisses on Ollie's neck. He continued kissing Ollie over his collarbone until he had one of Ollie's nipples in his mouth. Ollie sucked in a sharp breath when he felt Matt's teeth and then his soothing tongue.

Ollie went for Matt's half-hard cock over his boxer briefs and squeezed. "I need to say 'hello' to this magnificent thing." He shimmied Matt's underwear down to his knees and made to lower with them.

"In due time," Matt replied as his eyes flared with lust at the sight of Ollie's *Fleur du Mal* lace briefs. "I love these on you," he murmured and ran his hands over Ollie's ass and then slipped them under the waistband.

Ollie turned his face up and leaned in for a kiss, opening his mouth to Matt's warm tongue as he rolled his hips. It wasn't until nearly thirty minutes later, covered in a copious amount of Matt's cum, that Ollie had the chance to ask what Matt meant about the New Year's being a doozy.

Matt used the towel he had on the bed to mop Ollie dry. "Just that we have a lot to celebrate," he answered vaguely. "Now come on, let's have a shower." He tugged a groaning Ollie out of bed and into the bathroom.

"Okay, Lieutenant. Just so long as you plan on kissing me at midnight, I don't care what we're actually celebrating."

Matt turned on the shower and smacked Ollie's ass. "We're gonna party like it's nineteen ninety-nine," he beamed.

ACKNOWLEDGMENTS

I'D LIKE TO THANK John Stella, for being one of my biggest supporters, and the OG of beta readers. He has read every word I've ever written and has helped me to become a better writer.

Speaking of making me a better writer, thank you to Duney Roberts, who went through this manuscript when it was still part of Foundations, with a fine-toothed comb and made it shine! His insight into writing style, including gifting me with "Elements of Style" was life-changing.

Thank you to Julie Gallagher, my guide, my book guru, my sensei. She has helped me immensely in so many ways, and is the person responsible for making my manuscript and book cover into the book you just read.

And speaking of book covers … thank you to Sigrid Silberman for yet another beautiful design! She manages to take my gibberish and disjointed summary of the book and make images that convey the elements and emotion within the pages perfectly.

Thank you to my intern Erin McEwan, who has worked tirelessly on web stuff, sourcing images, and creating my (yet-to-be-sent) author newsletter.

Thank you to Ester Pescio for the Italian translations. She has no idea what kind of book she has hitched her wagon to, so don't tell her.

Thank you to my BookTok besties, Bernice, Unique, Barb, Sasha, Jess, and Stephanie2005, who make TikTok a fun place, encourage me with comments and DMs, and read and hype my books!

Thank you to my sons, who tell everyone they think would be interested (e.g., every LGBTQ+ person they are friends with/meet), that their mother writes queer fiction (though they call it something else).

And finally, thank you to my husband for your unending support.

www.ingramcontent.com/pod-product-compliance
Lightning Source LLC
Chambersburg PA
CBHW021046310726

48969CB00006B/1829